Police In 2052
Tales of a Schesis World: Book I
Written by: Zachary Churchill

Editors:
Trina James-Kneer
Deric Churchill
Revision 3

DISCLAIMER:

All characters, companies, politicians, groups, and events in this novel are not representations of any current persons, companies, politicians, or events in real life. This novel takes place in an alternate Universe and many years in the future. If there are perceived relations, they are completely fictional. This story is completely fictional in nature with no accurate real-world representation or personal relation to its author, editors, and artists. This story is exactly that, a fictitious story. It is told with the hopes that whoever reads it, can learn from it, apply it to their lives in positive ways, and enjoy its fictitious events.

CLARIFICATION OF DISCLAIMER:

The actions and events in these novels are not to be replicated in any manner. They take place in an alternate Universe in the future with no relationship to our Universe. The entire theme of the Tales of a Schesis World series is to show an example of the massive problems, personal and community wise, that result from any uprising or insurgency. The characters present peaceful alternatives to promote change. However, some choose a wrong path and this series is a foreshadowing of the horrors that come with potential uprising or insurgency.

"The poor know more than the rich. A statement said by a dear friend of mine. He lived the struggles of reality, just as the rest of the poor do. Nature is something they are forced to understand and abide by, or they will perish. When the rich and first world begin to tell the poor and less fortunate that they know their problems, that's when the virus starts. That's when the people begin to look for a cure."

Zaylee Tonitrum Ross

Appendix

Chapter 1: I Am The Law!

Honey colored hair, bundled into a circle, sits attached to a middle-aged woman's head. A glint of orange comes off her eyes but more reflection protrudes from her hair as the neon lights shine above and reflect its glossy nature. The desk in front of her obstructs her immediate contact with the man behind it. She stares at medallions splashed across the walls. Each one denotes a different public service that this office has provided for the city of Los Angeles. In big bold letters is 'LAPD' centered perfectly, though smudges of dirt distract from its alignment.

She straightens her posture. Each fold in her outfit moves with her. Boldly across from her, the man clenches his coffee mug. The ceramic touches his lips, as brown liquid pours into his open cavity. His neck bobbles in a smooth motion, forcing the liquid down into his gut. He places it back onto his desk, amid some papers.

"Looking over your paperwork, I have to wonder why a Cyberforce General would want to be a regular cop. With your skillset, you should be working with Icecave. So, why exactly do you want to be a cop?" he asks with distinct judgment. Zaylee replies firmly, "I have no ill intentions. I put in my application for two reasons and they were explicitly defined in my cover letter."

Mumbling, he responds with, "I see, the grey hat hacker wants an easy retirement job. Have to say, it isn't a great move. You should stick with your old job." he asserts.

Zaylee doesn't hesitate, "The blue glass armada operates without me because I have grown tired of the corruption within the government. I can't make a stand on behalf of the people so my best option is to serve the people directly." A smile peaks on the corner of her cheek as she continues, "I want to use my skills to help the people in anyway I can."

"Good enough. I can't hire you for our hack and protect division anyway, but I can put you on patrol. You could start as patrol and eventually be promoted to lieutenant status." he states. She looks at him with a slightly pleasing, but unapparent smile.

"That works for me. When do I start?" He grabs a piece of paper off his desk and glances across it. "You can report to your

FTO today. Get your approval from the ride-along and I'll start you on patrols tomorrow. We can work out payment details later." he confirms, apathetically.

"Who is my FTO?" she asks. The Captain behind the desk reaches his hand down. A red button pushes into its cavity. Static buzzes through it, "Jessica, report to my office." he says, before letting go of the button. Static buzzes again. "Yes sir." a girl's voice echoes back. The Captain looks away and parses through his papers again as Zaylee sits still until the door opens.

The creaking of hinges causes Zaylee to turn around. A tall, wide, and muscular woman pushes the door out of her way. Zaylee quickly stands up and looks at her. She is significantly smaller but it's not because she's short; this woman is just extremely tall. The woman stands still, awaiting orders, noticing this the Captain quickly realizes the delay in action is because of him.

"Jessica, take Zaylee instead of Dekima for patrol today. Just a basic evaluation and report back." he says. Jessica remains still. "Well, go." he continues. Almost immediately Jessica says, "Yes sir."

She averts her eyes from Zaylee and marches out the door.

-

Zaylee enters Jessica's patrol car. The engine roars, but it doesn't cause her to buckle like it does Jessica. Curious, Zaylee asks, "Can we buy our own patrol cars?"

After a moment, Jessica replies with, "You can, but it's expensive. I have the nicest car available for now, but I am the senior Captain on staff."

Zaylee stares out the windshield, "The price doesn't matter. I already own a white sports car. I'll bring it in if I get the job and see what the chief can do," Zaylee explains.

"What kind of car do you have?" Jessica asks. Zaylee locks eyes with her, "A 730 McDoodle." she answers.

"Wow." Jessica's face brightens up with astonishment as she speaks, "What did you do for a living?" Zaylee looks at the cars on the road, predicting their movement, as if she were driving. "I was a general." she claims. A look of confusion crinkles Jessica's face,

2

"And you want to become a sheriff?" Jessica asks.

"I worked my way up. I started higher up because I had a bachelors degree. But honestly, I had no idea what I was doing. Most of the cadets and lower ranking soldiers knew more than I did. I was a talented programmer and script kiddie though. So, I proved myself and made my way into special operations, hacking division. I made my way further, learning both the low and high ranks of the military. As a result, my pay increased." Zaylee claims. Still befuddled, Jessica asks "And your salary was enough to afford that vehicle?" Jessica continues to ponder, half paying attention to the road and half paying attention to Zaylee.

"Well, even as an officer I could have afforded it, if it was all I bought. They help pay for housing, food, and health care. They also give you tax advantages. I could have afforded it even with just a bachelors degree, but as I moved up, I made more and more. I applied my skills and was promoted. Eventually, the Cyberforce was developed and became a new branch of military. I was the very first general during the cyber war against Sweden, Russia, China, and Japan's rogue AI." Zaylee explains. Jessica nods, beginning to understand. Eager to talk more, Zaylee keeps going, "I had excess money and I always loved McDoodle's prowess of lightweight cars with medium engines to make a supercar. But as I served with the military, I learned how ridiculous those vehicles are. Everything from their company to model names are stupid."

Jessica turns to look at her as a red car pulls up beside them and slows their speed. Zaylee looks back and remembers her feelings of regret for buying such a car, "Their names are ridiculous and they always put some numbers and a stupid acronym by it. Typically, it's GT for Gran Turismo or Grand Touring. Some silly race acronym to sell more cars. They are children through and through. I've used thorium rail guns and I road in a TSR car, during China's expansion. Now those are impressive." Zaylee laments.

"You mean those thorium-salt reactor supercars?" Jessica asks curiously. Zaylee corrects her by saying, "I think you mean hypercars." After a brief pause, she continues, "But yes, those cars. We could have had them years ago, back in the mid 1900's, but morons remain in charge and allow other countries to catch up and use our thorium technology instead of capitalizing on it ourselves.

3

That low orbiting thorium space-blimp that has hundreds of modular thorium reactors powering it could have been ours and we could be winning this second cold war. But alas, all we care about is market control and money, rather than actual improvements. It's why the Chinese beat us and why they have TSR cars." Zaylee claims. But Jessica is only half paying attention, as her focus remains on the road.

Out of nervousness, because Jessica did not reply, Zaylee continues her rant: "One of these days the car companies will get what they are due. Who knows though? Maybe the Chinese will give it to them when they eventually take over the United States and our market. Then they will push those puerile electric supercars out of the market." Jessica becomes curious about her hostile demeanor towards the car companies.

Noticing this attitude she conveyed, Zaylee seeks to rectify her mistake, "I'm sorry. I get carried away. They are just cars. People in the states are so obsessed with them. It makes sense given all the land we have to traverse, but it doesn't make any sense to waste more money than what's necessary on them. I foolishly did and that's why I want to use my vehicle to apprehend speeding criminals." Zaylee claims. Jessica remains quiet and lets Zaylee continue, "I would like to impound all their vehicles and sell them back to every car manufacturer that allowed their customers to waste hundreds of thousands of dollars on unnecessary machines. We need excess money being spent on research, science, and the less fortunate, not frivolous machinery and technology. All they do is speed anyway." Zaylee explains, staring at Jessica. Only half paying attention, Jessica lurks forward in her seat, as a car rushes past them.

Its mute color fades into the skyline, almost going unnoticed, but its speed causes others to focus on it. The driver is leaning back, clearly intent on going faster and faster. He pivots through the cars, going around the slower vehicles so he can continue his rampage down the street.

"Speaking of speeding criminals, there's one." Jessica discloses, pointing towards the dash. Zaylee redirects her attention to the road, notices the man, and presses a button causing numbers to appear on the dash. An LED HUD displays numbers regarding the speeding criminal. It reads 'CA LICENSE #2Y355422' at a speed of

'140km/h'. She presses another button and lights begin to flash. "This is a code," Jessica begins to say but looks at Zaylee, waiting for her to finish her words: Zaylee obliges, "A code 3." The lag does not cause Jessica to stress or tighten her muscles, since she is familiar with rookies. She merely looks at Zaylee and says, "It's a routine traffic stop. You want to handle it?"

As the question lingers in the air, the man in the vehicle pulls to a stop on the side of the road, obeying the lights and sirens non-verbal requests for him to pull over. Zaylee sits up straight, "Sure." Jessica pulls the car over to the side of the road, behind the man's vehicle, and jerks it to a stop. Zaylee swings the door open and places her left cowboy boot onto the dirt. She plants it firmly and raises herself to a standing position and uses her hand to keep her hat on as she approaches the vehicle on the side of the road. Her fingers, still caressing the lip of her hat, lick it one last time before completely dismounting. The man waits in his seat with his hands on the steering wheel.

She bites her lip ever so slightly as she walks closer to the stopped vehicle and sees the window rolling down, descending back into its resting place. She peers inside the vehicle and notices the muscular man staring back at her. Out of reflex, Zaylee asks, "Do you know why you were stopped today sir?" The man looks back at her flippantly and bored. "I was going too fast." he replies. "You were going 140 in a 100 zone. That's dangerous speeds for everyone on the road, including yourself." Zaylee claims. But the comment does nothing; he continues to look bored.

"It's not like anyone got hurt," he replies with a short pause before following up with, "Look, I need to get to work. People depend on me. I'm sure you saw the fire department sticker on the back." he continues fervently. Zaylee looks angrily at him and then pauses, "License and registration." she demands while rummaging through her pocket for her tablet.

With a quick glance behind her, Zaylee notices Jessica behind her, watching. The man looks frustrated and vents audibly at her, "C'mon please don't write me a ticket." he pleads. As the words exit his mouth, he notices Zaylee's demeanor is ice cold. So, he hands over his license, which happens to be covered by a piece of paper; his registration sits atop his license, obscuring the information. Frustrated, he spews out, "Seriously, I'm a firefighter, I can't get a ticket. You're going to regret this."

Zaylee tilts her head back and looks at the back of his vehicle. On the opposite side of a sticker that looks like a bluish hedgehog is a sticker for his department.

She turns her head back towards him and smirks, "If you're a firefighter you should know why the speed is set at 100 kilometers an hour. Any faster and the mortality rate soars; most TC's that end in death are caused by driving too fast on the roads. You are endangering these peoples' lives." Zaylee says, as she looks out at the road. The speeding cars rush through causing his car to rock back everytime a car flies by.

A line of electric semi-trucks speed by, each one pushing them back aggressively due to their massive weight. Zaylee notices the logos of the semi-trucks and a taste of nostalgia enters her cranium as she sees a sign that reads 'How's my driving?'. But, just beneath that, is another sticker that has been plastered diagonally across it that reads, 'My driving is perfect because I'm mostly automated'. The thought makes Zaylee let out a chuckle, thinking back to how AI failed. But, the driver gets antsy, and Zaylee notices this.

"People like you are the reason why fire stations in California are overwhelmed with traffic collision calls." Zaylee states to him. Another car blazes by and rocks them with its sheer force. Zaylee's hair remains tight in a bun. She curves her cowboy boot and points it at his front tire. The tread is decent and the tire remains fixed in the loose dirt. His brake pads, a milky gray slab, show through the rim, but look like they are nearing replacement.

"C'mon seriously? You really want to cause beef with the fire department?" he asks. She looks at him with hostile intent, "Sir, you are getting a ticket because you increased the mortality rate on this roadway. Shady politics and blackmail only increase your chances of being served a higher fine and possible jail time. You cannot abuse these people and potentially kill them. I am here to uphold the law and prevent injustices from harming the people. You, driving the way you do, are an enemy of the public. You are a potential murderer and I will not let you go simply because you are a firefighter. Your injustice will not be tolerated." Zaylee says confidently. The firefighter sits back in his vehicle.

She stares at him, eyes rigid and unnerved, "Remain in your vehicle while I process your information." she commands him. He remains still and waits while Jessica and Zaylee go back to their squad car. They enter the vehicle and sit in their seats, the padding braces them and creates an unsavory dichotomy with the rigid plastic in the back.

Jessica looks at her, bewildered at what she recently heard, "I've never seen anyone uphold the law like that, especially a rookie. Almost every officer, highway patrol or sheriff, will let firefighters go because they don't want beef with them. You are the first I've seen who has told them straight and called them on their bluff. Usually they try to blackmail officers, claiming they won't save us next time there is an incident. And to risk all that, go against the grain, as a rookie?" Jessica scoffs, "You have some guts."

A tiny tweak appears on Zaylee's cheek, almost like a faint smile but not quite, appears quickly before she responds to Jessica by saying, "Well, I'm not like the rest. The people will not suffer under my watch and I will not oppress them like other cops do. I am here to serve and protect the people, not give special privileges to public service workers. I am a regulator of the law. I am an enforcer of the law. I am a servant of the people." Zaylee says to her. Jessica stares and looks eagerly at her, desiring to hear her words, because it's something new to her:

"I have been a stickler for the rules since I was a general. That is how true politicians act. That is what makes them a true government official. And it is true about cops too. If I am to be a cop, I will do it right. I will not tolerate any human that could do harm to the public. I have protected this nation my entire life. I intend to do it on terms completely for the people this time around. I will do it for the people, never the government."

Chapter 2: Buddy Cop

Zaylee sits across from Jessica and a woman of dark pigmentation. She presumes this is Dekima, Jessica's partner. But another woman also sits next to Zaylee, a younger woman with a device on her arm that is embedded in her skin. Along this new woman's eyes is a sideways triangle with one line where it reaches the surface of her lacrimal gland, at the end of her eyebrow, and the other leg of the triangle going underneath the eye, pointing at her nose. The triangle engulfs her eye, wrapping around it, because the center of the triangle is hollow, with the legs serving as lines that reach towards the center of her face.

The black coloring of the design on her eyes matches a metal clasp that holds her ponytail together, the remainder of her hair flowing down to her shoulders. Zaylee examines her more thoroughly now, curious as to her nature. She notices a smaller streak of black protruding down from her tear ducts, and, near her ankles, is another black metal cuff clasped around her leg. Its matte black coloring remains dull, even when she turns and the light strikes it, almost as though it were absorbing the sun's rays.

Upon meeting eyes with Zaylee, Jessica points over to the woman with unique designs along her eyes and says, "This is your new partner." Then she looks at the woman with the almost-frightening eyeliner and says, "Rayna this is Zaylee and Zaylee this is Rayna." Jessica claims. They look at each other and shake each other's hands. Dekima looks over at them, particularly glaring at Rayna, "I know you don't like it, but she will be the lead officer during your patrols, Rayna." Dekima claims. A touch saddened, Rayna pouts, "Ah man."

Seeking to avoid this circumstance, Rayna pleads, "C'mon Dekima, let me be in charge." But Dekima remains firm and says, "No Rayna. You cause too much trouble."

"Hypocritical coming from you." Rayna continues. "The trouble you claim I cause has a logical reasoning behind it." Dekima states, flashing her eyes at Rayna. The black triangular design on Rayna's face changes as her face turns to one of a childish pout. She folds her arms and leans back in her chair.

"This is why Zaylee is in charge." Dekima says, pointing at

her. Jessica looks at Dekima, listening to her, as the words continue to exit her mouth, "Anyway, Zaylee has more experience dealing with problems."

"Now go, you have a patrol to start." Dekima declares, shooing them away with her gesture. They both get up and push the chairs back from beneath them. They begin to walk together towards the exit. Zaylee's cowboy boots surprise Rayna by making very little noise as she walks through the halls, and she notices that they lack spurs on the end that usually give that distinct jingle.

Beside her, moving at the same pace, Zaylee becomes slightly annoyed that Rayna's work boots add a little more noise because of their steel in the front. Together, they push the doors open and are greeted by overwhelming heat. Zaylee stares out looking for their vehicle. Rayna briskly skips towards the vehicle, leaving Zaylee to catch up.

Rayna enters the vehicle first and slams the door. The sound ceases as Zaylee opens her door and enters. The two newly acquainted partners sit inside their cop car, its metal exterior catches the heat and confines it within, causing Zaylee's body to tingle as her sweat glands prepare to release liquid.

The metal car is coated white and black with defining characteristics to make it a cop car. Along the rear panel is 'To protect and serve'. Near the front panel, along the driver's door, is the word 'Police' written in large black letters. Just below that is the lettering 'Unit 451'. Rayna sits in the passenger seat, her body pressed against the torn fabric. Her long flowing black hair remains tightened in a ponytail by its black clasp, but Zaylee notices that its length is definitely considerable given the size of the clasp.

In the driver's seat is Zaylee. Her body presses against the torn and hot material. Each of her eyes has a distinct orangish line sprouting through the center of the brown. Unfortunately, her beauty is clouded by her age and the lines coming down beside her eyes. Even more so though, her beauty is overshadowed by the rancid looking interior.

A metal grate protrudes through the center of the interior, separating the front passengers from the back passengers, where the suspects are usually kept. Zaylee grabs the sensually flaming steering wheel; she clenches her fingers without letting go despite

9

the intense heat. .

"So, partner, where is this supercar of yours?" Rayna asks. With a shrug, Zaylee replies, "Sadly, it's at home. The Chief said I will need to make it through my probationary period before he can modify my personal vehicle into a cruiser." As the last syllable leaves her vocal cords, she begins turning the ignition. The vehicle clicks, failing to start. Rayna immediately opens her door on the passenger side and hops out. She ducks and looks at Zaylee, "Pop the hood." she asks in a monotone voice. Zaylee reaches down and grabs the lever. As she pulls, a click comes from the hood. Rayna turns away from Zaylee and reaches the front of the vehicle.

She ducks down and opens the hood. Fortunately, she is short enough that the hood stays open above her after being propped open. She stares at the feculent cob web infested engine bay and scoffs. A battery sits in the right upper corner near the bumper. Rayna grabs one of the terminals and places it onto the battery. A few sparks fly into the air causing Zaylee to exit the vehicle and walk over and stand beside her. "So, you're a mechanic too?" she asks.

Rayna clips on the other end of the battery cable onto her arm and begins gripping the bolt attached to her.

By clutching the bolt and activating a mechanism in her arm, she lodges the device in place and completes the connection, causing the electricity to soar through her arm and into the car's battery. Remembering what Zaylee had said, she replies "Yup" and gets out from under the hood. A few cob webs are wrapped around her wrist. She quickly removes them and drops them onto the floor.

"Try to start it." Rayna asks, slightly less monotone. Zaylee heads back into the car. The plastic key in her hand is moist to the touch from the sweat her body had started to produce. Despite the slipperiness, Zaylee jams the key into the ignition and turns it.

A rumble goes through engine bay as it starts up. Rayna unclasps the locking prop for the hood and slams the hood shut. Wind blows from its closure but her ponytail remains rigid at the clasp. The rest of her hair flows backwards as the air gets out of the hood's way.

She enters the vehicle and closes the door after she successful sits in the passenger seat. Slightly irritated from the experience, Zaylee asks, "Why can't they afford to have decent vehicles for the force?" Rayna shakes her head, "Stupid California politics. Nearly all of our cities have been in debt for over fifty years, unable to get out. Some of them charge their citizens to park on the streets overnight. You know, streets that every citizen in California pays taxes to maintain? But they still can't get out of debt." Rayna rants.

Zaylee puts the car into reverse and begins to pull it out of the parking lot. Her words exit her mouth just as she exits onto the asphalt, "Yeah. They also spend millions on football fields, solar panels, school gyms, public parks, and public service. It's a waste." Zaylee exclaims, attempting to get on Rayna's good side.

Noticing the lack of resistance to her diatribe, Rayna continues, "Public service. You know how understaffed San Bernardino, Los Angeles, Victorville, and other criminal towns are? We can't even do a proper bust, but you know, Claremont, San Jose, Newport, and Chino Hills, they can send out a fleet of six to ten officers for one homeless person or a domestic call. While all we get is every God forsaken drug dealer and gang banger breathing down our necks."

After taking a second salivate, Zaylee interjects, "The workforce is overwhelmed, sure, but looking at our schedule, we are going to be doing real police work not busting teenagers like those opulent and babied employees. Yeah, sure, they get homicides and class three felons once in a while, but on a daily basis like us?" Zaylee slides their vehicle over, maneuvering past a slower vehicle. She looks at all the parked cars on the street. Just beyond them is a plethora of tents and homeless individuals pushing shopping carts filled with assorted junk. Her mind changes the image for her into cleaner streets, with no homeless.

After taking in the scene, Zaylee continues, "Nah. They should send their extra units over here where they will actually be used and not bored busting the homeless all night." Zaylee rants agreeing with her. Noticing a pause, Rayna takes the opportunity to speak, "They wouldn't like the pay. Their cushiony insane salaries would dwindle down to our paltry pay and they wouldn't be able to afford their useless RV's, dirt bikes, and other unnecessary material goods."

Zaylee chuckles at her comment. "How do they even make

that much?" Zaylee asks.

"Overtime. Some of them probably don't, but hey I'd rather have their job than this one." Rayna claims. Zaylee looks over at her. "Yeah, I could definitely do some bored busting for what they make a year." Zaylee states. They both laugh. "Wouldn't we all? You could do so much good with that money rather than wasting it on stuff you'll never use." Rayna declares.

They both look out at the road, mesmerized by the dotted lines in the center of the street. Rayna stares blankly thinking about their conversation.

Her eye twitches up and then she looks at Zaylee, "Bored busting. You're a noobie. Where did you hear that?" Rayna asks. "I grew up in California. I worked as an EMT straight out of high school, like my father did, to make money. I've seen my fair share. I remember when I was kid, the shooting in San Bernardino happened by some religious radicals. My father was working at the time, and heard it on the scanner. He and his coworkers didn't think anything of it. They just thought it was another shooting since those happened almost every week in SB. Yet, of course, the media is selective and, in a round bout way, censored it. Only giving attention to their religious message. Things haven't changed, they've just gotten worse. It's why I'm here." Zaylee explains.

"Yeah, I know how that is. I grew up in P town. It was ghetto. Shootings and knifings every night, practically. I always wondered why the cops never busted the prostitutes on Holt and Mission. I guess the same goes for G Street in SB. The police just never have enough time to bust something that silly. They're always overwhelmed, while the rich cities sit right above P town, bored busting." Rayna rants with her. The radio begins to buzz, the static gnawing at their ears.

"We have a 415 off Magnolia Avenue." the radio says at it comes in clearer with each word. Zaylee picks up the radio. "Unit 451 en route." she says into the radio. Rayna looks behind as another cop pulls behind them and begins following them. "P town?" Zaylee asks as they continue moving towards their destination. "Pomona." Rayna confirms before following up with, "It's the blood pit right near North America's largest fair." Zaylee opens her mouth to confirm her understanding, "Oh. The L.A county fair. Wedged right below 'Lit Verne'." Zaylee says somewhat sarcastically. "Lit Verne? You mean La Verne?" Rayna asks, staring at Zaylee. Rayna pauses, "You must be one primeval woman to be using Lit still." Despite the insult, Zaylee doesn't take offense and just continues on.

"Yeah. I knew a guy who bragged about growing up on Evergreen in La Verne. He used to say that everywhere in La Verne was nice but then you go down Evergreen and all of a sudden, you're in the hood. Stupidest guy I ever met. Funny though." Zaylee explains. "Oh." Rayna mutters with a sigh and just continues listening to her, "It's like that in San Bernardino and Highland too. You can go to the north end where it's nice or in certain areas of downtown but then you make one wrong turn and it's nothing but bullet holes." Zaylee continues.

"Makes sense." Rayna reaffirms her understanding. "P town and Claremont are like that on their border line. It's primo pleasant living in Claremont, but make one wrong turn and you're in the ghetto. San Jose was that street. My guess is that all the cities are alike." Rayna clarifies. A police cruiser appears behind them, moving slowly, but clearly eager to move faster as it jerks back and forth. Eventually, it does, and blitzes past them.

Zaylee adds, "Huntington and Costa Mesa are like that too. It's everywhere. There is some reasoning to be had that it's because of affordable housing acts that requires a certain amount of low-income housing in each town. But the rich cities are jerks and tuck them away, in an effort to hide them instead of help them."

They arrive at the storage facility. Two large glass doors mark the entry way. An older woman stands outside and gestures for them to get out by moving her hand back and forth in an open position. Both newly acquainted partners exit the vehicle, their uniforms color giving a calm vibe with the, now, dusk skyline; their badges, once glistening in the sunlight, turn into simple aesthetic identifiers. Their reflective gear gives their badges a distinct shine every once in awhile, but the jostling from their movement makes those shines few and far between.

"Hurry up!" the older woman shouts, heading towards the gate. Zaylee walks at a brisk pace, almost like a jog, towards her while Rayna follows shortly behind. Upon reaching the older woman, Zaylee watches as her frail hands pull a tablet from the pouch along her waistband, "Watch." the older woman demands. A video begins to play on the tablet. Zaylee watches as a hooded figure uses a grinder on a storage unit. It slices through the metal, making a square along the unit's door. Then the hooded figure places the cutter on the floor and kicks the cut square out.

The video begins to speed up. A vehicle is now on screen, a black four-door sedan. Although its lights are off, the rough image of it can be made out. It propels forward and slams through the gate and into the parking lot beyond. The black vehicle drives off into the unrecorded portion of the street, noticeably weighed down. She pushes a button on the tablet and it goes black before she shoves it back into its pouch-like home on her waist. She points out onto the storage lot, "He's here right now, stealing more stuff." she states.

Off in the distance is a hooded figure holding a gun shaped object at a storage unit. White frost sprays from it and onto the unit. It begins to color the unit a matte white. Zaylee pulls her weapon from its holster. The sound of velcro is the only audible thing on property they hear. Rayna stops and pulls out her own tablet. After clicking a button, metal screeching occurs near the trunk. The screeching dissipates and sounds of propellers greet their ears as a drone flies into the air, its gun distinctly visible and frightening in the night sky. "What's that?" Zaylee asks, "A drone?" she continues to question.

"It's Tommy." Rayna answers. "He's an enforcer drone." she continues. "Ah." Zaylee audibly sounds in reply. "I was told you used special hardware but I thought that meant your arm. Why do you also have a drone?" Zaylee asks while continuing to walk down towards the hooded figure. "He records, adds support, and helps out where he can. But I can solve all my problems with my hydraulic gauntlet." Rayna replies, as she uses the tablet to make Tommy follow them. "Didn't you have drones in the military?" Rayna asks. "We did but they were more for remote hacking and surveillance, not as a flying beretta." Zaylee answers, staring at the flying drone. Its plastic housing gives it a comical look, but the weaponry beneath changes Zaylee's view and causes her to be impressed, "Tommy is pretty cool though; I loved playing with air force drones." Zaylee vocalizes quickly before refocusing on the situation at hand. They approach the hooded figure. As they get closer, they get a better view of the criminal.

Half of the door is frozen from his gun. He places his gun on the floor and picks up a hammer. The metal hammer smashes into the frozen lock section of the unit. Frozen steel remains fall onto the concrete below. "Freeze!" Zaylee shouts intentionally being ironic and forcing herself not to giggle at her own comment. He stops in place and puts his hands in the air. Red and blue lights exit Tommy's housing and begin to flash, while a siren begins emit out of a porous opening just beneath them. "Get down on your knees and put your hands behind your head." Zaylee commands.

He immediately obeys. Zaylee approaches him and slaps metal cuffs onto his wrists. She stares at him and kicks a piece of the frozen lock, "Looks like you've gotten smarter. Using ice is much quieter than that grinder." she declares. Tommy's propellers buzz in a unique fashion, giving off a purring sound. It sinks down to Rayna. She puts out her hand and rubs her fingers along his nose. The purring gets louder. "That's a good boy, Tommy."

Zaylee pulls the criminals hands down to his waist, "But you still have to go to jail." she declares. "Seriously?" he asks. "Quiet." Zaylee replies before reciting, "You have the right to remain silent and refuse to answer questions. Anything you say may be used against you in a court of law. You have the right to consult an attorney before speaking to the police and to have an attorney present during questioning now or in the future. If you cannot afford an attorney, one will be appointed for you before any questioning, if you wish. If you decide to answer any questions now without an attorney present, you will still have the right to stop answering at any time until you talk to an attorney. Knowing and understanding your rights, as I have explained them to you, are you willing to answer my questions without an attorney present?" Zaylee asks.

"I will not answer any questions." he replies. As he finishes, Zaylee pulls him towards their patrol car, his body lacking a natural equilibrium due to the handcuffs. Tommy follows behind them and Rayna opens the back door of the police cruiser, allowing Zaylee to place him inside the vehicle. After he enters and they slam the door, Rayna says, "Not bad for your first bust." Zaylee smiles, "Thanks."

Chapter 3: Drugs

Zaylee and Rayna stand near a body. It is sprawled across the floor with a large puddle of blood seeping into its host clothes. The right arm has been shot off and lays a meter from the body, the tendons ripped and strewn across the blood laden tiles. Close to the body's chest is a pump action shotgun, fittingly surrounded by bullet casings. Beyond the initial corpse, shotgun shells, assault rifle rounds, and 9mm rounds are dipped in the crimson dried blood. Yellow tape creates a border between the scene and the outside world. A slight breeze knocks it back and forth, letting those who are allowed to pass, that it is not an immutable border.

An ambulance is parked in front of the house. Two medical personnel walk up with their trauma bag to the scene. Zaylee's arms remain folded. She watches as one of the medical personnel walks towards them and walks over to meet him. His blue outfit has a pin tagged to it, defining him as an Emergency Medical Technician. It is made into an acronym, 'EMT', and the medical symbol of a snake is wrapped through the center, coalescing with the shield-like pin.

His large boots, along with his partners, make a distinct noise with each foot step, not dissimilar to Rayna's boots. The sound grows in decibel until he eventually finds himself standing behind the yellow tape. His partner stands behind him, looking at Zaylee. He pulls out an electronic nicotine dispenser and inhales deeply before puffing it out and sighing. On his shirt is a similar pin with one difference: this pin reads 'Paramedic' instead of 'EMT'. The young EMT stands extremely close to the yellow tape and stares at Zaylee.

"Are we allowed to come in?" he asks her. Zaylee looks at him, "No. Not yet." she says to him. Rayna comes closer to Zaylee, "He's kind of cute." Rayna whispers so that only she can hear. The EMT stares, with eyes fixated on them, his green iris flickers at her, alluring Rayna towards him, "What's your name?" Rayna inquires, forcing the question out. "Trey." he responds. They share a brief look before he looks back at Zaylee, "If we can't go in, we need to leave. There are other calls we can attend to."

Zaylee locks her black pupils with his green irises, "You cannot enter the scene. Declare them dead, as required, and you can leave." she says. He looks at the scene, noticing a few dead bodies. But, as he stares over near a wall, a look of befuddlement appears on his face, "I can't declare him dead." he says while pointing at the man leaning near the beige wall. "May I enter the scene?" he asks.

"No. Declare him dead from where you are." Zaylee informs him. He, and his partner, begin dissecting the scene, peering through the wreckage of what was most likely an all-out brawl between two rival gangs. Their eyes trace up and down. Immediately Trey's partner notices pink gunk on the wall and immediately utters "Yup, he's dead." He then jerks himself out of the scenario as quickly as possible, horrified that he just saw someone's brains on the wall. Trey watches as Zaylee and Rayna walk towards the body on the floor before leaving the scene.

Rayna ducks down and kneels on the ground. She stares at the gun and pushes some of the blood with her gloved finger, caking her hand. Upon noticing the consistency, she stands up and walks into the house. Quickly, Zaylee follows behind her and watches Rayna dissect the scene, staring around the kitchen. They both notice bags of white powder around the house. "Most manufacturers and distributors aren't stupid enough to do their own product." Rayna responds, while pushing aside some ladles that are hanging from the ceiling. She reaches the counter and moves a red circular bowl that is on the countertop. As she continues to look around, she notices a body lying face up. She lifts it up making the side of the body visible, its bullet holes clearly visible through the torn shirt.

"Maybe it was a dealer squabble." Zaylee adds. "Possible, but these were mostly goons fighting goons. Where is the other dealer?" Rayna ponders aloud over the dead body. His back is purple from the blood pooling down. "Dependent lividity." Rayna says succinctly. Zaylee looks over, noticing the body but, as she scans the room, she notices the head of another gang member several meters from its original placement. Flies buzz around its rotting flesh, a single yellow maggot crawls in his hair. "Decapitation and decomposition too. Gross." Rayna coughs out in between breaths, as she tries to avoid the rancid smell.

Zaylee pauses, "All we need is rigor mortis and incineration, then we've got all the definitive signs of death." Rayna shakes her head at the comment as Zaylee begins kneeling to get a better look

17

at the floor. A black metal gun lies thirty centimeters away from a criminal's hand, indicating it had slid out of his hands at some point during the commotion.

While she begins to assess the scene, trying to put the pieces together, Rayna peers into the trash can, opening the lid. Its horrid stench slowly seeps into the room. Zaylee looks at her, "We're not waste management, Rayna." She stands up and looks around the room. Air circulates from the trash can; Zaylee gets a big whiff of vinegar. "You smell that?" Rayna asks. Zaylee nods her head, "Yeah."

"That's heroin. Bad heroin." Rayna states. "Wasn't this a coke deal?" Zaylee ponders. "It was, but one of these guys was boosting H. We'll need to keep an eye out next time we bust some dealers. The cartel will only push H that smells like brown sugar. This must just be a junkie deal gone wrong." Rayna claims, closing the lid.

—

Zaylee and Rayna drive northbound on interstate 110. Zaylee can see concrete parts far out in the distance, to her east, broken and shambled, with a sign that is labeled 'Irradiated Zone'. The closer they get to interstate 10, the cleaner and more maintained the city looks. In front of them is a car broken and beaten. The hood is smashed in. Pieces of fiberglass cover the floor leading up to the vehicle. Inside is a woman, limp in posture. Her hand leans out of the vehicle with drips of blood coming down.

Wailing sounds come from the inside. A crying toddler sits in the back. The EMTs head towards the vehicle. A blonde EMT with green eyes heads straight for the woman in the driver's seat. He grabs her hand and follows her thumb down to find her radial pulse, proximal to the wrist. Upon finding it he grabs her finger. "Which finger am I holding ma'am?" She opens her eyes and looks at him. "Ring." she replies, somewhat surprised and with fluttering eyes that can barely stay up. "Correct. Now, can you move your index finger for me?" he asks, and when she opens her eyes, he shines a light in them. She pulls back but then she extends her index finger. The man looks at his partner, "Responds to verbal, GCS twelve, pulse is

18

forty-five and thready. Her pupils are not reactive to light, they are constricted. Possible opiates in her system." he says. His partner begins to write into his tablet.

Zaylee approaches the EMT, "Trey, right?" she asks. "Yes. But I'm busy." he replies pulling out an extrication device. As he works, Zaylee looks over her and says, "Push naltrexone. Twenty-five milligrams. Fifty if she doesn't respond."

The woman looks at her, angrily, "No, don't get rid of my high!" she shouts incoherently at Trey.

"Fifty milligrams. She's had it before." Zaylee declares. Trey looks at her, "How do you know that?" he asks. "I was an EMT. I need her sobered up so she can give me some information." she replies. "Yeah, but then I can't use morphine or fentanyl. The heroin opiates will block the receptors." he condescends, looking at Zaylee. She stares right back at him: "There are alternatives. Fentanyl reacts negatively with heroin, but Acetaminophen or Ibuprofen should work." Zaylee responds quickly.

They move her body slightly and attempt to slide a backboard behind her but it doesn't fit. They converse with each other as Zaylee increases her voice, "I will be coming aboard your ambulance. Given the situation, she might be a jumper." she says, looking at the woman still in pain. Zaylee counts on her fingers for a second before saying, "You'll need Rayna and I for the restraints. She'll start fighting once you push the drugs out of her system."

He shakes his head, "First time we'll actually have the appropriate number of people to restrain a patient." Lowering his voice, he mutters, "Seems like a waste of resources." he replies under his breath. He slides a black and green vest behind the patient; colored straps line up the vest. Both responders reach around and tighten the device down around her chest. Zaylee looks in the back of the vehicle and sees the toddler, "Rayna, grab a backboard from their rig." she commands.

She brings back a long yellow board. Trey and his partner transfer the patient in the driver's seat to a stretcher. "We need the jaws of life to cut this open." Zaylee says. "Typically, LA fire does that." Trey says. Rayna chuckles at both of them and walks towards the vehicle, crossing her non-mechanical arm over onto her mechanical one. She clicks a booster on her cybernetically modified

19

arm causing a hydraulic noise to purr from the device. She grabs an opening from the broken window and pulls herself up atop the vehicle. Her foot stands on the mangled door while her hands remain gripped to the top of the vehicle. She clicks the booster again; the purring gets significantly louder.

Rayna begins to pull the entire roof off. The puffs of air from the device in her arm propel out at a faster rate until, finally, the metal tears, almost entirely. She folds the top of the car over, like a quesadilla and shoves it down to be flat. "That good enough?" Rayna asks.

"Perfect." Trey says. The other responder looks at Rayna, "I didn't know they let Koreatown's cyber freaks on the force." he says. Taking offense, Rayna grits her teeth, "Watch your mouth. Or I'll throw you into the irradiated zone." Rayna says. He ignores her comment and hops into the back of the vehicle behind the toddler. They check her pulse, motor, sensory response, and capillary refill before strapping her seat to the board. After checking the numbers, they make sure everything is secure.

Now that her neck is secured for the maneuver, they pull her out and place the backboard on the secondary bench in the ambulance, locking it into place with her associated vest. They make sure she is strapped in properly as Zaylee hops into the vehicle, with Rayna right behind her.

After the responders give the go ahead, they all restrain the patient to the stretcher. Upon completion, Rayna hops out of the vehicle. Zaylee looks back and sees Rayna waiting, "You can follow in the patrol car." she says to her. "Affirmative." Rayna replies. She begins to walk towards her vehicle.

Trey's partner holds the addict's arm and pushes a needle in. She flinches as the needle digs in. A flash of blood appears on the capsule above it. "IV is in." he says, as he grabs a bag from the top cabinet. He begins the drip line and the naltrexone makes its way into her system.

Zaylee looks at the patient, "Can you answer some questions for me?" she asks. The patient looks at her, coming down from her high, and clearly agitated. "Fine." she responds. "Who is your supplier?" Zaylee asks. The woman coughs slightly, "My husband. He gets all the drugs; I don't know who from." she answers. "And

where is your husband?" The patient rolls her eyes, "At home."
Zaylee looks at Trey, "Do you have her identification card?" she
asks, causing him to say, "Here you go." She looks over and sees his
hand, the blue veins catching her eye. She grabs the card from his
hand, "Thanks." she says.

Trey looks at Zaylee, partially entranced by her picturesque
and uniquely colored eyes but mostly thralled by her intellect, "So,
you wanna grab something to eat after this?"

—

Someone flicks the blinds of a house as Zaylee dissects its
crumbling and decaying structure. It is a simple house sitting on the
corner. Their police cruiser sits outside, just beyond the cement, with
its tires gripping the asphalt. As the heat of the car envelops Zaylee,
she stares at the lawn. It is well maintained but a unique plant takes
up most of the landscape. The plant has a matte green center with a
yellow housing around it. Multiple large leaves skirt from each side
with the same pattern. Inside of the home remains quiet, although
the house looks like it has a story to tell, because a torn apart back
gate sits to the left of the home.

A lone car sits in the driveway but its light brown coloring
fails to glisten in the sunlight due to the deteriorated nature of it.
But, despite aesthetics, the symmetry remains; the van doors align
with its box-like shape.

The now acquainted partners, open their doors and exit the
cruiser. The blinds, in the front window, cease flickering and
immediately close. Zaylee places her boot on the curb but doesn't
step further; she waits while Rayna swings her body over the hood
of the vehicle and eventually finds herself standing side by side with
her partner.

"Well, there's one thing that never changes." Zaylee says,
Rayna looks at her, confused. Zaylee continues, "My dad had one of
those vans when I was little, an Astro van." Rayne reminisces and
says, "Yeah, Astro vans and trucks with large cages in the back to
haul scrap. That's the old school immigrant life." The imagery of the
trucks flashes and neurons connect for Zaylee, causing her to
remember another vehicle that stood out as culturally distinct.

"Then, you have those churches with their ten passenger

vans. Mormon vans we used to call them. Although some other churches, like Korean churches, used to have them too." Zaylee says, voicing her memories while stepping onto the grass, crushing its beautiful green nature. "Well, it's time to get to work. Rayna, swing around back. If you hear any commotion, come back to the front." Zaylee commands. Rayna nods her head.

Zaylee looks at the yard, the mostly green plants with a yellow edging to them trigger a memory for her and she finally recognizes what they are. Weary now, she grabs her remote and pushes a button, causing Tommy to exit from the back of their patrol car.

It hovers in the air above and Zaylee grabs the tablet from her belt, pressing the follow button on Tommy's controls. It begins to follow Rayna as she reaches the back gate.

The door's red coloring gushes down to the golden handle. Zaylee approaches, brushing a few of the plants out of the way. She presses the white button in its housing near the amber drywall. Instantly a ring is heard throughout the house, a chime of familiar, but annoying, nostalgia. Zaylee raises her hand and begins to pound on the front door, "Open up. Police." she commands. Ruffling sounds echo through the door but she can't make out where they moved to. Zaylee utters loudly, "We have a warrant. Do not make us break your door down."

She hears footsteps from inside, similar to when sweaty feet walk across a tiled floor, until, eventually, they reach the door and begin to unlock it. The chain hits the door with a thud. Suddenly, its handle spins and it's released from its closed position. Behind it is a middle-aged man with spiked but uncoalesced hair. His skin is darker, like Rayna's. Zaylee spots a kitchen to her left with talavera ceramic tiles lining the counter that matches the tiling on the floor that she heard his sweaty feet walking across.

The unique flower tiling brings a smile to Zaylee's face and reminds her of the many meals she had with her grandmother. The smell of beans and tortillas spirals in her thoughts, creating a placebo taste on her tongue.

She immediately shakes the thought and looks at the man in front of her, "I'm here to talk about your connections with dealers in the surrounding area." Zaylee says. He slowly tries to shut the door, but Zaylee places her hand in the way, laying it flat upon it. She uses force and pushes him out of the way. As she makes her way in, Rayna comes in through the sliding glass door in the back, holding a teenager by the shirt. Tommy follows her inside the house, his camera lens glaring red at the teenager. It watches as she places the teenager upon the couch, his shirt smoothing its wrinkles out as Rayna lets go. Tommy's crimson lens color fades back to its normal black and silver hue. "This your kid?" Rayna asks. "Yes, it is." he confirms. Leaning down to the boy's level, the father's face tightens with anger as he says, "¿Qué piensas, idiota?"

Rayna shakes her head, "That's no way to talk to your son." she says. She remains standing in front of the sliding door. Zaylee looks at the gentleman near the doorway, "Have a seat and we will continue talking." Zaylee commands. He walks over and sits near his son. A multi-colored blanket on the couch crumbles upon the impact. Slowly it takes the shape of his body as he lets gravity push him onto the couch. Zaylee stands in front of them, just beyond a glass table. Multiple pipes sit upon the table with drugs inside. The gentleman looks nervous and Zaylee bends over and tips one over.

"Weed?" Zaylee asks. "I have a medical condition." he invokes. "Don't they all." Rayna replies. Zaylee grits her teeth, "I don't care that you are doing drugs; what you are doing isn't illegal. What I care about is that you're circumventing California law by growing Tiger's Tail, which is legal to grow anywhere on your property without permits, and it produces THC. I remember, before weed was legal, smart people use to grow Tiger's Tail to produce THC. However, the act of selling and having massive quantities is illegal, without a license." Zaylee explains.

Rayna tilts her head, "You do know pharmaceutical companies have to make their money right?" Rayna coyly remarks, being as facetious as she can with her words.

Zaylee ignores the comment and adds, "I don't care about your drugs. What I care about is that you are circumventing taxation and I care that you have a child to take care of. Yes, we all know that you cannot overdose on weed, but you can still do harm while being intoxicated. And you should never be intoxicated when you have a child to take care of. And you should be paying your taxes so you aren't imprisoned." Zaylee claims. Rayna stares over at him, pondering deeply about how to give a heuristic perspective to him that he would understand.

"Withdrawals. Gum disease. Paranoia. Impairment of psychological development. Just to name a few." Rayna adds. "It doesn't kill. You can't die from it." he says defensively. Zaylee scoffs, "The withdrawals, paranoia, and lack of motor response, given certain dosages, could make it difficult to take care of a child. I'm not saying you can't, I'm just saying, for the best possible care, you shouldn't have drugs in your system. However, if you are competent enough to take care of your children, the second-hand smoke can stunt your children's psychological development. At least it isn't heroin like your wife though." He gives a grin, revealing his eroded teeth.

"Meth too, huh?" Zaylee asks. He immediately closes his mouth. They sit in silence for a minute before he justifies himself, "I do drugs to stunt my brain because I hate my intellect. And because she keeps stealing my stuff!" The emotion causes him to get out of his seat. Zaylee gives him a hard gaze and he sits back down. Rayna mocks him, "Yeah, I'm sure that's the reason." The derisive comment causes him to face Rayna directly, "I use it to stay awake so, when my wife falls asleep, I can steal my stuff back." he explains.

Zaylee chuckles, "Then, once she wakes up and you're coming down off your high, she steals it back?" Zaylee asks, smugly. He places his finger upon his chin. The grime on his finger smears and smudges onto his cheek. Boredom washes over Zaylee's face and she says, "Thankfully, we are not here for your drug usage. We only scolded you so that, hopefully, you'll stop and take better care of your son." Letting the thought linger for a few seconds, Zaylee reaches for something in her bag, giving Rayna the opportunity to top off Zaylee's comment by saying, "Drug charges are petty. We should be helping addicts get better, not punishing them." Still, waiting for Zaylee to open up her application on her tablet, Rayna places her leg onto the table in front of them. She plants her elbow on top of her knee and uses her hand to support her head from the bottom of her chin.

Before Zaylee gets the chance to show him the details on her tablet, Rayna snarkily utters, "There was a multi-homicide situation at a manufacturers house. None of the dealers are using their own product but we found traces of heroin in a trash can. We came here because we ran a TC with your wife. She was loaded up on heroin, with one of your children in the back." He tears a bit and says, "I know."

Zaylee places the tablet in her lap and puts her hand on his lap to comfort him before saying, "We will see what we can do about the charges on her and the possible charges we could write against you." she takes her hand off, just as he begins to get ecstatic at the notion, and says, "But only if you give us information regarding your supplier." Zaylee demands. The man looks hesitant and unwilling to divulge information; he stares down at the floor, then back up at Zaylee, "Cops are allowed to lie to get what they need. I must know, are you lying to me?" he queries frantically. He continues staring at her, nervously. They look at him, partially understanding what he is saying, but neglect replying.

"I need to know. Statistics run through my head. Adderall gets my brain going. Unlike the meth, I can maintain concentration with it. I know that when I was younger, blacks got more attention, even though they were a lesser portion of the population. They we less than ten percent of the population of California, while we" he points at Rayna and Zaylee, "the Mexicans and Latin, were pushing forty percent but not once did I hear them complain that there was like no Mexicans in Hollywood films. They only cared about putting blacks and Asians and women in film, while we got ignored."

Both Rayna and Zaylee nod, intently perusing his pontification with reservations in mind. His words again pour out of his corroded teeth and into their ears, "Our suffering against the police got ignored too, while the African race with less people got all the attention in all forms of media. American democracy, it's for everyone, but it's not equal. But guess who took over L.A and California? Who became that majority? That's right, us. But now that I'm a majority, still ain't nobody care what you do to me. So, I ask you again, what are you going to do to me?" he asks with a look of pain singeing his face.

He begins stumbling over his words, "Cause what you do to me, it won't be televised, it'll be ignored. No one cares cause I'm just the majority now you know, unless it's televised. And because I'm not white, black, or new wave feminist, no one cares 'bout me. The

Asians, Latinos, Hispanics, and us, we get ignored. What's a democracy when your larger populations are ignored? It's a curse and you're the wielder of the punishment." he says, pausing. "It will never be televised. So, do what you will, because you can get away with punishing me, without consequence." he condescends, a tear starting to form.

Zaylee stomps once to ease his qualms, and his ears perk up, "We are not like the rest. No group is superior to another. No group should ever be ignored. It's about stopping anyone who commits a crime and helping those that are wronged. We are the justice in a world of the injustice." Zaylee answers.

Rayna leans over, pressing on her elbow onto her knee, "Who cares who statistically attacks which race more than another? Who even cares about race? Losers. Losers with no control over their life argue all day every day over who cops hurt more or who is more oppressed. Turns out, we're all gimokes for not realizing that we're all oppressed by the ones who are feeding us this. So yeah, I am similar to you, in race, but who is to say my culture is not different? Could I not be from a lineage in another part of Central America or even South America? You generalize Americans, yet we are the only true Americans. The ones who care about freedom, religion, and nothing else." she states poignantly.

Riding off her oxytocin rush, she continues talking, "This nation stole our name. It did the same to the Indians. But what good does complaining do? We live and we die. We are born here now, and we still live off the land. No matter the race, we are born American's." Rayna says, pulling her hand off her knee.

Still angered and full of vigor, Rayna continues, "Once you start pointing out race and congenital factors, you become just as racist as them. There will be another cruel tyrant, there always will be. Sometimes they are of our race, sometimes they aren't. The point is that people are evil, and always will be. Your fixation on congenital factors merely proves your ignorance." Rayna retorts. His expression turns, expressing an epiphany, but also dejection and disorientation. Zaylee looks at her, a little scared of her passion, "Where did that come from?" she asks.

"I've been watching too many online vids lately from this girl who claims to be a prophet of God. I can't help it." Rayna replies.

"Alright." Zaylee responds. He stares at his hands with a wide smile on his face, then places them down to his side. His smile turns to a slight frown when he makes eye contact with Zaylee. "So, are you lying to me?" he genuinely asks.

"No." Zaylee succinctly states. In unison, Rayna corroborates her view by adding, "We are officers of the people and not the law. If the law helps the people, then we apply it as necessary. But we're not about enforcing more injustice." The druggie turns his head, out of shame. Noticing his behavior, Zaylee seeks to alleviate his pain, "Although I disagree with your habits and the negative impact they have on your children, we will see what can be done to help your situation, I can promise you that, but only if you help us." Zaylee confirms.

"Swear on it. Swear yourself to secrecy." he demands fretfully. "I swear." they resound together.

Chapter 4: Nodus Tollens

There stands in the center of a backyard, multiple smashed clocks. Their guts, springs and plastic, bathe the floor. In between their guts is a battered chair. Upon that chair is a passed-out female, strapped in. Saliva pours down her chin, dripping onto the floor. Droplets splash on the concrete beneath her. Around the yard, bottles and red cups mix with the dirt blending together to create a party flavored smoothie, with leaves as the whipped cream topping; everything blends together without distinguishable parts from each other within the landscape. A breeze blows through the yard, pushing their police drone, Tommy, a bit. Despite the movement, its lights continue to circle blue and red, throwing its colors onto the walls behind them, unabated by the wind that is pushing it around.

Another person lays face down in the dirt near an empty bottle of vodka and multiple red plastic cups. Blood seeps from his side, wetting his red shirt and mixing with the dirt creating a type of organic red clay. A small jagged pocket knife sits near his torso. Its blade covered in scattered shades of blood. Most of it has dried and is crimson in color but some of it remains bright. More bodies sit around the yard in various mangled and limp states. Their bodies sit as if they had fallen from the sky. One lays atop a large DJ speaker with dual thirty-eight-centimeter woofers and a drain hole shaped horn for the higher frequencies.

Zaylee and Rayna stand near the edge of the cement, taking each factor of the scenario into account. Rayna nudges Zaylee with her elbow, "What in the world happened here?" she asks. There's no reply. Still looking over the scene, Rayna mutters, "I don't even know where to begin."

With some effort, Zaylee pushes forward, causing some dirt to circulate as her cowboy boot steps forward. She looks over the scene and puts a black glove on her left hand before leaning down and picking up an empty beer bottle. She tilts her head over and catches Rayna's eyes, "Didn't you go to college?" Zaylee asks. "Yeah but I didn't go to Cal State Stabby Stabby." Rayna claims. Zaylee leaves silence in the rigid and alcohol spritzed sky. Rayna fills the void with a succinct conclusion: "SB was too far of a drive."

When the last syllable of drive ceases to be audible, the

female strapped to her chair begins to mumble. Zaylee points at her, letting Rayna know to approach, before walking over to her.

Rayna places her left hand on the girl and begins to shake her. The motion causes her head to bob back and forth. Saliva launches in every direction until she gains control of her neck, stiffening her body and regaining control of her body. Zaylee tells her Rayna to stop with a quick jolt of her hand and says, "Good. You're awake." Each eye struggles to open as the muted sound of Zaylee's voice enters her ear. Eventually she makes full eye contact with Zaylee, "Huh." she mumbles incoherently.

With a quick shove, Zaylee pushes her back into the chair. Her arms fling back to fight her, but Zaylee had already stepped back. Tommy continues to record the entire situation, but now turns on its siren; the high-pitched wail pierces the sky.

"What do you want?" she asks incoherently. "I want you to tell me what happened here." Zaylee asks. Rayna pulls another chair next to her and sits across from her. Hydraulic pressure noise reverberates from her arms to the woman in the chair. The girl, upon noticing she is strapped in, perks up and begins to pull at the plastic fasteners. "Get me out of this and I'll explain." she commands Zaylee. "It'd be easier to take you to jail in your chair hun." Rayna states.

"Fine." she replies. After tilting her head back, she explains, "We were having a party okay. The owner of the house" she pauses and jerks her eyes to someone across the yard before she vomits, "That would-be Charly, over there." Zaylee and Rayna look at him, then back at her, causing Zaylee to wipe away some of the dribble coming out of the strapped woman's mouth with her gloved hand.

She looks at one of the guys and declares, "He's a homie with the blacks. That guy over there" she says while pointing her eyes at the stab victim on the floor, "He's a homie with the Mexicans. They have beef. He stepped on the wrong turf and got stabbed." she claims. Rayna nods her head believing the story.

"What are the name of their gangs?" Zaylee asks, not breaking eye contact with her. "Look I don't know. All I know is his street name is Taco." she states. Zaylee holds back her laughter, and Rayna turns her head and mutters, "At least it's better than Bubba." Rayna says while looking off in the distance. Zaylee looks over at her, "I know, right? What happened to all the good gangster names; Jack Diamond, Machine Gun Kelly, Ronnie Biggs, Pretty Boy Floyd, you know? Now they name themselves Guzman and it just sounds like Guzzleman. Or juicy this or that and all I can think about is the gum." Zaylee says to Rayna.

Amused by the discussion, Rayna tries to be comical, "Now, we got Taco over here and I bet his homies, Frijoles and Carne Asade, are building up steam back at the crib loading up their AK's for 'war'. Cause you know you can't step to the homie, Taco. You might get e.coli." Rayna says. Zaylee audibly laughs from the comment. The woman spits the rest of her vomit onto the floor, the bright red blood clearly visible in the emesis, "This isn't a joke."

"Sorry, we got carried away. It was just funny that his name is Taco." Zaylee says. "It's more common than you might think." the party girl illuminates. Rayna attempts to lighten the mood, "Hey, I grew up in California. We're all Mexican here. Well Zaylee's only a quarter but it still counts." Rayna claims. The noise of glass breaking comes from inside the house. Bodies shuffle through the house. Both officers grab their weapons and point them towards the house. Tommy points at the house similarly to the officers, its siren still blaring. Its weapon lowers down out of its housing; the small gatling minigun shaped weapon sends its message of warning to the individuals in the house.

"Come out with your hands in the air!" Zaylee yells. There is no response. A loud explosion comes from the house; sharp winds pass by Zaylee. She immediately pulls down on the trigger of her weapon. Fire ejects near the barrels end but it is nearly imperceivable to the eye, the recoil does buckle through Zaylee's arm though. Bullets fly into the building from all directions as the rotation noise from Tommy grows louder and louder.

There is a slight lull in noise as the gunfire ceases for a few seconds. Only the sound of Tommy's siren continues. Rayna looks at Zaylee, "Shouldn't we call for backup?" she asks. "I'll page it in." Zaylee states, clicking a button her radio and requesting backup. Rayna looks over and says, "I doubt anyone will come, they're always busy running other calls. But it's worth a shot."

Gun shots come from the house, so Tommy immediately begins to start up its gatling weapon again. Zaylee stares into the window and begins licking off shots at shadows in the house. The screen door swings wide open and slams into the wall beside it. A large male exits the door aggressively, nearly tearing the door off as he exits. The gang member gets a grip on the situation quickly and points his weapon out at Zaylee. Rayna spins around Zaylee, who is firing through the window and does not notice the large man pointing his pistol at her. After turning around, Rayna fires two shots into his head. Blood spurts onto the screen door. His large body slams onto the floor with a loud thud.

Zaylee drops her magazine out, letting it fall to the ground. It jostles diagonally until it sits laterally on the floor. She grabs a metal magazine from her pocket and slides it into her gun with one fast jerk. A shadow splays across the room inside the window. Zaylee notices that another assailant is standing behind a wall. She hastily fires two rounds into the upper portion of the wall. They burst through the drywall, leaving smoldering pieces of plaster on the ground.

His body slides down the wall, using the blood to ease his descent. A gaping cavity remains in his skull, pouring blood out of it, similar to pouring wine out of a bottle. The second bullet had missed and had crashed into silverware along the kitchen, creating a domino effect. The ruckus from within begins to subside; the pots eventually settle on the kitchen floor. Zaylee makes her way in, keeping a defense position as she moves; she peers around a corner, brushing her cheek against the drywall. She quickly tilts around the corner and flashes her gun down the hall. But there is no enemy to attack; only dead bodies lay in the hall.

She pulls out her tablet and gives a command to Tommy. It begins to search through the entire house, making sure it is secure. Tommy circles around with its sirens and lights off. It comes back and a report appears on the tablet. 'No hostiles detected' it reads. She places the tablet back into her pouch and begins to walk out of the house and back outside. Rayna is making her rounds along the sides of the house. She fires two shots in quick succession.

Zaylee quickly runs over to where the shots came from and points her gun. As the picture comes into view, she sees Rayna holding a female up against the wall, her hand gripping her throat and her elbow pressed against her chest right between her breasts.

31

Rayna grits her teeth and pulls the female off the wall, holding her free form in the air. Her legs dangle and kick violently as Rayna tightens her grip. She begins to squirm rapidly, slipping ever so slightly out of Rayna's hands. Readjusting, Rayna quickly slams her into the wall, breaking off parts of the drywall and leaving an indent in the wall the size of her head that gives a decent view of the next room. Slowly, as Rayna's grip tightens on her neck, she stops squirming and drops her weapon. Free of all muscle control, the woman becomes limp. Rayna, noticing this, throws her down and into the grass of the front yard. A large red mark remains on her throat in the shape of a thumb and a hand grip.

"Well, that was fun." Rayna cheerfully states. Zaylee sighs in relief, "You left her alive, correct?" she asks with Tommy hovering up above behind her. "Of course. I try my best not to end anyone's life." Rayna states. She points to a spot on her arm where green buttons are flashing, "These tell me if their heart is still beating by monitoring the heartbeat as I hold them tight, provided an artery is nearby. Since I was holding her neck, the jugular was right there." she claims, pressing a button on her arm. The green buttons stop flashing on the LED screen and the words 'no signal' appear in its place. "We can leave her for now. Let's get back to business." Zaylee says. They walk back around the corner. The girl in the chair has fallen over, but remains alive and uninjured.

Zaylee looks at the woman and walks slowly towards her. As the dust settles from her movement, she reaches down and picks her chair up. With a clock in Zaylee's hand, she looks at the party girl, "Care to explain all these clocks, I'm quite curious." Zaylee asks. Rayna looks at her as Tommy gets closer to better record her answer, "Really. That's what you're interested in?" she asks sarcastically, staring at Tommy and then back at Zaylee. Noticing her focus is back, Zaylee reiterates, "I want to know. We run these gang calls all the time. When was the last time you saw a backyard like this?" Zaylee asks. Rayna shrugs in agreement. The girl looks at her, making eye contact.

"You really want to know the truth?" she asks. Rayna scoffs, "Duh. Why would someone ask a question and then not want to know the answer?" Rayna says rudely. "Pregnancy?" Zaylee asks. "Not now Zaylee." she replies quickly. Rayna looks at the girl and grabs her chair, gripping the wood and denting it, "Answer the question." Rayna demands. "Fine. But just know that I am telling you the truth." she claims.

"Time travel is a possibility. A new boss found scribbles of an old cartel boss, Fuego, regarding worldwide eugenics or something and how Fuego wanted to go back in time to stop bad things from happening." the woman begins to explain. Rayna becomes visibly irritated by the comment, and remarks, "Fuego is gone. And so is his reign of terror." The woman chuckles, "Think what you want." Rayna turns her head, "No, he's dead. They confirmed that it was his body."

The girl laughs, "That body had no cybernetic modifications. Fuego was more machine than man."

"ENOUGH!" Zaylee screams, "What is this about eugenics?" Zaylee interjects. "Apparently the boss said Fuego was interested in time travel because Hitler was sent back in time to kill all the Jews before they took over the world. But it didn't work out right. She went through multiple different time frames. Egyptian, Roman, the Middle Ages, and so on, but she didn't understand what was happening. Finally, though, she made it to the era she was supposed to, and she was a guy there, like her body changed into a dude. And, so, he rose to power. Once there, he gave Germany new tools, techniques, and technology while making himself a dictator, to destroy the Jews before they ever got into power." she explains. Zaylee looks at Rayna. She looks at the woman.

"And where do you fall into all this?" Rayna asks. "I was supposed to be sent back in time to end the other cartels, making our Sinaloa Cartel the sole provider for the entire lower portion of the states." she responds. Rayna scoffs. Zaylee remains displeased, "Cuff this liar. And get her some help for her drug addiction." Zaylee commands, pointing at her. The woman looks at Rayna, "I'm telling you the truth!" she shouts.

"Yeah, and I make ten million a year posting gaming vids online with repetitive music while I show the world my titties. This police thing is just my side job." Rayna says while untying her from the chair. She grabs some metal cuffs and slaps them onto her hands. The metal circle encloses around her wrists. It clicks a few, before tightening down on her wrists. While watching Rayna cuff her,

Zaylee asks, "How do your hands feel?" Rayna stops tightening but holds her hands together. "It's a little tight." she replies. "Do it again until she's comfortable but can't escape." Zaylee commands. "Ugh." Rayna groans, unlocking the cuffs.

Rayna begrudgingly slaps the cuffs back on and asks Zaylee, "Aren't we supposed to be helping bust a dealer anyway?" As Rayna tightens the cuffs, Zaylee replies, "After we book her and get some food we will continue." Rayna picks the girl up and pulls her towards Zaylee, causing the girl's feet to drag. Due to the littered yard, the girl's feet accumulate beer cans and other assorted trash.

Zaylee turns around and walks out of the yard, Rayna follows behind her with the girl in cuffs. Through the movement, trash is moved around the yard by the girl's feet. They approach the police car, Tommy's propellers slow and he drops into his compartment in the trunk, and Rayna ducks the girl down and into the vehicle. Zaylee rubs the scar on her neck and Rayna notices as she slams the door shut and they stand outside of the vehicle.

Rayna asks, "So, what's up with that scar on your neck?" Zaylee removes her hand from her neck and replies, "It happened back when I was in the military. They said that I had an injury to my occipital lobe and that they fixed it. But I was under for the operation so I don't remember everything that happened. I do know that I have this lump in the back of my head now and this scar." Rayna shakes her head, "I wonder what they did to you. I bet they didn't tell you the truth."

Zaylee chuckles a bit, "You and your conspiracy theories about the government Rayna. Unlike you, I trust doctors, government or not, because of their Hippocratic oath." She pauses, and lets some silence breathe through the conversation, "I don't think they did anything to me. They fixed me up and got me operational again. If it wasn't for them, I never would have led the blue glass armada." As the last word exits, reinforcement police arrive on the scene in army fashion on the lawn. They exit their vehicles and approach the house.

Captain Jessica walks towards Zaylee. "What happened here?" she asks. "We apprehended a gang member, her associates fired upon us. We returned fire until the suspects were terminated." Zaylee asserts concisely. Jessica walks to their squad vehicle and peers in. Her partner stands nearby and scans the girl. "She is a member of the Sinaloa Cartel." her partner discloses. Jessica picks her head back up and looks at Zaylee.

"Let her go." Jessica demands. "What?" Zaylee responds, confused. "The Mayor and Police Chief have said all Sinaloa Cartel are to go free." Jessica replies. Rayna looks over and nudges Zaylee, "This is Los Angeles. They accept bribes and the Mexicans aren't stupid enough to care only for money cause they know power is where it's at." she whispers. "Are you kidding me?" Zaylee queries angrily, getting into Jessica's face. Her partner shoves Zaylee away, "Back away officer." she commands. "And who are you?" Zaylee queries.

"Dekima, a Lieutenant, and your superior officer." she answers. Jessica gets in between them and sighs, "Look Zaylee, I don't like it as much as you do. But if you want to keep your job, you will let her go. If the Mayor finds out you have a gang member in custody, he will lose his bribes, and you will lose your job." Jessica replies. Zaylee locks eyes with Jessica, creating a tense situation. "Go get some dinner." Jessica replies as she hands Zaylee a fifty-dollar bill. "It's on me." Jessica continues, as Zaylee hands the fifty dollars back.

"I will not accept bribe money." Zaylee replies as Rayna interjects and yanks the fifty-dollar bill from Jessica. "Fine, but you still have to let her go." Jessica declares.

Rayna opens the door and the criminal exits the vehicle. She turns around, showing her cuffs to Rayna, with a wide smile on her face. Begrudgingly, Rayna pulls out a key and unlocks the cuffs.

The criminal walks away, down the street, with a huge grin still on her face. Zaylee opens the driver door and enters. Seconds later, Rayna follows suit, and now they are both sitting in the vehicle. Zaylee turns on the car, "Really Rayna?" Zaylee inquires. "It's L.A. This has been going on for decades. Killer Crips, Los Zetas, all of them paid off public officials. Now it's the Sinaloa Cartel and some Columbian cartel but they pay them off just the same." Rayna replies. "Whatever." Zaylee says, pulling out her phone. She pulls out her phone and scrolls until she finds Trey's contact.

The phone dials and Trey answers, "Hey". Zaylee quickly

asks, "Hey, do you want to get dinner?" There is a pause, allowing Zaylee to lower the volume so Rayna can't hear Trey's reply. "Okay, so, Out-n-in?" Zaylee asks the phone. There is another pause. "I'll see you soon then." Zaylee says, closing her phone. "He's going to meet us there." She grips the steering wheel tightly, the leather touching her fingers.

They continue driving down the street until they see an Out-n-in. Palm trees stand outside, basking in the hot sun. They pull into the parking lot and Zaylee pushes onto the brakes until the vehicle comes to a complete stop. She puts it into park and stops the vehicle. They exit their car and walk through the parking lot, eventually entering the Out-n-in. They see Trey already sitting by himself at a table with white bench seats laced with red designs. In the center is an umbrella, where the top follows an alternating pattern of white and red. They approach and sit next to him.

Zaylee sits beside Trey and Rayna sits on the opposite side. A robot rolls towards them and takes their order. The robot rolls away towards the kitchen, eventually coming back with several burgers and orders of fries. It slides the red trays in front of them. The smell of thousand island dressing hits their noses and they dig into their food. The French fries have a slice of cheese melted on top of them with thousand island dressing poured around it. Their burgers are filled with lettuce, tomato, and onions. Each bite drips the sauce down on the red tray below.

They finish eating and their red trays sit on the marble with scattered food upon them. Their plastic utensils sideways along the ceramic dishes. Rayna stares over at Zaylee, "Those gangsters are all the same. They either try to lie their way out or gun you down. Usually both." Rayna explains. She twiddles with a fry in one hand before continuing, "It's the way of the world. Manipulation and force are tactics of the weak trying to get the upper hand. People like gangsters get away with so much crime so they think they can get away with more. So, they'll do heinous things, and when they get caught, they'll just use the rich's flaw of greed to get away with it. They forget that the only thing that matters in this life is helping others and loving God. Power and money are worthless." Rayna explains.

The robot rolls towards them, using the inductive flooring

that powers it to guide along. It fails to notice Zaylee and Trey holding hands. "Pay when you are ready" it says autonomously, dropping a receipt gripped to plastic on the tabletop. It turns and rolls away as Trey smiles at Zaylee. His eyes shining through her, melting her heart like butter. He pulls out his wallet and drops a twenty-dollar bill on the table. The pressure from his fingers thins it out over the plastic housing. Rayna drops a fifty on top of his twenty and slides off the cushion saying, "Thank the govt for the meal, can't let their corruption go to waste". They all follow suit until they are all standing. As if told to act in synchrony, they walk out of the diner, swinging the door as they exit, talking and enjoying each other's company the entire time.

As they get closer to the parking lot, Rayna leads the way back to the police cruiser. Each foot step brings them closer, echoing their footsteps. Trey's steel toe boots click with each step on the floor, almost in synchrony with Zaylee's cowboy boots.

A loud whine comes from an alley near them. Trey and Zaylee's ears perk in the direction of the cries. They look at each other, slightly perplexed at the situation. They begin to walk down the alley. Allowing the high pitch whine to get louder, they approach the unknown source and the whine apexes as they get closer, giving them a direction to head in.

Rayna catches up to them. "What are you two doing?" Rayna coyly remarks. "Sh!" Trey says quickly pressing a finger on his mouth to signify quiet. The whine echoes even louder through the grim alley. Trey, pinpointing the noise, opens a nearby dumpster. The piercing scream seems to slam the dumpster handle wide open without Trey's help, as if the noise itself was helping

Trey open it. Peering over the side he notices a baby, squirming in the rubbish. Its face, dirty; its clothes, torn.

Zaylee peeks over near Trey's head and looks in. As she does, Trey extends his arms and grabs the child amid the black bags of garbage. He pulls the baby close; the stench pierces Zaylee's nose, but Trey pays no notice the smell. Eager to help the child, he places its head on his shoulder without a second thought. The cries continue to become more and more quiet as he begins to bend his knees and sway back and forth.

"How could someone do that to their baby boy?" Rayna

37

states with fervor. Trey rocks the baby back and forth, cooing, before he succinctly says, "It happens more often than you think." Zaylee moves her hand in between the baby's hair, soothing the young boy. He begins to fall asleep on Trey's shoulder.

Now that the baby is sleeping, Trey explains, "Humans, whether you choose to accept it or not, are lazy, evil, and cruel." Trey proclaims. "I have faith that they can change." Zaylee attests.

"Babe, monkeys, birds, and penguins can all take care of their young. Humans refuse to because they want to maintain a first world lifestyle with all the assets and comforts that come with it." he declares. Zaylee remains quiet, staring at the brick wall behind them. She leans on the green dumpster and peers in before reaching around and closing the lid, but the rancid smell remains.

Trey utters fervently, "They won't even get pregnant because culture has them believing in a certain type of beauty. So, they get modifications, surgeries, and wear all kinds of makeup, making others feel ugly for being poor or having bad genetics. And, when they get pregnant, if they can't afford, an abortion, they dump the child out." Zaylee scoffs, but before she can comment, Trey continues, "You see, even if they overcome the falsehood of culture that has them falsely define beauty, having a child is a burden to them and they claim they aren't ready or capable, but even animals can take care of their young. They are giving an excuse so they don't have to take care of the child. Whatever excuse that might be so that they can give into the mutilated culture that the rich have thrust upon us." Trey explains. "People are the problem with this planet, babe. They care more for objects and culturally accepted beauty than life. It's pathetic." Trey elucidates. Zaylee looks at him with a question on her face.

The stench of the alley protrudes into their nasal cavities. Zaylee tries to keep her face straight but the fumes bounce around, almost playing with her tastebuds, causing her to hold back some vomit. Trey, however, does not look perturbed, and, to cease the questioning that he knows is coming, he continues, "Typically, we find at least two babies a month, just abandoned. Not even at a hospital, fire station, or police station. No, they just dump them wherever. Not that abandoning your child at one of those places has any properties of being okay. Only those who have been raped, are vegetables, or are dead can't take care of a kid. Only they have a legitimate excuse for abandoning their child at a public service center." Trey says, pausing.

"If animals can take care of children, without our level of thinking, then these humans truly are just lazy and selfish. That is what happens when you don't have God's moral compass guiding you." he finishes.

"I will prove you wrong Trey, people can be good without God." Zaylee repudiates aloud. Then she lowers her voice slightly and mutters, "But I love your passion; you truly challenge me." Rayna leans in, "Rawr, cougar time." she says loud enough for Trey to hear.

Zaylee shoots her a look and Rayna asks, "Is this some Freudian Electra complex? I mean, he's an EMT like your dad." Trey smiles for a second while looking at the baby, not paying attention to their conversation. Zaylee sternly looks back at Rayna, "It's not some complex but it could be love. All I know is Trey challenges me to think differently. If he stops though, I'll drop him like that." she declares, snapping her fingers. Trey smirks and continues to coddle the baby.

Rayna hears the baby's cry as it pierces her ear. The noise echoes through the alley as the baby holds the cry for an extended period, curling its lip as it finishes its long cry. After the sound fades, Rayna perks up, "You know, in a way I never thought about until now, people who abandon their baby are saying that their ancestors are better them. Think about all those people that grew up without running water and were just hunters and gatherers. They took care of their young in a hostile environment with very few tools. It really says something about the state of the world's culture when you claim you can't afford a baby. You have to be quite a selfish individual, or you're just so ignorant that you'll let others think for you. Not sure what's worse." she echoes through the alley.

Trey loosens his lip as he does some baby talk and then replies, "You know, you're right about that. The selfishness of this world has gotten extreme. There were times during world wars where people were having six to ten kids." Zaylee nods, "Yes, well, as fun as this philosophical quandary has been, we should take this baby to the hospital. I don't think this alley is the best place for a baby." Trey nods in agreement as the baby boy wraps his fingers around Trey's thumb.

Chapter 5: The Chemist

Los Angeles' skyscrapers shine in the sunlight, creating a picturesque imagery in the smoggy sky. Zaylee and Rayna stand outside a rundown cruiser. Its paint flakes onto the floor below. The bumpers rust is wildly apparent and crumbling onto the floor. Her cowboy boot kicks on the back of the rusted bumper causing orange dust to cover the ground. Her boot slides along the vehicle, grinding into the rust. Rayna twists her left arm to the side; the hydraulics begin to squeak out air. She grabs her arm and clicks along her forearm. The hydraulics twist, making a pleasing noise to Rayna's ears.

Zaylee looks over at Rayna and asks, "Why don't you sell your hydraulic technology and make a profit off it?" Rayna sighs, "This life is not about money. It is as Christ said, it is easier for a camel to go through the eye of a needle than for a rich man to enter heaven." Rayna remarks. After looking at the device in her arm, Zaylee mutters, "Well, your technology could help people too."

Rayna mulls the thought over in her head as she runs her fingers along the cold metal device, then looks down at some of the tubing connected to it and answers, "Hun, this technology is dangerous in the wrong hands. I use it to send the message I want to send, not to let rich folks become richer by profiting off my success."

Their conversation ends abruptly as a police vehicle roars down the street. Rubber burns under its rims. The sirens scream, making other drivers aware of its presence. Nearby vehicles slide to the side of the road. The curb brushes against their tires. Sirens continue to ring in their ears as it rushes down the road. One block, two blocks, then three. The noise continues in their ears before fading out. Another police car blazes down the road, then another. Three police cars cover the road together, following in formation.

Swat vehicles rush down the street behind the police cruisers. Their big black metal exterior edges forward, pulling downward from the engines power. Rayna neglects her hydraulics and begins to stare at the vehicles rushing down the road, "They are finally going to apprehend him." Rayna says with a pause. "The last supplier." Rayna utters pithily.

"There is never a last supplier." Zaylee claims. The hydraulics cease their noise, its connected hand presses on the cruiser, imprinting itself on the hood. Rayna's eyes look at Zaylee, imbued with an aura of questions ready to be relayed, and her arm firmly planted on the hood. Zaylee quickly realizes her stare. "It happened before, decades ago. History will repeat itself, so long as the factors remain available. Chemists and growers who run and supply pharmacies end up becoming drug dealers. They make more money." Zaylee explains. Rayna sighs, "Ah."

Zaylee begins rumbling, "It's an effortless way to make money. They started it with medicinal marijuana. Everyone had a card, yet dealers could easily make a hundred thousand a year selling privately. There are no taxes and no middle person. The cash they make is the cash they keep. It was ridiculous because anyone could acquire a card, for something as stupid as a headache. Or they'd roll down to Venice and pick one up for cheap. But now that basically every drug is legal, they will always continue to sell outside the market. Because some people are greedy. They want a bigger slice of the pie and they don't want to deal with the government."

Rayna pitters through her words and adds, "That and they don't have to talk about their addictions and stop their habits. They can just take dope till they croak. No rights revoked, no kids taken away, they just get high." Rayna says while twisting her wrist around. Buttons beep along her arm. A bright green LED lightens up hairs around them; the dark hair on her forearm buckles with the light. Zaylee scoffs, "Ridiculous world. A paradigm never changing. We'll help it change. One person at a time." she adds. Her head tilts up while her body adjusts to show confidence. A smile shoots across Rayna's face as she watches this happen.

Their radio begins to blare. "Unit 451, we have a 415 at Loyola High School." a female voice proclaims through the scuffed-up radio. Rayna twists her hydraulics, "Time to get to work." Rayna says as she finishes tightening her hydraulic arm, pointing it upwards towards a puffy cumulus cloud in the sky as she turns towards the vehicle. The depreciated police station sits in the background as they enter their vehicle; the worn-down, once beautiful, panes of glass on the building are tarnished with spray painted gang logos. Zaylee turns on the car and stares at the vandalized trash cans in front of them, trash spewing out of them. They pull from the lot, watching cars turn in and out of the lot across the street. She spots a sandwich place; her stomach replies with a growl.

She turns right onto the street, ignoring her stomach. Light redirects from the glossy black pavement and into all four of their eyes. Simultaneously they pull down their visors to create a border between them and the sun. Its rays splash onto their visors, creating the desired effect, but some of the light still makes it way through. Unabated by the distraction, they continue down the street. It bustles with activity; people line the streets, pushing each other. Some stop when they see their vehicle, out of fear. But they have little time to analyze the situation.

Street sign after street passes them by. A big sign, labeled 'Venice' in white with a blue background, swings side to side. A red light shines barely slipping through the sun's intense rays.

The light turns green. Zaylee continues forward, turning right onto Venice. They pass multiple brick walls on their right, similarly splattered with graffiti. Barred up companies sit on both sides, just beyond the brick. As they head further down, the buildings continue but the brick wall ceases. Chain link fences now sit on every side, guarding companies and their property. They continue until they see a gated fence on the right. A large football field sits just beyond the fence. Even further is a three-story gymnasium, but it has been ravaged by age and graffiti, much as the rest of the neighborhood. Zaylee cringes at the site, "And to think I went to this High School." Zaylee articulates with disgust before following up with, "My dad thought it would be such a great idea since he went there and they had finally opened it up to girls."

Rayna jovially runs her fingers along the cold metal of her covered up arm, "It was only a matter of time before the kids and their cans tagged it up. Just like their bodies. Holes and paint. It's what they love. It's cultural. Don't hate it because you didn't grow up with it." Rayna replies. Suddenly they reach a beautifully designed building. Its walls are almost orchestral and are pleasing to the eye; the Victorian style of the structure is beautiful to their eyes. Zaylee suspires in relief, "This is what I remember. It was like Princeton in

43

the ghetto." Zaylee states. Rayna also peaks up and similarly gasps in admiration, "It was a college. St. Vincent's, I think." Rayna attests. Continuing her sidetracked discussion, Zaylee says, "Yes, and it's the oldest school I know of in SoCal."

A car skids out of the parking lot and speeds down the street. Zaylee flips a toggle switch. Its metal lodges itself in the 'on' position. The siren's blare pierces their ears. The engine roars, demanding its wheels spin faster and faster. It propels forward, picking up speed as each ounce of gas launches through, exploding them down the road. Rayna gears up and pushes forward, negating the force of acceleration that was attempting to lodge her into her seat. A look of excitement plasters across her face. The car in front of them drifts around the corner; a cement curb just barely misses the tire. Zaylee pulls the emergency brake up and begins to slide around the corner. She aligns to the road and puts the emergency brake back down while pushing down on the accelerator.

"This is Unit 451, in pursuit of a red sports car. License plate number 9GDK1278." Zaylee voices into the radio. "Affirmative Unit 451. Back up will be enroute in five minutes." a voice replies quickly. Zaylee looks confidently back at the road. She pulls behind a vehicle, using it to break the wind. Abruptly, she pulls around the vehicle and into the left lane. A burst of speed launches them closer to the speeding vehicle.

Cars move out of their way to the side. They slow themselves to a stop near the curb. Zaylee blows through all of them regardless. She maneuvers around those that fail to move out of their way. The car gets closer in their line of sight. A shiny red paint job and lowered suspension marks its sporty nature. As they approach, the car propels forward at a faster rate. It grips hard, leaving white smoke in its wake. Zaylee forces her acceleration pedal down to the floor, the boot applying the pressure as Zaylee commands. Both cars continue down the road, blowing through stop signs and intersections, guiding themselves through with ease.

The red sports car turns a corner. Zaylee continues through the street, taking her vehicle to the top speed it can reach. She pulls the emergency brake and slides around the corner, attempting to follow the now disappearing red sports car. Spinning through another corner, she disengages the brake and propels forward, launching them back. But, as they both look for the vehicle, they see it is nowhere to be found. "NO!" Rayna shouts, punching the dash with her arm and creating an indentation, "We can't catch anyone with this pathetic vehicle." Rayna pouts.

In a soothing voice, Zaylee professes, "It's depressing because they probably spent a few hundred thousand dollars on their vehicle, yet someone could put together a faster car for under fifty thousand." She continues slowing the vehicle to the speed of traffic and begins turning off the sirens. Zaylee's soothing voice terminates and picks up a hint of disdain as she continues speaking, "We're talking two thousand horsepower of mean. Then, only the TSR cars can compete with them. But just like the ignorant socialites and their aspiration to own overpriced supercars, the government fails to understand the same thing. I have proven it's capable. I took my supercar and made it faster by replacing its overpriced junk."

Rayna shoves her feet on the dash, "We can't even do our job. For a century, they just keep getting away. God, I am glad they don't televise it anymore." Rayna states, taking a deep breath and sitting back. While folding her arms, she says, "We need someone intelligent in office to fix these problems before the people become aware." she continues. "Faster, lighter cars with better drifting, and the like just beat us down." she continues to whine. Her upper lip scrunches to match her nose. "It's not fair!" she shouts, again pounding the dash. Dust flies into the air. Plastic falls from the dash and onto the floor.

Zaylee peeks to the right, down a residential block. She smirks. The vehicle jerks as it turns around, making a U-turn, fully submissive to Zaylee's orders. She turns left down the street, speeding up and turning on her sirens. Rayna looks down the street and notices the red sports car sitting in front of a house. Zaylee slows a tad as she drives onto the lawn and places her car sideways behind the sports car, blocking its escape. Rayna exits the vehicle with a smile on her face.

A blank face greets them in return; the man stares at the gun pointing directly at him. The metal glistens, similar to the badge on her vest. Zaylee's cowboy boot softly pushes into the ground. Grass gives way under the pressure. She steps out and, as she does, the man raises his hands into the air.

"Look, I give up. You got me." he claims. With a stern bravado, Rayna instructs, "Put your hands behind your head and get down on your knees." while simultaneously approaching him at a brisk pace. Zaylee follows suit, staying roughly two meters from him. "Open your vehicle." Zaylee orders. "But she just said-" he tries to state. "OPEN your vehicle." Zaylee orders using a decrescendo in decibel, starting loud and finishing quieter. He obeys, unlocking the car via a radio frequency remote attached to a key that's embroidered with a graphic of a horse; Zaylee approaches his vehicle, opening the door.

"Now back away." Zaylee demands while maintaining monophonic power of the discussion. Rayna continues to point her weapon at the man. He goes back down to his knees and places his hands back on his head. She stares into the vehicle and notices the smell of paint thinners coming from the vehicle. "Ether." she says to herself. The vehicle is jam packed with, what looks like tubes, beakers, and cleaning supplies. In front of it all is a large blue container, labeled 'meth'. Its transparent nature allows Zaylee to see-through it. The box is filled with bags upon bags of what looks to be cracked glass.

Zaylee scoffs, "Really?". She turns to look at him. "They raided them! I had to take them. I was the only one they wouldn't suspect." he tries to defend himself. "No. Why are you manufacturing methamphetamine and labelling the box? Are you some kind of moron?" Zaylee clarifies. "It's easy money." he claims, as his face blushes out of embarrassment. "You're turning a little pink there. I think I will call you pink man." Rayna remarks. Zaylee points a finger at him, "It's too easy, that's the problem with it. Every little chemist in High School or College thinks they can get away with it but you always get caught. You aren't built to be a criminal; you are built to help the world. Anyone can be a criminal. Anyone can be stupid with money. It's the ones that use their intellect for good that don't end up in a jail cell." Zaylee begins.

"Did you ever stop to look at the idiocy occurring around you? It's not hard to make and blow a few hundred thousand on a nice car. If you're evil, you can make money by abusing others." she asserts, pointing at his vehicle, "You want what you cannot have, but what you cannot have is not worth it. It's just what you've been taught to want. You just ignorantly succumbed to their culture. You see, not even the houses are worth it in California. They are overpriced pieces of garbage on a land that destroys itself with constant fires and earthquakes. It's just land. It's just a car. You can find a better house and a better car elsewhere for cheaper. What you do with your life is more important than any object you own. Regardless of location of usage of said object. You can't save a child from her abusive father by buying yourself a supercar." Zaylee projects, walking around him in a circle.

Rayna chuckles, "Then why do you have that fancy car of yours Zaylee?" Images of her sports car circle within Zaylee head and she's reminded of memory when she took her car out to the track and raced. The jerking of the vehicle whipped her side to side in the car, but the vehicle gracefully turned around each corner. She recalls how the electric motor powered the first initial acceleration until the gas kicked in and gave her that final push.

Zaylee looks at Rayna, "I know the truth because I made the mistake of buying a sports car." As the sound moves through the air and hits Rayna's ears, vibrating the bones within and she processes the words, she leans back on his car and lets out a sigh.

The red paint glimmers in a few areas as a ray of the sun makes it mark on the vehicle, coming through the trees above. Rayna looks down the street and sees all of the trees that create a border between the sidewalk and the asphalt. The picturesque scenery moves with the wind, but some leaves fall onto the street below.

A few cars drive down the street, picking up the leaves as they speed by. The leaves slowly settle onto the ground below and Rayna exclaims, "You know, you can learn things without having to experience them. Just pray and God will teach you. It's how I know that spending money on frivolous things is pointless. I read my scripture, prayed to God, and, most importantly, applied logic. With just an ounce of logic hun, you can learn that their overspending takes away from the less fortunate. You can still sell your car and give to the homeless, make amends for your sins."

Zaylee looks at Rayna and notices the compassion in her words but she thinks back on how she already did that and sold her beach house, donating the money to a homeless shelter company

47

that buys old churches and schools to use.

Upon opening her mouth, the words fall out, "I keep my car as a reminder of my mistakes. I have no need for forgiveness from a God that does not exist, but I know I always have room for improvement. My car reminds me not to return to my old ways."

The younger drug dealer shakes his head, befuddled by the conversation that is going on. He lifts his hands and waves them, "Sorry, but what exactly is going on here?"

Rayna stands up, leaving an imprint of her rear on the vehicle. She tweaks her hydraulic implant and looks at him, "Just a little lesson for you while you spend the next few years in the slammer." She moves forward and Zaylee notices a golden cross necklace moving underneath her clothes.

The criminal looks at the floor as the necklace becomes flush with Rayna's chest once again. "I'm sorry." he pouts. "I will never do it again! I want forgiveness!" he shrieks, the tears running into the grass below. Zaylee calms down, feeling a hint of sorrow for him, "I believe you, but you must face your rehabilitation." Zaylee says while slapping the cuffs on his wrists, "Then, when you realize all the lives you facilitated in ruining, you can help the world with your knowledge." she continues.

Rayna opens the door to their squad car, "Only those who give all of themselves to God truly know how to reach the greatest light." Rayna eloquently orates, making each syllable distinct. He ducks his head, entering the vehicle.

Chapter 6: Chrematistic Popularity

Zaylee and Rayna drive down Hollywood Boulevard. In the distance, they can see an empty red carpet guarded by silver poles, that hold a barrier together. Rayna rolls down her window; the breeze of Los Angeles enters their vehicle. She watches an older female lieutenant talk to a homeless person. His bicycle and shopping cart are sprawled behind him. Multiple police cars are parked on the street by the homeless man and five officers stand near the lieutenant.

"Bored busting at its finest." Rayna states. Zaylee slows her vehicle down and looks at the officers harassing the homeless man, "Typical. They can't find any real crimes to solve so they focus on homeless people. No wonder people hate the police." Zaylee says. The lieutenant turns the homeless man around and slaps cuffs on his hands. Rayna cups her hands around her mouth to amplify her voice, "Get a real job!" Rayna hollers. Zaylee pulls her back by her shoulder.

"Why Rayna?" Zaylee asks. "There is real injustice and real crime going on out there. The police should do their job." Rayna claims. "But you are the police." Rayna shakes her head, "And? I am merely a citizen with a duty to fulfill. They fail to fulfill their duty and they fail to help the people. Busting homeless people, really?" Rayna comments sarcastically. Zaylee shakes and retorts, "I guess, but they are still your partners. We rely on them, firefighters, paramedics, and EMT's for safety. It's one of the main reasons they get out of tickets."

"You're defending them now, why?" Rayna questions, while Zaylee parks the car. She hits a button and Tommy pops out of the back, "Well, I ticket them, and I'll arrest them, but why would you want to create tension with the person mending your wounds?" Zaylee asks. As usual with Rayna, she utters "Ah." while opening her door. Zaylee mutters, "I just don't know the solution." As Rayna closes her door behind her, the conversation ends. They both step outside onto the pavement; the red carpet awaits them.

—

Tommy circles above a long red carpet, the serenity of night balked by the hysteria below. On the right-side Zaylee and Rayna stand in front of a metal fence. It separates the crowd from them. Beyond them and out in the distance is the linked skate-way that celebrities use to get around the complex without being hassled by their fans. Back on the red carpet, walk two fancily dressed individuals. One female and one male. The female wears a short red dress that matches the carpet, her breasts look as though they are about to fall out of her dress though. The male is wearing a tuxedo that accentuates his straight-lined jaw. Flashes of white light pour down the carpet walk way, emanating from the phones of every bystander. Rayna nudges Zaylee and points at the man.

"He even waddles like a penguin." she jokes. Tommy continues to follow over them. Its lights flash but fail to be noticed in the barrage of lights below. The camera mounted on his belly records actions going on in the crowd. An announcer sits slightly to the right at the end of the carpet. Their elevated platform is graced by a sign dangling from their table. It reads 'VidTube Media'. Atop their table sits two microphones pointing towards two announcers.

Each microphone is oval shaped. They have gray metal sheets covering them, with scattered holes, to protect its glowing innards. Connected to the microphones by a metal extension arm is a meshed object, almost entirely porous in nature, with a circular housing. Their headphone cords dangle to their laptops that sit near their microphones. A banana centers the back of their laptop's screens. Noise starts to bellow down the carpets path. Tommy and the rest of the audience remain doing the same actions. The noise bellows over them, distinct and human in nature.

"Zachary and Megan's new sci-fi flick was a major success at the box office, despite inconsistencies with reality." the female voice bellows. "Yeah, but it's to be expected. Ninety nine percent of sci-fi films have inconsistencies with them and no film or book is perfect. The other tubers have gone over those flaws and spent lots of time predicting what's next, making big bucks by pointing out the obvious. But I think Zach did an excellent job this time around, despite being overshadowed by his sister, Courtney Ignot's, success." a male voice replies back.

Rayna yawns, "This is boring. All they do is insult people when their 'art' sucks just as bad as everyone else's. It's all subjective." Rayna says.

Intently honed in on the situation, Zaylee offhandedly asks, "Then why did you agree to come?" Rayna, eager to get more of Zaylee's attention, explains "It's fun to watch them. They are like little kids who think they are better than everyone, but they are actually worse. Teaching the next generation what beauty is. They give ammo to the ignorant, enforcing what it means to be beautiful and, therefore, insinuating that others are ugly."

Zaylee succumbs to Rayna's efforts and questions, "Ah. So you have fun, stimulate those emotions, and get a kick out of making fun of them?" Asserting herself, Rayna replies "Yeah, I do. What else is there to do in life? I like to make fun of the critics. Their job is easy and I know for a fact they can't write, learn, or understand anything real. They just use anger or agreeance to gain a following, when in reality, everything they talk about it culturally influenced opinion. Biased bigots, the lot of them."

"Well, you're not wrong. You're on the right path but abusing others for yourself is a path that will lead to more negativity." Zaylee preaches.

Preparing an avalanche of words, Rayna swishes her tongue around before sermonizing, "Their mentality is one of inevitable destruction and they have nothing useful to offer the world in its coming years. We must focus on removing them if we are to focus on bettering society. Because it doesn't matter how the path is spoken or told, it simply matters that the path of God is told and followed. If it takes a hundred years for someone to rise up and say it right, then let it be that way. But I think there is a storm coming. Black skies, gray clouds, and thunder to wrought the fallacy and false culture they have created. I can feel that the more people continue to talk about how she saw Jesus, the more people will band together, and begin to understand the need."

Zaylee irks at mention of religion, "Humans have potential without violence or God. Don't you go taking Trey's side now. I'm going to prove him wrong. We can solve the problems in society without violence. Just look at Nelson Mandela, Gandhi, and Thomas Moore. They achieved laudable goals without the use of violence." Zaylee states. Rayna grows confident, "Gandhi caused suffering by putting a drain on economics. It's rudimentary logic. Even though they were kind, and had good intentions, people still got hurt. When you want to teach the world, people are going to get hurt." Rayna explains.

Another celebrity walks down the carpet. Her skin, almost all showing; her dress, barely on. Beside her is a man, bulky and tall. His blonde hair flows down the side of his shoulder, like a waterfall. As he approaches a group of cameras, he rips open his shirt and shows his abs, grunting as he does. Rayna and Zaylee scoff. "So fake. You're just lean. Drink some water!" Rayna yells.

With a flick of her hand, Zaylee calms Rayna. They continue to watch as lights propel constantly from their cameras. A few of the individuals aren't press and are using their phones, while they fall giddily in love with the celebrities that walk past them.

Rayna looks at Zaylee, "What were we talking about? Oh, yeah. The problem is that society takes sides. We deem their side as morally good, when they are all really morally ambiguous, depending on interpretation. However, there are truths that are provable as morally good, regardless of interpretation, simply because of their results. And the prophet has given us them."

"Oh, really now? Care to explain?" Zaylee inquires. "Societies throughout history have grown by following certain paths and have been destroyed by following other paths. We can look at history and learn that the United States is on its path to destruction. We follow the wrong leaders and promote the wrong intentions, Satan's intentions. Ignoring religion for a second though, there are specific actions that are provable as good because they maintain the integrity and growth of a nation. In the subject of philosophy, these things can be proven as good through axioms and through results from biology, political science, physics, and mathematics." Rayna explains.

After perusing the data just given to her, Zaylee inquires, "So, we should just make cookie cutter copies of previous nations, simply because it worked before?" Upon asking this, she does not give Rayna time to respond and answers her own question, denoting its rhetorical nature, "You know that there is a problem with that mentality. Our species has become more advanced. We can't just revert and use the policies of old."

Rayna, visibly irritated, explains, "It's not about the policies of old. It's a requiem of philosophy, mentality, and Schesis. We must make this world obsolete with proofs of something better. It just so happens that this world has devolved from the past and the past is now more advanced than us, philosophically speaking. Their primitive ways, while primitive, are more effective than anything we can think up because they are imbued into the very fabric of the Universe: nature. And who created nature? God." Rayna explains as a noise explodes in the crowd, distracting them, "Sorry. We need to focus." Zaylee declares, while pulling out her black lined tablet. An image of Tommy appears on the home screen. She swipes up and Tommy's camera appears, giving them a visual of the situation.

They begin to jog towards the two celebrities, who are being bombarded by unruly and obsessed celebrity zealots, whose giddiness has overwhelmed them and make them act irrational, which makes Zaylee think about how maybe Rayna is a religious zealot. In between catching her breath, Rayna inquires, "You didn't hear a word I said, did you?" After a few more steps, Zaylee reaffirms her assertion in a slightly irritated tone, "No. We need to focus Rayna." She looks down at her tablet to see Tommy shooting cylinder devices into people that get too close.

Tommy flies overhead and buzzes at the celebrities. A man reaches his hand out and tries to grab Megan's red dress. Tommy launches a cylinder into him. The electricity buzzes around the device in his chest. He falls to the ground and the device turns off but the cylinder glows green. Zaylee watches all of this on the tablet. A notification pops up confirming that the device did not put him into cardiac arrest. Tommy continues to move forward over the celebrities.

Their faces cringe out of fear. Down the carpet is a female carrying a weapon. The crowd separates, screaming as they notice her weapon. A metal ball births out of the weapon and into the air, expanding into a net as it flies. It descends over Tommy and the celebrities. Immediately a laser exits Tommy and slices up the net. The nets two hemispherical parts fall to the ground, charred and burned. They become trampled from the oncoming crowd; the chaos continues and everyone continues to scatter. A shrivel comes from Megan. Tommy's propellers spin fast, expressing anger. It moves quickly to Megan and launches a cylinder into a male touching her.

53

He falls to the ground. The other members of the crowd trample over him. His grunts of pain go unnoticed as the river of humans continues to flow. Tommy pushes ahead of the two celebrities, leading them to a metal door. The icy metal greets his fingertips, but does not stop him from pushing it open. Beyond the door is a staircase. Zachary leads Megan through the door and up the stairs. Tommy makes his way above, flying and ignoring the stairs.

They stare at Tommy, floating high above. The look of fear and anxiety leaves Megan's face upon climbing up the stairs and separating them from the chaos; Megan's pulchritude begins to return. Tommy watches, as they both make their way up the stairs. Its camera shows Zaylee what is going on. Megan notices that the propellers begin to hum distinctly in a manner of happiness. "It's so cute." Megan proclaims, stopping to stare at Tommy. It rocks backward, as if smiling. "C'mon." Zachary says. "We're losing money by just standing here; I have another show to shoot you know." he continues.

"Right." Megan replies. They both continue to make their way upstairs. Another door greets them. Its handle is similarly as cold as the last, but it is likewise obedient and turns at Zachary's request. The wind blows in, hitting Megan and Tommy. The door blows wide open and holds itself under the pressure. A metal rail of the skate-way hangs over the side of the building, Moon rays flicker and reflect off it. At the edge is a flat board laying in-line with the rail. Beside the rail is one extra board.

Zachary runs over and hops on the board. Its metal clasps bind over his fancy dress shoes, removing part of their shine. He presses a button on the end of the board, air begins to exit the board. It pushes forward, the air launching it down the rail. A metal hook keeps it tied along; a cord extends down the rail with the board. Megan picks up another board. Multiple zealot hostiles reach the top of the stairs.

Tommy looks at the door. It stands in front of Megan. The hostiles rapidly approach. Tommy begins launching electricity ridden cylinders into each approaching hostile. Bodies slowly amass upon the rooftop from Tommy's escapades against the celebrity-crazed individuals. Megan hooks in the power plug to her board. The remaining tension retracts into the board. She snaps it onto the rail. Tommy's lens continues to project a bright red while it continues to launch cylinder after cylinder into approaching humans.

Finally, Megan slides down the rail. Tommy launches a canister onto the rooftop. It begins to haze.

Soon, the entire rooftop is covered with the haze. A few people are foolish enough to walk through but they quickly fall back to the stairwell and vomit. Tommy follows Megan and Zachary above the skate-way. They begin to slide down. The air modifies their movement, correcting their descent and allowing them to slide down the rail. Megan's hair flows from the downward motion. She pulls her red dress down, realizing that her underwear is visible to the crowd below.

Another barrage of camera flashes bombards them, echoing out from every fan's phone. They speed up in attempt to get away. Pneumatic sounds protrude from the rail. Tommy moves faster attempting to keep up with them, its body tilts as it flies in their direction. Easily, Tommy catches up with them. The wind smashes into Zachary's face, pushing his cheeks back. The end of the rail approaches them quickly. At the end, Tommy sees Zaylee and Rayna waiting. It purrs in excitement and pushes ahead of Zachary and Megan to hovers in between their arms.

Rayna extends her arm and pets Tommy. Its nose pushes into her hand. She pulls it in front of her, "That's a good boy Tommy." she exclaims. Zachary reaches the end of the rail first. He quickly detaches from the rail. His board follows his exit, retracting its cord into its housing. Shortly after, Megan reaches the end of the rail. She likewise dismounts from the rail. The leather like cord zaps back inside the housing.

"I'm glad you two are okay." Zaylee declares. "The skate-way got us out there in a pinch." Zachary responds. Megan cringes, "Yeah, but not before they got pictures of my underwear." she adds to the discussion. "It's alright, that'll put you on the cover of Celebriitiies webpage for sure." Zachary replies. "I know, no publicity is bad publicity. But I just wish we didn't have to deal with creeps like that." Megan answers.

Rayna jests, "Creeps like that are what pay for your overpriced toys." As the she finishes, she picks up one of their boards. "Hey, I'd like to see you do what we do." Zachary ripostes.

"Yeah!" Megan agrees ecstatically.

Rayna begins to jerk her body back and forth, throwing her arms in multiple directions, "Oh no!" she yells. "Help me! I'm being attacked by my fellow actor. My life is in danger!" Rayna continues to scream sarcastically. She falls to the floor and begins to roll around, as if she was being attacked.

"He's stabbing me in the butt. Oh no! Don't stab my butt." Rayna cries, while grabbing her butt. "Ugh." Zachary moans. Tommy purrs sporadically, as if laughing. The lens continues to record Rayna on the floor. The celebrities don't react so she stops and looks up at them, "Well, what are you waiting for? Throw dollar bills at me like I'm a stripper." Rayna coyly remarks. They remain quiet.

Rayna looks at Tommy and mutters, "Maybe I should have taken off my clothes first and acted like I've had sex with other famous people, then divorced them for their money." It nods in reply, as if it were laughing. The celebrities throw Rayna a death glare, causing her to lock eyes with them.

"You know, once you are dead, everyone will forget you. And you'll be lucky if the only people who remember you are the homeless who use your tombstone as a place to hold their beer." Upon hearing the comment, the celebrities scoff and walk away.

Chapter 7: Koreatown

Each wall of the underground garage is solid cement. Chilly air makes the room rigid, stiff, like being wrapped up by a bodybuilding vampire. Zaylee's hair stays wound atop her head, as usual. Its honey color glistens off the dull lights hanging from the garage ceilings. Two workers stand around a slick white sports car. Every curve adds a little more seduction and enticement to the vehicle. Sparks fly from a saw entering its side. Zaylee remains calm as her vehicle is sliced up. Another, taller and older, female walks in her direction. She walks past her and towards the workers next to the car. They stop their saw as she gets close.

"Is this car from impound?" she asks the worker. The worker lifts up his welding mask. "No, it's Zaylee's, the new officer. She just got off her probation period." he replies. She nods. "It looks just like Laci's." she continues. "Oh God, I would never touch a psycho twin's car." the worker adds. "Didn't you deconstruct Fuego's car after he died?" she asks. "Yeah, exactly why I won't touch anything related to it ever again. The F-mobile was full of so many bombs, I thought it was going to blow up and make the rest of L.A irradiated."

The older woman, now at the car, looks at it and runs her fingers along the side. Zaylee stares at the back of her head as she caresses her vehicle, mumbling to herself, "Nosy cops. They always believe they are important and in control. They're always getting into other people's business." Zaylee mutters quietly. The older woman looks back Zaylee, partially overhearing what she had said.

"You have something to say officer?" the woman asks. Zaylee tightens her posture and looks dead at her, "Ma'am, I was only saying that I'm glad I'm not like you." Zaylee poignantly exclaims, attempting to offend her. Unphased by the comment, the woman declares, "You have been causing problems since you got here. I heard you let a meth addict go simply because of personal ethics. You'll be out of here quick."

Zaylee looks at her, hostility brewing in her eyes, "I am a servant of the people. Obviously, you are not. You only seek to serve yourself." Zaylee ripostes. The woman scoffs, "A servant with a four hundred and fifty-thousand-dollar car. What a joke." As she begins to walk away, happy with her insult, Zaylee grabs her hand, "No. You will not play this psychological ignoring game with me just because you think you have power over me." The woman's face goes blank.

With ardor, Zaylee retorts, "I worked my entire life. This car is my only thing of value and it is a reminder of my mistakes. I am allowing it to be reconstructed into a police cruiser so that I might better apprehend criminals, speeding and escaping, alike." The woman stares back at her, "Ballsy. No wonder you survived so long." she says, brushing Zaylee's hand away vigorously.

In an instructive voice, she commands Zaylee thusly, "Now, get going officer. Rayna is waiting." While saluting her, Zaylee replies "Yes, lieutenant." In a final word, she forces Zaylee to walk away: "Dismissed." Obsequiously, Zaylee walks away from her and out of the garage. Multiple beat up police cruisers sit outside of a run-down police station. Graffiti is splashed across the walls, as no building was immune to the ever-present gang writing, and this infuriates her, but she reminds what Rayna said about culture and calms a bit.

Her eyes navigate along each cruiser. A young girl with brunette hair is leaning against a police cruiser: it is Rayna. Each one of the young girl's hands spread upward, a needle sticks into the air. She begins stretching her muscles allowing the fluid to flow through them, allowing the liquid to empower her arm.

Each muscle booster installed in her arms bulges with implied intensity, granting her control of her hydraulic fist. Her arms fall back to her sides, she clicks the dial installed near her thumb. The muscles saturate and swell opposite to their normal size. Zaylee gets closer to her, standing roughly a meter away, staring dead at her and folding her arms. "What?" Rayna asks. "What do you mean 'what'? Do you really need to refill in front of the station?" Zaylee queries.

"You never know what could happen. Labeling this building as a police station makes it a target. We should be stationed out of abandoned locations around the city. It's the intelligent thing to do." Rayna responds.

Zaylee nods, "Uh huh, sure" she sarcastically remarks as she clicks open the police cruiser. The shaky and beaten down door opens with a creak. Every hinge has become tight with age and requires force to open. Paint flakes off due to Zaylee's fingers collision as she pulls it shut with a quick thrust. Rayna follows suit and makes her way into the passenger seat, unabashed from Zaylee's comment. The crumbling fabric housing grinds down into her back. "Man, this piece of crap is uncomfortable." Rayna says. Zaylee ignores her comment and grabs the steering wheel, pulling it to the side.

She slips the key into the ignition. It jams in, refusing to turn over. Zaylee starts fooling with the key, pushing it up and down. Eventually the key slips in and the car turns over. "Thank God." Zaylee exclaims. She thinks back to when Rayna started the engine by linking up her robot arm, "Remember when you had to fix it?" Rayna nods, "Yeah. These cars suck."

Setting the car in drive allows Zaylee to bolt out of the parking lot and onto the street. Buzzing comes from the radio, "We have a 415 in progress on the corner of Wilshire Boulevard and South Western Avenue." a male voice echoes once through the vehicle.

They continue their progress on the street and turn East down Olympic. Zaylee grabs the plastic radio device and presses on the side, "Unit 451 enroute to 415 off Wilshire and Western." In the distance is a sign on the corner designating Elden Avenue. She makes her way into the right lane to turn right down Elden.

As they merge onto Elden, a police car behind them bolts around, without signaling, causing Zaylee to vent her frustration aloud, "No blinker. Typical." The police cruiser cuts in front of her, speeding up and eventually cutting around the corner without signaling and without lights or sirens. "Oh no." Rayna says contemptuously. Zaylee begins to honk her horn at the police cruiser. The palm trees, being the only thing present on the street of Elden, pay the sound no mind. The two partners continue down the decorated street that is Elden Avenue. Zaylee notices the empty sidewalk and how the shadows of the palm trees blanket it.

A massive truck drives quickly down the road the cruiser had just bolted down, and slams into the cruiser pushing it back into the middle of Elden Avenue. It spins over the curb, onto the sidewalk, and into a palm tree. Its hood and bumper crunch up against the brown stem pointing high into the sky. The truck, with its hefty grill, remains undamaged in the center of the avenue. Car parts lay spread across the avenue in different shapes and sizes. Glass and plastic shards sit, waiting to press into a poor soul's feet.

Zaylee pulls her cruiser over just before the crashed cruiser. The old female officer, that caressed Zaylee's car just minutes prior, crawls out of her damaged door that lays to the right of her arms. As she crawls, blood pours down from her face and into her hair. After a bit of crawling, she sits up, using the curb to support her back. Zaylee immediately recognizes her as the lieutenant that scolded her earlier. She steps over to her, allowing her cowboy boots to crunch the plastic and glass. Rayna follows her over to the vehicle.

Shaking her head, Zaylee says, "Stupid." Now, standing above the woman, she continues as their eyes meet, "This is why we have signals and laws. If you're going to blow through a red light, you need to code 3, or at least pay attention." Zaylee continues. Zaylee grabs her radio and clicks the side, "We're going to need emergency services on the corner of Olympic and Elden. We have an officer down." she says into the radio. "10-4" the voice replies back. They walk over to the lieutenant and stand close.

"Did you see..." the lieutenant begins to mumble incoherently trying to gain control over her faculties. Rayna curls her hand over her ear, "Did we see what?" she asks derisively. The lieutenant pulls herself up off the curb towards her cruiser, so that she can lean on it, "That guy just rammed into me." the lieutenant claims, grabbing her side and cringing. She lifts her hand up and sees it's covered in blood.

Zaylee lets the radio fall to her side and says, "You should have had your lights on." After uttering the last syllable of 'on', Rayna follows up, "We tried to warn you." Uninterested in the conversational drivel, the lieutenant demands, "Arrest him." Rayna and Zaylee look at each other. Zaylee then looks back at the lieutenant.

"I'm sorry lieutenant. This was not his fault. It was yours." Zaylee says. "ARREST HIM! Look at what he did!" she screams out, pointing at the wound bleeding on her thigh. She forces herself to cough. Within seconds of collecting spittle in her mouth, she launches the blood onto the floor. Then the lieutenant bangs on her

60

vehicle, "And my car. It's destroyed." she states.

With a hint of pride, Rayna explains, "Oh hunny, that's American steel. We drive reliable, but breakable, Asian or German cars. Steel is the one thing American cars are good at. It's not his fault." The man, finally having parked his car, jumps out of the cabin, which is about a meter off the ground. He sprints over to the officers on the side of the road.

"I'm so sorry officer. I didn't see you turning." he proclaims with empathy. An ambulance pulls up beside them. Zaylee pulls him aside, "We will need your information sir. Insurance, registration, state identification, et-cetera." He takes a look at the officer bleeding before processing the words Zaylee just spoke and replies, "Of course." as he rummages through his wallet and hands his information to her. "Do you know if she will be okay?" he asks, still worried.

"I've seen enough accidents to know that she, most likely, will be okay. She could have back problems, a concussion, or other damage, but she'll live and return to her normal life within a week or two. That injury is not enough for her to bleed out. Only a hematoma in her head could, but that's unlikely. And there's no aortic dissection, which means her main artery didn't burst upon impact, so I'm pretty confident she will be fine. Neither of you were moving at too fast of speeds and, at the angle you hit her, it just slid her car over. It'll be painful, but this is why we have traffic laws in place. She was speeding, not signaling, and not following normal protocol. Some cops eventually have to learn the hard way though. It sucks, but that's life. She'll be fine." Zaylee claims, looking through his information as she speaks. A look of relief covers the gentleman's face.

An ambulance vehicle pulls into the middle of the street. Its sirens continue to blare, making it uncomfortable for the nearby citizens. A medic steps out of the vehicle and into the street. Curiously, Zaylee wonders to herself how many other medics besides Trey are in the area, although she doesn't mind it too much that he's not here, since she trusts in emergency medical personnel.

She notices a black plastic box with metal latches clenched between the medic's fingers, dangling down towards the ground. She walks over to the woman, her box swaying in line with her movement. Zaylee's eyes officially meet hers, she lifts her arm up and waves, wanting to thank them, but she is interrupted by Rayna, "Time to go, Zaylee." Rayna firmly states, grabbing Zaylee's free arm. She pulls her towards their vehicle, causing Zaylee to turn one hundred and eighty degrees.

They enter their vehicle and continue down Elden. The leaves upon the palm trees sway in the wind. Rayna rolls down the window and places her hand on the rubber insert for the window. Her hand clasps around the door. The metal quivers under her grip, pressing inward.

As they continue driving, Rayna starts rapping out of boredom, "Wasting money, money." After a short pause, she repeats the chorus and heads into the verse: "Wasting money, money. Screw the economy, I hate poor people." she continues to rap. Zaylee, her mind thinking about Trey, sarcastically remarks, "Really Rayna?" Rayna's face lights up, "Oh right, we need your McDoodle for this to be a real rap video." Rayna replies.

"Quit it." Zaylee demands, turning the corner. Tall buildings surround the street. Most of them are white in color, akin to marble. As they approach Western Avenue from Wilshire Boulevard a red light allows them to absorb the environment. A tall and putrid green building greets them on the corner. Despite its rotting green color, it looks like it used to be somewhat elegant. Running up and down the building is the words 'Warehouse'. The same writing is posed across the front except with a 'The' in front of it. Zaylee notices the writing. "Strange." she declares.

"What is?" Rayna asks. "Californians always put 'the' in front of everything. 'The 10 freeway', 'the 110', 'the 101', and 'the 5'." Zaylee answers. The red street light flashes off, and begins lighting up green. Traffic begins to move forward, urging them to move and keep up. Their vehicle turns right, turning off the yellow blinking signal light automatically upon turning.

Along the left side of the street is a group of individuals in a circle. Each of them is wearing a distinctive style of leather clothing. One of them is wearing a trench coat and watching pedestrians along the sidewalk. Puffs of smoke exit his body, a circular red burn lights up the end of his white cigarette. The rest of them are wearing similar clothes, in varying leather jackets and black cotton shirts, and each of them has similar body permutations. Stiff black steel clasps along their arms, tightening to their wrists. The same black steel wraps around the female's hair, tightening it into a ponytail, identical to the clasp that Rayna uses except that the edge of the clasp is lined with a crimson color on a few of the individuals. Zaylee assumes this is to denote leadership or capability.

Zaylee turns on the vehicle's lights and siren. Its high pitch scream is ignored by the group, which is now circling around, moving in and out around its epicenter. Their arms flay back and forth but the black steel clasps stay clasped, unaffected by the motion. Zaylee presses a button on the dash causing Tommy to pop out near the trunk. Tommy analyzes the situation and similarly activates its sirens and lights. Red and blue neon circles near its propellers. It approaches the group from above and, as it approaches, the neon reflects off their shiny metallic apparel. Zaylee gets her tablet out, pushes a few buttons, and Tommy's video capture is replicated it.

On screen are touch screen options for attack maneuvers. Her new view of the scenario widens giving both Zaylee and Rayna an aerial survey of the area.

On the tablet, in the center of their group is a girl. Blood drips from her mouth. Open cuts line her body along with the black and purple hematomas. She reaches a hand up into the air, begging for, what looks like, help. Zaylee pulls the car near the group and places it in park. She quickly exits and pulls her taser out, pointing it at the group. The man in the trench coat drops his cigarette and stands between her and the group. Rayna slowly makes her way out but doesn't pull out any weapons.

"Back away from the woman!" Zaylee demands, pointing her taser at him. The man looks at her, nodding his head in the air, "No." he replies. "Do it now or I will use force!" Zaylee continues, Tommy's red lens pushes forward in his direction, indicating its aggression. Upon lowering its gatling weapon, the man's facial expression turns to fear.

Flicking his cigarette away, he pleads calmly, "Hear me out." while staring at Tommy. Zaylee nods and Tommy's lens goes to a slightly less bright red. He pulls out another cigarette and lights it, after blowing a puff of smoke, he states: "This woman raped a man."

Zaylee becomes flummoxed by the comment and lowers her taser ever-so slightly. He continues, "The judicial system will not enact punishment, so we are doing it on their behalf."

Tommy gets less than a meter from his face and points his gatling at him. He begins to raise his hands into the air, cigarette still in-hand, "But if you truly wish to arrest me, do so." he continues, finally extending his arms fully into the air, ash falling down on the side of his coat. He gets on his knees and places his hands behind his head, dropping the cigarette onto the floor as he does. Faint lights protrude from his arm, similar to the lights on Rayna's arm.

Rayna gets closer to him, "Stand up." she commands. He stands up and Rayna looks into the crowd at the bloodied girl, "Back away and I will arrest her." she explains, walking towards the group. She flexes and activates her hydraulics. The group separates, allowing her entry. The golden cross necklaces briefly wobble off their chest as they move back. Rayna moves into the circle, kneels down, and picks up the woman with significant force, holding her in the air.

The beaten girl's feet dangle before Rayna lowers her onto the sidewalk. The diagonal angle of her feet aligns horizontally with the ground, stepping in a puddle of her own blood. Rayna deactivates her hydraulics and slaps silver handcuffs onto the accused rapist's wrists.

"Thanks Rayna." the man in the trench coat states. "No problem, Vero." she replies, while lowering the rapists head into the vehicle. Zaylee holds her taser off to the side in a confused look and claims, "Rayna, these citizens took violent measures against a citizen. Regardless of criminal action, we must apprehend them as well." Rayna looks back at Zaylee, "I didn't see anything." Rayna replies before turning her head. "Did you guys see anyone do anything?" she asks, staring at the group. "Nope." they reply in unison.

"It's on Tommy's camera and my camera. You cannot let them go." Zaylee says. Vero steps forward, his coat bellowing from the movement, "This is the only punishment she will face." Vero claims. Zaylee retorts quickly, "I don't believe I was talking to you." Hearing this, Rayna steps in between their locked eyes, staring down Zaylee, "Our system is corrupt. If the judicial becomes corrupt, it is the citizens duty to break their corruption by any means necessary, it is what our founding fathers intended." Rayna replies. She takes the accused rapist and tosses her into the back of their cruiser, slamming the door and locking her in.

Rayna walks towards Vero and stands next to him, letting him take over from where she left off in the discussion, "It's in the constitution. These judges and lawmakers have abused us for decades. It's time to take a stand. To send a message that we're done being controlled." Vero continues.

Zaylee looks at Rayna, almost tearful, "What is this Rayna, your tribe?" Zaylee asks. "These are my people – these are God's people, and we will stand against those government officials that ignore justice. You don't know this, because I wanted to keep my motives a secret, but I joined the force to break it down from within. The chief worked with judges and let my parents' killers go free." Rayna attests, full of fury.

Zaylee claims from experience, "But warfare does nothing but breed more tension and less solutions." Vero shakes his head, "There is no other way that will make them listen to our message. Our coryphaeus will handle the supreme justices, senators, and congress, but we must do our part to fix our world and bring God back." Vero explains.

A member of the group shouts, "Yeah! The woman that puts out these vids saw Jesus. She knows our plight and the people need a protector and a prophet who knows our struggle and will rally us against corruption." a person in the group says.

Tommy looks at Rayna, his propellers purring in a distinctly melancholic manner. Nearly shrieking with emotion, Zaylee states, "I don't care for your prophet. Powerful people rise and fall, such is the way of life. Those that advocate violence only make people suffer more. Even if it was the founding fathers intended, I'm sure they wanted to mitigate bloodshed."

Rayna sighs, "The world is already bleeding. Those in control have made it bleed. We need a new philosophy, a new style of thinking. She is our answer!"

"ENOUGH!" Zaylee shouts. They look at her with shock, unable to speak, "I was a general for years. Violence must end for real peace to begin." Tommy moves up and down, simulating a nod.

Vero takes charge, "Peace was never an option with these people. Their stubbornness, their greed, their desire for power. These will not go away with passive-aggressive actions. We have actual proof that Jesus existed and they still deny it, saying there is no God. We will not simply protest with words like others, for they have failed to achieve greatness; they have failed to bring about change. We will act where others don't; we are above the fear of death because we have God!" Vero claims. Rayna lifts her arm to be horizontal. The lights beep, "Our technology cannot get better with their iniquities and their lack of belief. We need freedom and God to return." she states.

Still trying to uphold her values, Zaylee says, "Regardless, I must arrest them for their actions." She begins to approach Vero with her cuffs in her hands. Rayna gets in between Vero and Zaylee, "No." Rayna pithily states. Zaylee looks at her with sorrow, "I don't want to arrest you, Rayna." Rayna raises her arm, clicking on the hydraulics. "I dare you to try it." she tempts.

Zaylee attempts to approach, but Rayna pulls her arm back, ready to swing. Quickly Zaylee steps back, pain of sadness welling up within her. Zaylee looks at Tommy as he quivers and backs away from Rayna. One of the members in the crowd takes his necklace off and wraps the golden cross necklace around his hand, throwing it into the air and yelling, "We run Koreatown now!"

Another member turns towards the warehouse wall with a spray can in hand. Zaylee turns around and walks into the street, Tommy follows but Rayna stays with Vero. Zaylee notices Tommy's sadness and says, "I know boy, but we should get used to this. L.A cops have an extremely high turnover rate." she says. Tommy eventually makes its way back to its home in the back of the vehicle. Zaylee walks around the driver's side and opens her car door to enter the vehicle. As she pulls onto the street, she reads the freshly sprayed graffiti on the wall.

It reads 'Cyberpunk Squad'.

Chapter 8: White Sunshine

The Chief's desk is well organized; a stapler, a tape dispenser, and a cup of pens sits near the edge, resting firmly. Zaylee sits in a chair across from the chief, gripping the arm rest, her nails grinding into the wood, leaving an indentation. Her fingernails are painted black and are visible in between each tap of her curled hand. A clipboard wobbles as it makes its way into the Chief's hands. Bound tightly by the clasp is a substantial amount of text regarding activities around the station. At the header of the paperwork is a larger text reading 'Officer Rayna'. Below Zaylee can see that it describes recent events regarding Rayna, in Koreatown.

He flips the frontpage over. As it dangles over the clipboard, he says, "It's depressing to see Rayna leave the force like that. I don't know what has gotten into officers these days, talking about prophets like we live in the time of Paul."

After speaking, he drops the clipboard back onto his desk, in between the stapler and tape. The thud from its impact reverberates and shakes the pens in their container. "Constant violations and refusal to apprehend suspects properly, all claiming that the justice of Jesus is at hand. It's maddening." he claims. Zaylee looks at him and says, "I'm not sure either, sir."

"Well, I guess you will have to work alone for now; we're short staffed as it is." he declares as his chair slides back making a singular screech. He reaches out his hand towards Zaylee, "In your fancy supercar, you will be assigned as the priority unit for high-speed pursuits" he attests. Zaylee nods, "I will try my best sir. There is peace and order to maintain on the streets." she says, letting go of his arm. The chair slides behind her, making way for her exit. A rush of air comes from the hall as the door opens. While walking down the hall, Zaylee nods at the other personnel.

She exits the police station, opening the doors to the heated inky asphalt parking lot. With each step forward, her pair of new cowboy boots jingle from the addition of spurs. The metal jingles repetitively as she walks through the parking lot to her vehicle.

A shiny metallic white sports car with deep black accents sits, parked, in front of her. The aggressive looking exterior breathes an aura of power and an atmosphere of strength. Police lights sit above her vehicle with multiple different sirens eager to flash while the cage divider partitions the rear seats, ready for criminals. The cage divider is colored a Stygian black, accentuating the similar coal colored grill bumper lodged horizontally on the front. The pitch-black grill serves to protect, ram, and otherwise usefully assist its driver.

She pulls out her keys and presses the center button on a custom white-gold casing. Clicks echo from her car, like music to her ears. She tugs the door handle upwards and uses leverage to unbind the butterfly doors, allowing the hinge to thwart gravity and launch the door vertically as if pointing to the heavens themselves.

The black leather on the front seats greets her nose with its aroma, like the sweetest rose tainted with a hint of scotch. She inhales deeply, enjoying the smell while the seat continues to tempt her to enter. She places her right foot into the vehicle first, followed by her left foot. Her body seats itself onto the leather, pressing with pleasure against it as it conforms to her torso. The main key jostles in the slot, indicating a non-perfect fit due to wear and tear.

A single click turns on the car's electrical systems. As she turns the ignition, the engine begins to purr. Like strings being pulled on a harp, Zaylee smiles. She pulls down the lever and places the car in reverse, gripping the plastic housing allows her to change gears but she pauses on the 'R'. "My grandpa always said that 'R' is for Race." she says to herself, smiling as she remembers him. The car begins to roll in tandem with the pressure she applies on the accelerator. Due to its sensitivity, Zaylee backs off the peddle, and slows the speed so that she can exit the lot safely. Amid the deacceleration, she looks at her radio from the center console, all its lights had activated when she turned on the vehicle, creating an existential experience in the cockpit of her supercar.

The police in the parking lot stare at her car in awe, their faces drooped out of astonishment. They pause from their daily routine to watch her pull from the parking lot. The low supercar uses its suspension exceptionally elegantly until it exits the lot, gripping close to the sidewalk, causing a subtle screech to echo out. She pulls into the street, grabbing her radio as the car grips the asphalt. The light on her radio turns to red, "Unit 451 on patrol." she says, releasing her fingers off the button.

She exits the lot and begins patrolling. But nothing seems to be happening; the flow of traffic seems to be normal, with the pedestrians calmly going about their business on the sidewalk. She leans over the wheel, "Huh, slow day." Zaylee says to herself.

Eager to spice up her day, she pulls into a bakery and gets a sandwich to eat. After sitting down and eating, she enters into her vehicle again and heads back onto the street.

The lights of L.A flicker in her cornea, allowing her to notice their reflection in her mirror. After some more patrolling, the radio bursts with static before a voice bleeds through, "Unit 451, we have 510 approaching Vermont Avenue, a red Morgan Stinger and a black Buscemi Venular. Your vehicle is suitable to pursue and I see you are on South Hoover Street. Please confirm."

Zaylee picks up the radio, "Confirmed, on pursuit now." She turns the corner towards Vermont Avenue and eventually maneuvers onto Vermont Avenue. She turns on her lights and siren; the siren pierces the air and the lights flash brightly due to their pristine bulbs. Cars move away from, allowing her to speed up down the street. The radio buzzes again, "Unit 451, we still have a 510 Northbound on Vermont Avenue. They are moving at a high rate of speed; you will need to speed up." the voice says. She continues to accelerate as she spots the speeding vehicles; they have slowed down as they approached the police station. "Ha. They slowed because they saw the station." she says to herself before picking up her radio, "Unit 451, vehicles are in sight, over."

The two vehicles speed up dramatically and propel away from her as they hear the siren and see the lights. But the siren volume quickly fades as her quick burst forward causes the engine's volume to quickly murder it. She puts her pedal down to the floor, the vehicle continually accelerates, forcing the air across the breadth of her vehicle.

Drivers on the street pull to the right of the road, allowing her to approach the suspects. The imagery was common to Zaylee, as this was the current protocol for other drivers on the road when she activated her lights and sirens. Beyond that, she sees the red and black sports cars roar in the distance, to the north. As she slams the accelerator down, the engine in front of her screams deeper and deeper due to the shifting into higher and higher gears Zaylee

69

beckons the car to complete; the gear shift's leathery feel clings to Zaylee's fingertips, her flesh gripping it, pulling the shifting mechanism into fourth gear.

Her vehicle blows past the vehicles that are currently steering to the right; they are unable to pull over in time due to her rapidly approaching nature. The speedometer's red arrow ticks past 260km but the cars in front of her keep pushing forward, in between cars, and blowing past lights with no regard for the citizens around them. Many of the pedestrians bellow out curses as they avoid the heedless racers.

The two supercars slow down and jerk right, onto an interstate. She quickly follows them up the ramp and onto the gray concrete interstate, slowing only as much is necessary to turn right and follow the loop. The sirens continue to blare and she picks up speed once again, the engine hitting 10,000RPM's with ease on the tachometer.

After the initial jerk from her acceleration fades, she picks up her radio and presses down on the button, "Suspects are heading North on Interstate 110." Zaylee says. "Confirmed unit 451, air support is inbound, ETA five minutes." a female voice replies, before it cuts back to static. She catches up, finally reaching optimal viewing distance for a scan. But the vehicles in front of her have no plates; the paper dealership plates are the only visual read she can get on the car.

Her system blurts out a blue window pop-up, 'Unable to scan suspect's vehicles', it reads. Her eyes trace over the screen, noticing the pop-up. She clicks on the screen, removing the pop up with her right hand's index finger.

She now sits right behind the two supercars, her lights still circling on the top of her supercar, and the sirens blasting across the freeway, angrily commanding the supercars to stop. But the adversaries notice her approach, and attempt to accelerate. To retaliate, Zaylee floors her vehicle's gas pedal, pushing the speedometer arrow over the 400km mark.

Their two supercars struggle to maintain the same level of acceleration, which creates a gap for Zaylee to protrude in between them. But the red Morgan Stinger pulls closer to the Buscemi Venular, closing the protrusion. The giant jet-like engine in the back of the Morgan Stinger catches her eye, its enigmatic engine is chrome and lined with two turbos flowing across the engine block, blocking it from view.

Its engine revs like a musical instrument, with a distinct pattern that was programmed by the manufacturer. The sounds of the supercars make the scene seem as if an orchestral entourage was blocking Zaylee. She watches them, glaring with vexation and rage. By deaccelerating for a second, she glides behind them and immediately speeds up, slamming the grill on her car into the back of both their vehicles as they close the gap between them that she once occupied. As she pulls back, she notices that she has scratched up their rear bumpers, detracting from their once alluring paint-job.

Zaylee grabs a different radio looking device and clicks it on. "Pull over." she demands into the microphone. Simultaneously, her voice amplifies through her vehicle's speakers. Both cars veer to the right, giving the appearance that they are pulling over, but they immediately redirect and exit interstate 110. Zaylee does not fall for their deception and follows directly behind them.

As she exits onto the street, their loud vehicles can be heard pushing down the street. The Morgan Stinger and Buscemi Venular complete their turn, but Zaylee gets clipped ever-so slightly by another vehicle, which causes her to veer to the side of the road.

Both vehicles she was pursuing dart off with two new vehicles following closely behind them, causing her to do a double-take. Zaylee stares at the vehicle that swiped her, its paint lined with artistically drawn blue lightning bolts on the side. The hood is covered with race logos but she reads a sideways defining label reading 'Cyberpunk Electric Squad'. Sparks fly out from under its hood but Zaylee ignores the vehicle and looks back at the street.

A sign on the right reads 'Mulholland Drive'. Knowing the road, Zaylee vigorously applies pressure to the accelerator, causing her tires to spin in the back, burning her rubber treads down. The Electric Squad vehicle accelerates instantly applying its torque to the ground and taking off, following the supercars Zaylee was chasing off the interstate. As the vehicle passes her, the tires on her supercar finally catch and launch her forward at a higher rate of speed.

She looks at the lightning bolt graphic wrapped vehicle ahead of her and smashes down on the accelerator as hard as she possibly can, forcing the vehicle to launch forward at an insane rate, and causing pain to lurch onto her toes. The red speedometer arrow ticks past 100km after a mere three and a half seconds of acceleration.

She approaches the new vehicle, its discordant noise hits Zaylee's ears. The car's engine slowly ceases and its driver pushes to the side of the road. Zaylee ignores it and accelerates forward, continuing to burn gasoline. She drifts through Mulholland Drive and its windy turns; the bosom of her vehicle torques through each turn with ease. As the car increase in speed, she grips the gear shift and uses it in tandem with her emergency brake to slide through each turn. The trees on the side emit a peaceful aura for Zaylee, despite the insatiable thrill of the chase.

At a tempo of 240km, she pushes through each turn abraded by the maneuver; the friction of her tires slows her speed upon each swivel of the wheel. She slides sideways through a turn and notices the four vehicles directly in front of her are fighting each other by slamming into one another.

Two vehicles are of the same type of model as the Cyberpunk Electric Squad and the other two are the ones that Zaylee was chasing before. The cars are pushing against each other, throwing electricity and sparks as they collide with each other. Zaylee straightens out to gain more momentum; her supercar frenzies frantically trying to align itself onto the road to gain speed. She pushes forward, lunging towards the vehicles at a frightening rate.

A short epoch passes; the scene is magnificent to Zaylee and, so, she freezes the image in her mind to remember it later. In an effort to cease their dangerous behavior, she prevaricates ahead of all four supercars, leaving them behind her. She grabs a lever at the top of her vehicle, pulling down on it opens up a compartment below her trunk. A metal ball hits the asphalt with a thud causing it to expand horizontally across the street. Spikes stick out along the expanded ball.

The four supercars, unable to avoid them, race over them, popping all of their tires.

Their cars grind down, eventually spinning all of their rubber out until they come to a stop. The Electric Squad's wheels spew out some foam, halting the deflation of their tires intermittently. Zaylee slows considerably, then pulls her emergency brake, allowing for a complete 180-degree spin. She forces the pedal down, moving her supercar forward at a slow but steady rate until she reaches the four burned out supercars, coming to a complete stop right in front of them. A few of the drivers in the cyberpunk cars have departed from their vehicle and advanced on the Morgan Stinger and Buscemi Venular that lie still on the roadway, their rims the only thing left bracing them.

The electric cyberpunk drivers are holding out handguns with a red wire attached to a pack on their chest; they fire off rounds through an electrically driven handgun.

Zaylee thrusts open her door, stepping onto the asphalt below. She pulls out her weapon and points it at the cyberpunk members, "Stop where you are!" she shouts at them. They look over and then look back at the hostile drivers, ignoring her. They continue firing assemblages of bullets towards the Morgan Stinger and Buscemi Venular.

Their bullets leave metal holes in the side of their vehicles. The drives of the Stinger and Venular sit pushed up against their doors with their hands over their ears and fear etched on their faces.

Zaylee pulls out a grenade from her belt and throws it at the approaching cybersquad members. After throwing it, she turns around and ducks behind a vehicle, putting her hands over her ears. An explosion goes off and electrifies the air. The cybersquad members fall to the ground, limp from the shock. Zaylee puts her weapon away and walks over to them.

As she looks them over, she mutters, "Your electric powered weapons recoil too much. And you fail to capitalize on Tesla technology, like the grenade that has you incapacitated." Zaylee ducks to their level and starts cuffing them, but her berating does not cease, "If you make bail, let Rayna know you won't win against true Justice." A non-cuffed cyberpunk member coughs and tilts her head towards Zaylee, "You cannot dispense justice. Those two have run over citizens, permanently handicapping them, and they just get away with it. You can't stop them." she says, condescending to her. "We will see about that." Zaylee says, kneeling down and cuffing her.

More police swarm in behind Zaylee's vehicle. Eventually, they park, exit their cars, and slam the doors behind them. They approach and pick up the cuffed cybersquad members on the floor. They walk them over to their vehicles and place them in the back. A male officer approaches Zaylee, standing in front of her. Noticing him, she states, "Captain Kiff, the remaining two street racers are behind their vehicles. I will arrest them myself." Upon hearing Zaylee, the two street racers walk back from their cars and look at the Captain.

Captain Kiff looks at their information on his tablet, "Unnecessary." he succinctly insists. Zaylee looks back at him, "Unnecessary?" she repeats with a question. "These two have diplomatic immunity. They are free to go." Captain Kiff replies, before turning around. "No, these two broke the law, endangered our citizens. I don't care if they are the President of another nation, harming or allowing the potential to harm citizens is a federal offense and a crime against humanity. The UN laws should have some way to extradite or prosecute these felons." Zaylee claims confidently. But the Captain makes no effort to recognize Zaylee's comment, and continues to focus on his tablet.

"Are you feeling green today Captain or are you always this sick in the head to let murderers go free?" she asks.

Kiff sternly remarks, "Watch your tone." Zaylee scoffs as he shakes his head. He puts the tablet away in his bag and looks at Zaylee, "You will stand down and do as I say." A look of refusal splashes onto Zaylee's face, "I will do no such thing. If I let them go, they will eventually kill someone." Zaylee continues. Captain Kiff turns and looks at Zaylee with intense magnitude and power, "You will do as I say or you will be fired." She remains silent, and Captain Kiff walks away. She contemplates everything as she walks back to her vehicle, and leaves, frustrated.

Chapter 9: Cheaters

"Unit 451 on patrol and ready to receive." Zaylee says into her radio device with more monotonicity, given how repetitive the statement has gotten for her. She places the radio back into its slot as "10-4" comes out of the speaker. Zaylee pulls the lever again and puts the car into drive.

She pulls her vehicle out of the lot and begins her patrol, turning left. Immediately she heads to one of her favorite streets in Los Angeles: Olympic Boulevard, which just happens to be one block North of the police department. She felt blessed that she could work on the cherished street from her childhood. She remembered how she had gone to the Electronic Entertainment Expo near Olympic for a decade with her father, once he left EMT work to become a programmer, and how much she loved that opportunity to learn about coding.

Thoughts begin to correlate, creating a cogency of atmosphere that bred, what she believed, was Los Angeles. The neon lights around the street flash inside her pupils meshing with reality as they trigger in her retina; the stop lights neon ambiance flows through her. She re-imagines the scenes of the Expo; advertisements, repetitive speeches, violence, blood, sex, and drug enhancements flood her neurons. She believed it to be the perfect analogy of Los Angeles, except with more palm trees, millions more palm trees, everywhere.

A car rushes around the corner, notices her vehicle strapped with lights on its roof, and immediately tries to turn around, but it gave away the location it was heading towards by making such an abrupt move. Multiple cars are out in the distance. She watches metal sparks fly as they slash into the lead car's tires. With his punctured tires, he ends up stopping in the center of the street. The driver cringes in fear, gripping his steering wheel tightly.

The cars that followed him spin in different directions around him, while a green car slides in front of him, right near the hood. Tears drip down his face upon seeing two huge Mantis blades protrude out from the nearby cars. They swing, slicing up the front of his car. Pieces of the hood slam onto the ground with a loud thud.

The crosses draped around their necks jolt forward as their

car slows from hitting his car.

Zaylee quickly turns her vehicle towards them, revving the engine as the instant electric torque hits the wheels. They continue to slice up his car by ramming their cars into his. One of the bladed vehicles stops completely and the driver gets out of it, slamming the door behind him.

He pulls the Mantis-blade off his car and shoves it into his gauntlet. After the blade locks in place with click, the blade starts to heat up. He lunges straight into the side of his door, shoving the blade through the metal. He slides the blade down, the heat easily slicing the door in half. The flaming door collapses onto the floor, crashing into the asphalt, putting a cut into the street. He reaches in and yanks out the driver, slamming him onto the side of the car. Zaylee drives up quickly, stopping her vehicle behind the criminals. She opens up her door, draws her weapon, and places her hands on the top of her roof, pointing the weapon at them, "Freeze!" she shouts at them.

He stares over at her with a face etched in hostility, "Never!" he shouts, turning back to face the man. He shoves his Mantis-blade into him, breaking his ribs upon insertion and causing his shirt to catch fire. The heat grinds down on the bone but fails to slice all the way through. He pulls it out and drops him to the floor, Zaylee grasps the trigger, creating a pop that echoes down the street. The man falls to the floor mid-run.

The rest of the Mantis-blade wielding criminals begin kissing their crosses and praying as they run to their cars and drive away, zipping away at the fastest possible speed. She walks over to the demolished car, putting her weapon back in its holster.

Zaylee reaches the downed man, a hole sits in his chest from the blade, but she realizes that he is barely breathing, since the blade singed part of his diaphragm. She pulls out the radio on her belt, "I need backup at my location, an ambulance as well." she says, placing the radio back down into its slot afterwards. The man she wounded with her pistol lays on the floor, still breathing. Noticing this, Zaylee asks, "Why did you do this?" The man fiddles with the hole in his shirt from the bullet before answering, "He beat a child while drunk, killing her, but the mayor pulled some strings and let him go." he says, spitting out blood onto the floor.

"You can't enforce justice that way. All you'll end up becoming is a judge of dread." Zaylee says, relaying her perceived epiphany from before. "Besides, do you really think you can catch all the criminals?"

He laughs, "It's not about catching them all. This isn't a video game, it's real life." he says, pausing to catch his breath. "It's about the one you let go." he continues, pushing himself off the ground. Zaylee points her weapon at him, "Stay down." she commands. But he keeps his momentum going forward. "I said stay down!" she shouts. He turns around and spits out blood to the side, although some remains on his cheek and moves as he speaks, "What are you going to do? Gun me down for doing what the police couldn't?" he jests.

"No, I just, well." she tries to reply. "You just what? Want evil to continue running society?" he asks, turning away and looking back at his car. He opens the door and sits down, attempting to catch his breath. Zaylee looks at the man on the floor with a hole in his chest, the heat from the slice helped slow the bleeding. She looks back over at the criminal, who is starting is car, "Your weapons are pathetic! You need more heat!" she yells. "Ever heard of acetylene? Use that instead of propane and you'll be able to cut through bone!" she blurts condescendingly. The criminal drives away, purposely heading towards Zaylee with his window down.

She points her gun at him as he smiles, causing her to insult him, "You aren't even a competent criminal. I can do what you do better, teach you how to fight with real skill. But that's not a lesson you need to learn, you need to learn how to have faith in humanity." she says quickly to him. "Hmph!" he rudely grunts at her, before speeding off.

Zaylee kneels down and gets close to the wounded man, "I will do what I can." she says, motioning her hand towards his chest. "This will hurt." she confirms, planting her hand on his chest. She applies pressure to his wound and the last of the bleeding stops, but he is still wheezing. Slowly, he ceases to breath altogether and perishes in her arms, but with his last breath he says "He was right, I am a criminal."

The last sentiments cut through her heart, leaving a stain of confliction; her mind fights against itself, attempting to retain her semblance of order and justice.

After gathering her thoughts, the ambulance arrives and she lets them take care of the deceased individual. As she glints an image of them doing CPR, she hops into her car. A singular tear flows down her face but she wipes it away and focuses herself, channeling her sadness into a more manageable emotion.

"Unit 451 back on patrol." Zaylee says into the microphone. "10-4 Unit 451." a voice replies. She puts her radio back into the slot near the console. She looks at the road ahead, endless to the eye. "I will prove Trey wrong." Zaylee says to herself, "Humans can be good without God. Because God doesn't even exist! I will prove that humans are good without religion. That we created morality" she continues as she stares at the environment along Olympic Boulevard. Multiple people walk down each side of the boulevard. Every single one is different.

Some are wearing suits and some are wearing culturally cut tank tops with logos of their favorite video games or streaming shows. Others are wearing dresses and some are wearing very little. The dynamic of L.A screams heavily along Olympic. The electronic signs and media literature plastering every open spot on the buildings.

Zaylee was enjoying the scenery; even the advertisements brought a smile to her face. They reminded her of a childhood long ago and helped her avoid the recent vigilantes and the loss she just incurred.

As she pushes further along Olympic, she spots a homeless person with a shopping cart. He is pushing it down the street with all his belongings inside. He stares at her different, and unique, cop car as she passes by.

Zaylee, having realized the man's situation, and desiring to stimulate some positive emotion within herself, turns around at the designated U-turn. As she turns her vehicle around, the man watches her and presumes she is going to stop him. Her car approaches the scraggly gentleman slowly. He stops where he is and pushes his cart to the side. He walks over and sits on the curb, waiting for her to approach.

She parks her vehicle and exits. Each cowboy boot hits the pavement in her endeavor to reach the gentleman, the spurs jangling as she moves; she walks towards the man sitting on the curb, causing a metallic noise to echo from her boots as she does.

He stares up at her, "Yes, officer, how may I help you?" he asks through his cavity ridden teeth. His hair rough, jagged, and flowing down over his eyes, but the green color still shines through. Staring in his eyes, she asks, "Sir, you're homeless, correct?" The sun glares down on them, striping the pavement below. "Yes ma'am." he replies, looking at her in her brown eyes. He notices a tiger stripe splitting through one eye and marvels at its beauty.

"How did you become homeless?" she asks, pointing her boot out towards traffic. The question stirred deep within him, polarizing his rage that he had been keeping under the surface, "My wife took my kids. The judge demanded I pay absurd child support and alimony to her. But she was the one that cheated on me. And I didn't even get visitation rights." he explains, while staring at the loose gravel in the street. Zaylee moves closer and sits in the street beside him. She points her eyes, just like her boots, out towards traffic.

Zaylee thinks for a second and says, "There should be more equality in the courtroom. I'm sorry someone was cruel to you. We shouldn't perpetuate cruelty within the law, but that's just how the system is right now." She then seeks to care for him and asks, "Do you still have your job? Or at least a place to stay?" she asks him. "No. My wife took everything from me. The house too." he replies with sullen eyes.

"All I wanted, through all of it, was to see my kids." he says, as he begins to cry. Each tear splashes onto the gravel.

"You could get a job to support them and maybe change the Judge's decision," she explains to him. He wipes his tears away and mutters through his sorrow, "I was forced to quit my job because I was going into debt having to continue paying mortgage, alimony, and child support. If I can't see my kids, what is the point of my suffering?" he asks, while looking at her. "I can give you a ride to a shelter for the night." Zaylee says.

"What I really need is a better job, so I can pay all that she wants. I want to see my kids. Hold them. Hug them." he says, beginning to tear up again. "I want to show them that I love them." he says, with tears streaming down his face. "Every kid needs a father. Someone to help them when they struggle." he confers.

"But now, all I do is get cited by cops for loitering and being homeless, or 'supposedly' stealing a shopping cart." he states, while putting his fingers in the air to physically express the quotations when he speaks the word 'supposedly'. As he returns to his normal stature, a crumb falls from his beard and onto the ground below.

Zaylee remains interested; her eyes never break contact with his. He begins gesturing out to the tents on the street, "I don't understand it. L.A is full of homeless people. Why me? I was a good citizen. I paid taxes. I never broke the law. I was always a good father and a good worker. Then, a judge comes in and wrecks my life and I have no recourse."

He looks at her car and gestures at it, "Just look at your car, you can enforce those corrupt officials will with, what's the word? The word for no punishment?" he asks. Zaylee singularly and pithily remarks, "Impunity." He exclaims, "Yes, that." After a brief moment of excitement from the word, he returns to his normal sullen disposition and laments, "How am I supposed to contest the ruling? I can't afford a lawyer. I'm just an average citizen, not even close to rich." he claims. "In fact, I don't have a single dime to my name. Yet, Beverly Hills sits with thousands of vacant bedrooms, only serving to feed their rich owners ego's. Sure, they claim to help others, but why do they have more than they need?" he ponders rhetorically, attempting to magnify the issue even more.

She sympathizes but corrects him, "Our enemies might be the government and criminals. We must bind the former with the law so that we may better apprehend the latter. But we must do so from within the system." she explains. The man laughs, "And what about the narcissistic rich folk who act like they care but are basically go around throwing burritos and rolls of quarters at me? They could actually help us, give us a place to stay, but they throw scraps at us, like it's some kind of joke. And then they say they worked hard for their money so they deserve it! Like I didn't work hard for my money when I worked." he asserts.

Zaylee looks at her vehicle with regret and then back to the homeless man, "My vehicle helps me better apprehend criminals. I would sell it to help you, but it's kind of a reminder for me. I do know of a place that I donated to when I sold my house that could help you with housing and food though." she explains. They make eye contact again, "What is food and housing without my children? All I care about is them. My wife doesn't, and was pissed when she found she was pregnant, yet she gets the privilege of seeing their beautiful faces everyday." he says, walking towards her car. He runs his fingers around its fine white exterior and mutters, "I understand your reason for this car, and that's what separates you from the others that waste their money on Buscemi's, Horses, and other McDoodles. But if you contrast that to what the money could be used for, to help people, are you not still labeling people as unworthy?" he asks.

Defensively, Zaylee retorts, "Well, some citizens own extremely fast vehicles. I would not be able to apprehend them without it, and it's cheaper than a helicopter. However, I'm not your average cop; I am willing to bend the rules, if it helps the people. Much of the police force culture declares that the people are criminals. It's kind of ingrained because of the law and it's difficult to suck the poison out of the system out because of it." she declares. He looks a tad confused and so Zaylee continues, "Any cop who denies having a quota is just trying to save face in the media. We have to criminalize society to meet the police chief's demands. The cops that have busted you have done so because of his orders. Particularly because you are an easy target. But, like I said, I am not like them. The people are my friends, who I must protect." she explains to him. But his face stays sullen.

His face twitches, "It's not like you are telling me anything new. The poor have become smarter. Because of the rich and powerful that oppress us, we were forced to adapt. If you want to do something, fight the government. None of this religious crap will help that these folks are spewing either cause God doesn't exist, otherwise he would have stopped these legalized criminals decades ago, and punished the rich that lord over us. What ever happened to regular old public service of removing corrupt individuals, you know?" he asks.

"I am servant of the public, but I do believe in the sanctity of our origin too: capitalism, competition, checks, balances, and democracy. We will find our way back. The people just need to work for each other, instead of against each other." Zaylee says. He smiles and then laughs, "People with power and money will never give up what they have. They crave more, always." he says with a grim smile of defeat. But Zaylee remains steadfast, "I think the difference is that they don't realize how much their power and money could help society." Zaylee counters. His face brightens up slightly.

Seeing his positive reaction, Zaylee continues, "The less you use your power and the more effective you use your money, the better off the entire nation will be. But, with more power comes more abuse. It's a shortcoming of life. But that's how you test a human, to see if they are solicitous of others, or only thinking of themselves. I say give them power, then we know who to target. Then prevent them from ever having power again. No?" Zaylee asks him with endearing eyes. "Yeah, that would be a nice place to live." he adds, giving a real smile. She smiles with him.

"What is your name?" she asks. He looks at her curiously, causing her to reply, "I can try to put in a word with the judge. They love politics more than compassion. Every public servant might be plagued with corruption, but I'm here to set the balance in a way that favors the people first and only helps the government if it'll help the people." she asks politely, explaining her intent. He reaches into his pocket and places his fingers inside. A black leather square makes it way out, crimped between his fingers. He opens up the wallet, revealing its contents. A singular card behind a plastic see-thru housing. He puts his fingers inside and pulls out the card.

"My name is Mike Hertindo." he says, as he hands her his California identification card. She places her hand near the card and crimps it. He lets go and Zaylee takes it from him. She places it close to her face and reads the information. The plastic computer on her side unlatches upon her touch. She opens up the computer and places in the appropriate information. Their fingers touch as she hands him back his card.

"Thank you, Mike. I will pull your information and see what I can do." Zaylee says to him. He looks at her and smiles, "Thank you, officer." he says with tears in his eyes. He turns to Zaylee and begins to reach in for a hug. Zaylee backs up a little, "I'm sorry. I can't give you a hug, it's our policy. They believe you will go for our gun." she states, as he puts his arms down. "Oh," he says sullenly.

She gestures towards him, "Rules are rules and it's like we

said, they want us to believe our citizens are criminals, but I know you aren't. It's despicable. I know the majority is kind and caring, deep down. Especially the poor and unfortunate, since they are way more charitable than anyone rich or in power because they understand plight." Zaylee says.

Mike comments, "But, you're not. Why do they allow you to work for them? I can't see them tolerating someone like yourself on the payroll." Zaylee replies, "I was a high-ranking general. Hacking division." He looks eager for more information, so Zaylee continues, "We were the greatest cyberforce since the NSA's Patriot Act members." she laments.

Zaylee opens up more, "Not giving me a job would have landed them bad, and unwanted, publicity. They'll do anything to keep their image clean. Since I wear a camera on me, always. It's a personal choice by the way. I do it so they have no way of saying I forged paperwork or did something wrong. And they definitely will keep me on. They wouldn't want me squealing about their current dysfunction and so forth." she explains to him. She points to the camera attached to her shirt, "This is worth their job and mine."

"Oh." he replies, not understanding most of what she said. "Unit 451, we have a 415 near the 2700 block of Pico Boulevard just south of your location." the voice says through her radio. "10-4" Zaylee says while pushing down on the radio button. "Sorry, Mike, I have to go. I'm sure I will talk to you soon." she says. "Us millennials stick together."

Mike shouts as she walks away, "Not when they bang your best friend with your baby in the other room!" She laughs and says, "So, it's true, you can become a cuckold even without choice!" she replies to him, lifting her head over her shoulder. "Living proof right here." Mike says, pointing at himself. He moves his hands off his chest and begins to push his cart down the street. He waves his hands in the air as he walks down the street, moderately happy.

Zaylee gets into her vehicle and turns on the engine. It purrs. She smiles as she presses her foot down on the pedal. Immediately the car launches forward, widening her smile.

Chapter 10: Clerks

Zaylee enters her vehicle and turns it on. She heads down the street and turns south. Then she turns down Pico, heading West towards the ocean. Many restaurants line the street with their neon signs. Some are franchise, some are corporate, and almost none are private. Zaylee recognizes that most of the franchise and corporate ones have robots working inside with no humans. She makes note of the private businesses, happy to see that all the profits are going directly to a hard-working family, instead of feeding a corporate or franchise machine. Although the massive amount of franchise and corporate restaurants compared to private restaurants stirs anger within her; the corporations outweigh them more than a hundred to one. She remembers her childhood, back when Los Angeles' restaurants had a closer fifty-fifty split between private and corporate or franchise.

Near a corporate restaurant there are two people standing outside. A bright neon sign labels the restaurant as California Pizza Bar. She remembers that Krust originally owned their license but Nettle bought them a couple decades back. They became huge after that with properties all over the states. She stops the vehicle in front of the restaurant and sees a woman brandishing a knife at a male. Zaylee immediately puts her vehicle in park and exits, ejecting Tommy from her car. Tommy flies into the air, its sirens and lights blasting away.

She stares over at the woman and pulls her gun from the holster. The gun, now gripped within her palm, moves upward as she points it at the woman, "Put the knife down!" Zaylee screams at her. The woman turns and stares at the direction of the voice. The knife hits the floor with a clank. Zaylee approaches slowly, still pointing her weapon at the woman. She commands Tommy to point its weapon at the woman. While she is attended to by Tommy, Zaylee sheaths her gun and reaches into her pocket, hauling a pair of black gloves out.

Again, she rummages through the receptacles sewn into her pants, until she grabs hold of a plastic bag. The bag falls down onto the top of her police car, hanging just pass the grill on her hood. The woman, now compliant and aware of her situation shouts, "Officer, this man sexually harassed me!" Zaylee ignores her comment and seizes the knife by its handle with her gloved hand. She walks back to her car and shoves the blade into the bag on her hood. Its top clasps, preventing air from entering or escaping.

Zaylee looks at the woman, "No matter what happened, you cannot act this way ma'am. The law clearly states you are only allowed to protect yourself, by getting to a safe place where you can call the authorities." Zaylee states, telling Tommy to stand down and approaches her, "You should have called us originally. We could have resolved things in a peaceful manner. You can still file a report now, but I have to take you in for attempted assault with a deadly weapon." Zaylee confirms to her.

"He grabbed me!" she screams while the tears begin to flow down. "I'm sorry ma'am, I have told you I will do my best to take care of the situation, but, for now, I need you to calm down and come with me." Zaylee says as she walks in between the two strangers.

She looks at the manager, dressed in his formal attire, "I will need both of your identification cards please." Zaylee commands kindly. They both reach into their pockets and retrieve their wallet and purse respectively. She unclasps the latch on her bag and hands Zaylee her ID, while the manager begrudgingly demounts his ID and places it in Zaylee's palm.

She clutches both of their ID's and looks at their pictures then their faces, matching them up and ensuring she has the right cards. Upon confirming she has the correct cards, she pulls out her tablet and swipes them through the slot to confirm their validity. Tommy watches from a distance, hovering in the air beyond Zaylee's head. Both their names register, displaying all of the information about them. She returns each identification card to its respective owner.

Zaylee thanks them with a nod and looks over at the woman, "Now ma'am, I am going to have to place you under arrest." Zaylee informs her, while grabbing her shoulder and turning her around. The woman willingly gives up her other arm as Zaylee fetches her handcuffs, detaching them from her belt. Each metal band slaps around her wrists. The second band ties her hands together, pushing cold metal on her wrists.

By touching her skin, Zaylee gains enough leverage to push the woman forward. Simultaneously, while pushing the woman by the handcuffs, Zaylee grabs her head and ducks her into the cop car. She moves into the back of the squad car. Long strands of braided black hair flow with the forced movement as she makes it into her seat. Zaylee closes the door, activating the auto-lock system, and heads over to the other side of the vehicle to seat herself in the driver's seat.

Zaylee grabs the steering wheel and pulls away from the curb. She grabs her radio, "Suspect in custody, enroute to station." she says into the radio. "10-4 unit 451. Upon detaining suspect, please pick up Megan. She will be your partner for the remainder of the day." the voice replies. Zaylee tilts her head back and looks at the woman leaning against the window.

She notices that the woman is crying and apologizes, "So, I'm sorry that I'm booking you but it is the law and you were threatening to harm another. No excuse can prevent you from your punishment but I am not your enemy. I am here to be a mediator and friend to all citizens." The lady stares peculiarly back at Zaylee, "My friend?" she flippantly submits.

"Yes, your friend." Zaylee replies, before illuminating her intent by declaring: "You can tell me whatever you wish. You can tell me about your issue at work and I will do my best to alleviate your problem. Even if I cannot prevent your inevitable punishment, I want to help you solve the problems within your life." Zaylee continues. The woman looks at her flabbergasted by the comment, "Help me? You can't help me. We are scum to the police. You used to catch people selling and doing drugs and arrest them. Then, you all of a sudden change your mind, renaming jail as rehabilitation and killing felony three strikers. Yet my baby daddy is still in there. You ain't here to help me, you're just some hussy they hired to make sure they stay fat and rich." she says angrily.

"The other police are ignorant." Zaylee replies. Seething with indignation from her comment, "That's not police, that's those judges. They will burn your life just because you're not rich or powerful. It doesn't matter if you didn't do anything that hurt anyone. Nor does it matter if you did something you didn't have a choice to walk away from. You can't stop people from doing drugs and being ignorant. But what does it matter to them if you don't have money? If you're a nobody, they'll put you down, like you're some unwanted dog at the pound."

Zaylee sighs, "It matters because they need to make their money. They all need to make money but they are illogical. They'd rather pay for your food and cost of living for years, rather than just rehabilitate criminals properly. It's a system of ignorance, led by ignorance, and controlled by the ignorant. You can't blame us all. I am here to help. Talk to me and I will try my best to help you." Zaylee explains to her.

"Fine." the woman replies, reaching forward. Her hand jostles in the air before finding its place back at her side. Zaylee looks over the woman's exterior and notices that much of her physique reminds her of a Bolivian woman she met many years ago. The memory of Bolivia echoes through her head from her old history class and she remembers how it is named after Simon Bolivar and how he was the George Washington of South America.

She thinks back to how she learned that in college and how mad she was that public school didn't go into depth about him, given how important he was to history. But the memory fades and reorientates her mind on the situation at hand. To refocus and connect with the woman, she locks eyes with her, "So, who is this man that's been harassing you?" Zaylee inquires, before thinking ahead and saying, "Like who is he to you. And what pushed you that far?" Her words, while simple, are also bound with an attempt to rehabilitate her decision making. She rolls her eyes, "He is my boss. I've been working under him for like three years now. All he does is bug me to do things outside of work, like dates. It's constant texts and sexual advances with him. It's aggravating." she begins to explain.

Zaylee interjects, "All men and women do is text. It's millennials teaching their kids to act like them, it's pathetic. I grew up with those people and I know how disgusting they are with it. They lie and say they will love you forever. That you're special. Important. All to boost your confidence and they want you to realize that they were ones that boosted it, just to get in your pants. Not to have kids or a relationship, just to have sex, because culturally, the rich and powerful have declared that value of a female is in your body and not your mind. We need to change this culture and focus on logic because the rampant sex is disgusting and pointless."

The woman doesn't reply, causing Zaylee to continue, "The things people will do to be loved though. And the things people will fake for sex. It's a disgusting system that perpetually continues throughout existence. The long endeavor that is rarely sated. If you find a good guy, keep him. God knows I've burned through too many but I eventually found someone worth keeping around. A guy who doesn't lie and a guy who remains who he is throughout, while helping me learn too." Zaylee continues, referring to her personal life.

Still, the woman does not respond, so Zaylee spews more words at her, "But we have to focus on the problems as a nation. That's the only way we can make this place better to live in. There is no need for violence. If we vote, we can change the nation to be how we want it. We can vote in new politicians to represent us." Zaylee tries to teach her. She gives a partial laugh, "No need for violence? You can't be serious." she says, still chuckling.

She stares at the bottom of Zaylee's patrol car, tilting her head to look around. Perking back up and leans in towards Zaylee, her head sits diagonally in comparison to her torso as she speaks, "I can't afford to support my kids, let alone a lawyer. Then, when I filed a DV215, for a restraining order, the judge takes his side because of his rich Pasadena Nettle lawyers. He knows he can't fire me because I'll win in a civil case against him for sexual harassment, so he keeps me working for him, so I can be under his thumb. Now you can think what you like, but you got that white privilege bias. You can get things done because you are white. So, why on Earth would you want to help someone like me?" she says, increasing in negativity.

"Someone like you?" Zaylee asks. "A black." she answers. "You power happy whites and Latino's are always condescending because we're, like, lower class citizens who supposedly steal all your benefits by being a minority." she finishes. Zaylee stops her vehicle and parks it. She looks back at her. "You are a citizen of this nation. No congenital factor can ever change my perspective of any citizen, that includes you. Do not declare me white and associate me with the rest. I could be British, German, Italian, French, Swedish,

Finnish, Norwegian, Russian, or Irish. The government chooses to label them all as Caucasian but there is a difference among them. And yes, I do have Mexican heritage within me, as well as European. But your label is unwarranted and racist; you don't know me." Zaylee states.

"I'm racist?" the woman asks, sitting back in her seat and shaking her head.

Zaylee thinks, leaving only the roar of the engine to fill the void of silence, before she attempts to elucidate on the finer details, "Your comments are equally as racist as the white privilege or Latino majority you claim oppresses you. The culture of a race has skewed your view and you have chosen to lop everyone of a certain race into a category. You have stereotyped them. If you were truly using equality, you would know that it means differentiating people by their character, personality, and actions, without noticing congenital factors. Generally, those statements, like yours, are made so that you can escape the law and continue to riot and commit acts of violence so you can gain power. I have seen people who have murdered several innocent civilians, who were simply expressing their view. I have watched these same people help criminals escape. These criminals are defended by feminists and racial activists. They have the people all riled up and continuing crime for no reason. Actions like yours and the activists only stems more violence and harm to the people."

The woman in the back pauses before saying, "I believe what you do, we share the same message, but there is a need. There is a need for violence because these people will not listen to us otherwise. They haven't before and they won't now, even with proof of God right in front of them, giving us truth that we have never heard before. We are cash cows to them, working class slaves, tools for their wars and their objectives. We are cattle being led to slaughter. They will slice our throats and use our blood for their restaurants." she says while pressing her finger tightly on her neck and giving a slicing motion. After a few seconds to let the sentiment linger, she affirms, "God, I'm lucky I even have a job."

Zaylee remains quiet, and to fill the void, the woman continues, "Hell, they might take that away soon, and replace fancy restaurants with fancier robots. And you know what the worst part is? We can't even fight them properly. They will condemn us, enact martial law, kill us, or do anything they have to, in order to keep their power and money. The feminists and racial activists are just the same. They both ignore the greater good and the people in power allow them to. If we even think about stepping up, we are punished so that those in control can keep their fancy cars, houses, and ignorance. So, they can be right and we can be wrong. Just like right now. I will be unjustly punished, regardless of what you attempt to do. You cannot help me; they won't let you. But she has given us the truth, undeniable and beautiful, as words from God should be. So, even if we die, we die knowing we are right and they are wrong. There is nothing they can ever do to change that. The fabric of the Universe remains the same no matter a judge's decision, for it was God that built the Universe and gave her these truths."

Irritated but also sympathetic, Zaylee vocalizes her view, "What the judge did was wrong. I cannot change what he did but I can try to rectify it. Judges are supposed to dispense justice, not bias. I have faith they can change. They signed up to be judges for the people and not judges for their friends and the rich. I believe they can change. I'll try my best to help you with them."

Zaylee focus on the road, waiting for the woman to reply. She notices a semi-truck attempting to merge over and so she flashes her lights, signaling that she will let them. The truck glides into her lane and she reads the back of the vehicle, noticing that it is a refrigerator truck, probably containing ice cream or some type of perishable food. As her mind wanders through the various edible commodities that it could be, the woman gets closer and closer to the grill divider.

The woman begins spewing words: "People don't change. Thinking like that leads to instability and false humans who will burn a country pretending to be someone they are not. People can only learn and mature. And these people are children subject to the fallacies of ignorance. They fund big towers in the sky instead of medical research. They open another crappy burger joint instead of funding education. They apply excess fines through their lawyers and contracts, to feed the corrupt judicial system. They fail to make a more amicable work environment, that would allow for more innovation in their products. They want to keep what they have

90

instead of adapting and making the last thing obsolete." she rants on. Her saliva drips over the grill of the car as her anger increases.

"What is this rambling?" Zaylee questions while placing her car in park. She turns back to look at her, to better absorb the information.

"The people in power are against us, and against God, because they want to keep what they have. They shut down everything in their way and remove any potential for growth. Oligopolies, controlled markets, biased court systems, police brutality, culture promoted fallacy, and frivolous spending. You just wait. One day the Lord's servants will come for all the celebrities, judges, and police that wronged us. And you, you will be our enemy on that day. And on that day, they will watch you bleed out, happy that your power trip is gone." she says with extreme hostility.

Zaylee ponders aloud, "Who is this crazed woman you speak of? Why has she made you think this way?" The woman lets out a weak laugh at Zaylee's ignorance, "You need to watch more vids. She showed us the last testament of Jesus, written on bone and bamboo, a record from the past that showed that Jesus is real. Now there is change coming. She knows it all. She will lead us all. She is the prophet of truth and her truths will lead us to build a nation that is unstoppable in philosophy, technology, and progress." the woman replies.

The woman sits back in the vehicle, causing her body to coalesce with the plastic seat. The rigidity causes her to twitch in an attempt to become comfortable. Zaylee grips her wheel as the woman looks at the back of Zaylee's honey colored hair, that's wrapped in a bun, but looks like it needs a good wash to get out some of the debris from her various activities. Beyond Zaylee's hair, her view is blocked by the diamond shaped metal grate that divides the front of the vehicle from the back.

Zaylee starts conversing about the change this woman seeks, "Violence won't get rid of the problem. You'd have to take out those in charge and replace them. Riots will just make them go quiet and wait to resurface. They will eventually abuse the public once gain. You must use your rights as a voter and elect the right officials into office, so they can make the proper changes for our nation." Zaylee says, starting to question her own thinking paradigm, "But, how

91

would you know who would make a good replacement? How do you know they are not like the rest?" Zaylee asks herself.

The woman shakes her cuffs at the chains, the silverly metal glistening, "Hello!? You don't. But there comes a time when any replacement is better than none. Change is growth, maturity, and maximization of nature's gifts. If you pay attention and learn from your mistakes the world becomes a better place. Maybe even one where I can make a livable wage and provide a decent life for my children without having to live in poverty." she replies.

Zaylee looks at her, "The minimum wage has never been a livable wage. I know that corporations keep their workers in poverty to keep more of the revenue, but violence isn't going to stop them. You have to work to earn your higher wages, politically. You know, talk with your representatives and so forth." Zaylee replies.

The woman sits back down and scoffs, "We have tried to work for it politically for hundreds of years. The pattern is always the same. The rich elite brings us down, so they can become so rich, it's stupid. And if we increase the minimum wage, they simply raise their prices. Economics is broken by greed, and that greed comes from not having God as a guide. We need to send them a message that we sit idly by anymore." she replies. Zaylee stops and offers a caring glance, "What is your name?" Zaylee asks. "My name is Ciara." she answers. "If there is anything I can do to help you, Ciara, I will do it. No one deserves what you've had to endure." Zaylee replies to her, getting out of her beautiful police vehicle.

Chapter 11: A Computer Virus

Ah, my day off from the job, I say to myself. No more criminals to apprehend and just the peaceful hum of my computer, I continue. Huh? I say, confused. The Schesis show? I think to myself. I wonder what this is about. There are quite a few of them. Introductions? Ontology? Our greatest tools? The final frontier? What are these things? And why are they on my webpage? I wasn't looking for this Schesis thing. Although, this must be the prophet that Rayna and Ciara were talking about.

This must be a virus though, since I didn't click on anything. Let me check the add-ons for my browser.

As soon as I click the add-ons button the video for introductory one first and foremost begins. The audio begins to blare in my ear. It's a pretty voice, but the aggravation of it automatically starting is enough to overlook her voice. I click on the red 'x' in the corner of my browser. Nothing happens. Can I close this? I don't want to hear this.

I click on the close button of my browser again but it doesn't work. I try the hotkey to close the window, ALT + F4. That doesn't work either. I try another, CTRL + W, to close the tab, that doesn't work either. I smash my fingers into my keyboard, frustrated that it still won't close. No combination of buttons is closing it. This is one nasty virus, can't even close it without opening command prompt or task manager. Blah.

I begin to listen to her. Some of her words are interesting. The calamities facing the world? What is she referring to? She has a stack of tablets that she is showing the camera, made of bone and bamboo and with ancient writing on them.

I can see a young girl with black hair. A triangular mask attached to her face moves with her as she speaks, augmenting her features and beauty. I watch her lips close and open as she mouths the dreary words explaining the tragedies occurring around the world. Even though I cannot see her eyes I can see the passion on her face as she speaks about the world. I can tell that she truly cares about everything and everyone. She only wants to create a better place for everyone to live in and she's not dispirited, but she's miserable. She knows what must be done but lacks the power to do it. Only problem is that she believes in God.

Everything she is saying sounds like something I would say. The world is a corrupt place but there are legitimate ways to fix it for everyone to be happy without conflict.

I grab the armrest on my chair, physically representing my fixation on the video displaying on my monitor. The interface of my computer can still be seen on the bottom of my monitor. Its large one-meter 32K display adds an almost retina level of clarity that is indistinguishable from reality. My slightly off vision adds to its perceivable clarity.

It seems like this girl is effective at getting her message out. She has developed a virus to spread her videos. This virus isn't commonly coded either, cause the normal way to get rid of viruses didn't work. Seems to be written in Haskell. I wonder if this is what that woman, Ciara, meant. I guess I am now finding out what she was talking about. All this philosophy, but it's too much to soak in for one sitting.

"Hey babe, come back to bed." Trey says. An image of him laying down on the bed pops into my head. I imagine him sitting up and staring in my direction, begging me to come and sleep with him. It is nice to have the embrace of someone else. I haven't felt it in years. He makes me feel alive and the competition he has with me really motivates me.

"Not yet. I'm watching something." I reply. I'm not sure he will like my response but I really want to finish this video.

"But Zaylee!" he says, pestered by my answer. I knew he wouldn't like it. He responds like a little kid, it's so cute.

"It's important. I'll be there in five." I reply to him with a serious tone.

"Fine." he acknowledges.

I guess I will watch this later. I'll save these links so I can watch the rest tomorrow. And I will subscribe to her on ourtube. I click on her channel and then click the subscribe button. I notice that she has a post regarding upcoming content. It says that it will be released tomorrow and it will be the last of her introductory videos. That would be the opportune time to check out all of her videos. Since it'll be complete.

Right now, I have to focus on removing this virus. I click out of my browser. Now that I'm subscribed and have the links saved, I'll continue watching them all tomorrow.

I move the cursor towards an icon on my desktop of a coding program. With the wallpaper transparently covering the rest of the desktop behind it, I press twice on the mouse.

A coding program opens up after I click on it. The virus is encrypted. It isn't too large of a bit encryption. Only thirty-two bits. But it will take a few hours decrypt it. The program functions autonomously and will run all possible decryption codes until it finds the correct one. I'll be able to find out what exact variant of Haskell code was running. I am reminiscing about how I used to help the engineers and programmers with computer difficulties in the military.

I imagine myself towering over a few people sitting in chairs, in a dimly lit room, with computers in front of them. My three stars tightly fixed onto my coat. My hat sitting firm on my head. I walk in a tight formation over to them. I proceed to ask them if they have fixed the problem. They tell me that they have not.

I tell them they are relieved. My mouth lacking saliva makes the words seem powerful. As he leaves, I push the chair back and take his place. I immediately set down my hat and move my hands onto the mechanical switch keys. Pressing them down fills me with joy. The same joy as what I am feeling right now.

I had to manually do the coding for their projects. Now there are written programs to do it for me. But I miss doing it myself. I miss being able to use cryptology, maybe I should crack open the old math book but they won't let me do it with the department. But it's so easy. All you need is the right string of numbers and you can break any firewall, even a five hundred and twelve-bit encryption. Quantum computation works off a different series of computation, it has the chance to find it more quickly, therefore, making this old Haskell form of encryption obsolete. But Haskell is still a powerful language with much utility in its hacking capabilities.

Ultimately, no matter how far the encryption evolves, there is always something to override it. That is the nature of technology. I love that this girl talks about things becoming obsolete, yet the final frontier is technology. It's a beautiful philosophy that can be applied to every piece of the world, no matter how complex or simple.

Everything can become obsolete. Those that fight it are only fighting the inevitable.

The new quantum computation is why the pirating industry is thriving still. All they need is a string of codes from the entertainment or data crystal creator. So, quantum just follows every path possible until it finds it. Then, once they have discovered the string, they refer to the older days of piracy. They use that string to 'crack' the code and gain access to the media. Then all they need to do is find a Swedish or Ukrainian server to upload their file. Thus, the piracy continues and Hollywood continues to get angry. But I don't think they will ever stop the pirates. Maybe I could stop them but the Hollywood division won't let me participate and it'd only be temporary anyway. Eventually their hacks will become more elaborate and they will find a way to hack their property regardless of what I did. It's the way of the black hat. You only need a stronger white hat to stop them. Plus, what do I care about those spoiled brats.

Now what is she saying in this video? The United States doesn't fight war properly? I can't believe what I am hearing. I love the military. Their main job is to protect the people, their rights, and their money. But maybe she has a point, maybe. I mean, there were missions that were a waste and there were missions that actually harmed individuals. All we did was send people to their death. It could be view as a form of eugenics instilled by the government; a way to weed out the weak. A few commanders, lieutenants, and generals I knew desired only to enroll people, just to remove them from society because they were believed to be worthless. But as a group, the military did the people right. It's the only reason I stuck with them and applied my skills for them.

Honestly, I miss my military lifestyle. I miss the responsibility and the power I had to be reserved and intelligent with. It was my choice, my mission, and my objective to accomplish. I could do whatever I wanted, but I had to do it right. It was my force to lead, completely. I could easily do it in favor of the people.

This home and police lifestyle is not for me. I couldn't transition from soldier to civilian, that's why I joined the police force. Yet, that is still not enough. I want to be out giving commands again. I don't want to be in a subservient relationship to my superiors. I'm not sure following God like she wants would be helpful though, because that would still being some obsequious servant. I guess I have to bend to other's demands to get Trey to bend to mine. I'm basically making him happy so I can continue simply helping the people. I was never cut out for this kind of life.

The military was the only organization that actually felt intelligent to me. Now, she is saying that they are inferior? What she is saying makes sense though. Whenever we fought a war or went to other countries, we used our own resources when we should be using their resources. If there are people that are part of that country, generally they will fight beside us. That is people resource that we could be using, instead of losing our military members.

I lost many good men at the hands of our enemy, when I could have been using the enemies' forces against them. People will rise up to stop tyranny, they always do. You just have to give them a reason to and give them hope that they can win. I can do it again if I wanted, but humanity will change. Trey is wrong. They can all save themselves without my influence. I just need to think of a better way to do it, to prove that it's possible without God as I know it is. I need to get more involved. I need to.

But, if I do what I want to do, then the chief will definitely fire me. I can't have that; I won't be able to help the people. I can feel my eyes drooping. I am significantly tired.

I better be getting to bed now; I will get back to this later. Trey will be waiting; we have a big day tomorrow. I head over to my bed and see Trey waiting on his side. His long blonde hair flowing onto his pillow. I smirk as I jump into the bed. I grab his face and kiss him. He laughs and kisses me back. I hug him and he wraps his arms around me.

Chapter 12: Cheaters II

A deputy stands in the hall with a freshly pressed and cleaned uniform and looks at Zaylee, "I appreciate your attendance, Zaylee. I didn't expect you to come, given how trivial this case is." the deputy says. "It's my duty as a police officer." Zaylee replies, shaking his hand. "Well, no one thought you were going to come, after all, it's just some homeless guy. I don't know why you are so obsessed with him." the deputy continues. Zaylee shakes her head, "Unlike most officers, I care for the people, even the ones I have to arrest." She moves past him and towards her seat. Trey is sitting down already, waiting for her. She approaches and sits next to him.

"All rise." the bailiff says. Zaylee and Trey stand on the same side of the courtroom, beside the homeless man she talked to on the street months back. His looks have been altered to fit the courtroom. Black stripes his arms and most of his chest except for a line down the center. A white shirt lines the opening with a black tie looped through, then around his neck. His face has been washed and groomed appropriately.

His jet-black hair is combed and slicked back. He stands confidently but fervently awaits the trial.

The room has several large televisions hanging down from the ceiling. Zaylee quickly remembers how the courthouses across the nation have hundreds of televisions for various amenities they claimed were necessary. Trey tilts his head down and whispers to Zaylee: "Look at this. They waste the people's tax money on frivolities that were unnecessary. Juror rooms filled with 125-to-150-centimeter televisions. Courtrooms and judges' offices filled with the same technology, it's ridiculous." Trey whispers quietly to her before catching eyes with the bailiff, who stares him down. Trey re-orientates himself and stands straight and formal once again.

"Department sixteen of the Superior Court is now in session. You may be seated," the bailiff tells the courtroom. They all sit and await the Judge. He likewise sits down, "Good morning, citizens. I'm calling the case of Mike Hertindo v. Rebecca Smith to order." he pauses and looks at the defendant and plaintiff. "Are both sides ready?" he asks. "Ready, your honor." the lawyer standing beside Rebecca says. Zaylee, having never seen her before, looks over and observes her. She has red hair down to her waist, brown eyes, and pale skin. All of this is wrapped in a decadent dress.

The lawyer next to Zaylee adjusts her suit, buttoning it, and says, "Ready, your honor." Zaylee looks at Mike; some of his ethnic traits and mannerism remind her of Rayna. His olive skin easily puts him in the same Fitzpatrick scale as her. Although, Zaylee double-takes and things that he might be just a tad darker. The Judge continues, "Let's begin." The lawyer next to Zaylee looks at the Judge.

She calmly but fervently addresses the court, "Your honor and citizens of this great country, the defendant has been charged with knowingly giving HIV to my client, without making him aware of her disease prior to sexual intercourse. We will also prove that the defendant is guilty of kidnapping Jared and Lily Hertindo on the night of April 16, 2052." she says. She looks down and picks up a disc. "This evidence will prove that the defendant is guilty of all charges being pressed upon her, namely assault with a deadly weapon and kidnapping." she says, doing a slight bow. "Thank you, your honor." she finishes as she sits back down.

The defending lawyer stands up and begins to walk around the courtroom. His presence amplifies his words. "Citizens." he begins, moving his hand to gesture at the watching humans. "Your honor." he says, nodding his head as the words pour out, "Contrary to what they have claimed, under the law, my client is innocent until proven guilty. During this trial, you will discover that any evidence provided, will not be substantial enough to convict my client and are absurdities brought about by the delusions of a homeless man. She simply did not do what they claim." he continues to walk around the courtroom. Trey scoffs at him.

Rebecca's lawyer takes a step to the side and makes a circular motion with his hand, "This is just an elaborate attempt for Mr. Hertindo to get custody of my client's children." he exclaims, walking towards the prosecution table. He places his hands on the wood, "Isn't that true?" he proffers, staring dead eyed at Mike's lawyer. He pushes himself off the table and folds his arms behind his back, "By the end of this, I will have proven my client is innocent." he pauses and looks at the Judge. "Thank you, your honor." he states, turning back and walking to his seat next to his client.

"The plaintiff may call its first witness." the Judge says, looking at Mike's lawyer. "We call Zaylee Tonitrum Ross to the stand." she says.

The clerk looks at Zaylee, her brown eyes greeting her. The bailiff leads Zaylee over to the stand and places her inside. She remains standing, waiting for direction. "Raise your right hand." the clerk demands. Zaylee raises her right hand up, keeping her left near her side. "Do you promise to tell the truth, the whole truth, and nothing but the truth lest you face punishment for your lies?" the clerk queries. The sentiment of non-belief puts a smile on Zaylee's face but Trey frowns, letting Zaylee know he is upset by it.

Zaylee claims, "I do." The clerk looks at her, "Please state your name for the court." the clerk asks. "Zaylee Tonitrum Ross." she replies. The clerk declares, "You may be seated." Out of habit, Zaylee sits down in her seat with an upright posture, almost at a perfect ninety-degree angle. The prosecutor looks at Zaylee, "How do you know my client?" she asks. Thinking back, Zaylee explains, "I saw him on the side of the street, I pulled over, and began to question him."

"Why did you question my client?" she asks. Zaylee stays calm and in the same rigid position while responding with, "I presumed he was homeless, given his attire and shopping cart, and wanted to help." Zaylee answers. "So, for the record, everything you did to help my client get a job, and a home, was simply out of charity?" she asks. "Correct." Zaylee responds. The lawyer looks at the Judge. "No further questions your honor." she finishes and goes back to her seat. The Judge looks over at Rebecca and her lawyer.

"Does the defense have any questions?" the Judge asks. The defense stands up, "Yes, your honor." he responds and makes his way over to Zaylee, "Officer, is it true that you helped Mr. Hertindo circumvent the law to lower his alimony payments?" he asks.

Zaylee holds back a scoff and responds with, "No, I followed proper procedure and helped Mr. Hertindo restart his case against Mrs. Smith." The lawyer continues pacing, "Is it not true then, that you went over another Judge's head, to achieve your desires for Mr. Hertindo while getting the EMT known as Trey involved?" Zaylee remains quiet and the lawyer continues, "Do you deny getting him involved in the business of Mr. Hertindo and having him purposefully run calls related to him?" he cross-examines. Zaylee shakes her head, "I did what was legally in the boundaries of Mr. Hertindo rights. Nothing more and nothing less. I followed the law at every step. What Trey did is Trey's business; I did not ask him to get involved, he did it of his own volition." Zaylee explains. The defending lawyer scoffs, "Really now?" he mocks her rhetorically.

"Yes, really." Zaylee continues. "Did you happen to know that Mr. Hertindo constantly harasses Mrs. Smith? She was being paid for emotional distress caused by Mr. Hertindo on top of the other payments." he claims. A bout of sarcasm leaks out of Zaylee, "Emotional distress caused by someone who cheated while their child was in the other room?" The lawyer takes offense and yells, "Your honor!" The Judge, in a monotone fashion, commands "Officer, do not antagonize," he commands. "Sorry, your honor." she responds.

"Your actions caused Mrs. Smith further distress. Your intervention was not necessary. And, furthermore, the law does not need your input since you were not personally involved with any of the crimes committed by Mr. Hertinado." the lawyer says, playing off the Judge's comment. The Judge nods in agreement.

The lawyer lets out a bellow and wipes his brow, "No further questions, your honor." he states. "The witness is excused." the Judge declares. Zaylee stands up and walks back to her seat, her spurs clicking as she walks. The Judge looks around the courtroom, "Does the plaintiff have any further witnesses?" he asks.

Mike's lawyer stands up, "Yes, your honor." she says. "The plaintiff calls the hematologist examiner." A female stands up, in a white lab coat, and walks over to the witness seat. She stands in front of the chair and raises her right hand. "Do you promise to tell the truth, the whole truth, and nothing but the truth lest you face the punishment for your lies?" the clerk asks. "I do." she responds. "Please state your name for the court."

"My name is Patricia Pasteur." she states. "You may be seated." The hematologist listens to the clerk and sits down. Mike's lawyer stands and walks over to the stand, "Patricia, where do you work?" she asks. "I work for Giraffe Medical Group." Patricia answers. "Furthermore, I have been a certified hematologist for fifteen years."

The lawyer brings a test result sheet to her stand, "Have you seen this test result page before?" she asks. Patricia looks at the sheet, "Yes, I was asked to run a sample of blood and this is my results sheet. Although this does look to be a copy, the results are accurate to the official document." she responds. Mike's lawyer looks at her, "Have you run tests on this client before?" the lawyer asks. "Yes, I have. On multiple occasions, over the past three years." Patricia responds. "Was there any difference in results from the previous results?" the lawyer asks. Without hesitation, Patricia remarks, "There was."

"Can you please clarify for the court, what was the difference in results?" the lawyer asks. Rebecca's lawyer stands up. "Objection! This is a direct violation of HIPAA passed in 1996." he shouts. The Judge looks over at Mike's lawyer, "This is not a criminal proceeding, Ms. Pinzón. We have not granted disclosure on said documents." the Judge explains. Ms. Pinzón looks back at the Judge, "My client, Mike Hertindo, has agreed to disclose all medical information as long as it is relevant to the case. He has deemed this relevant." Ms. Pinzón explains.

"You may continue then," the Judge states. Ms. Pinzón looks back at Patricia, "As I was saying, can you please clarify, what was the difference in results?" she asks. Patricia looks directly at her and states, "Mike's results came up as positive for HIV." Ms. Pinzón pauses, "Thank you, no further questions." she says as she heads back to her seat. The Judge looks over at Rebecca's lawyer, "Does the defense have any questions?" The lawyer stands up, "Yes, we do." he replies, standing up and heading over to Patricia. He adjusts his tie and looks at Patricia.

"Patricia, is it possible that my client contracted HIV from his activities as a homeless person?" he asks. Patricia places a finger on her chin, "It's possible." she says, as she puts her finger and arm back down to her side. He places his hand on the wood of the booth and asks, "Is it true that homeless are notorious for being drug users?" Patricia collects herself and her thoughts before responding with "Yes, they are." Rebecca's lawyer paces the courtroom, "So could Mr. Hertindo have contracted HIV from sharing needles with another drug user?"

"It's highly probable." Patricia responds. The lawyer looks at the crowd and raises his arms up in celebration, creating a horizontal line from one arm to the next, perfectly horizontal and even with his shoulders and neck. He turns back around and looks at the Judge then at Ms. Pasteur, "Thank you." he says looking at Patricia. "No further questions your honor." he claims. "The witness is excused." the Judge claims. After she leaves and sits back down in her seat, the Judge looks at Ms. Pinzón.

"Does the plaintiff have any other witnesses?" the Judge asks. "Yes, your honor, we have one last witness." Ms. Pinzón answers. "The plaintiff calls Emergency Medical Technician, Trey Tucca, to the stand." Trey stands up and moves towards the witness stand. His uniform pinned with a metal badge, denoting his profession to the courtroom. He stands tall over the stand, the chair barely visible behind him. His medium flowing blonde hair accentuating his eyes. He raises his right hand, the veins slightly protruding from his arms, but the muscles in his arm aren't abnormally large, merely toned.

"Do you promise to tell the truth, the whole truth, and nothing but the truth, lest you face the punishment for your lies?" the clerk asks. "I do." he responds. "Please state your name for the court." the clerk demands. "My name is Trey Octavius Tucca." he answers. "You may be seated." He sits down, his uniform remaining straight and unwrinkled in his seat with his upright posture, mimicking Zaylee's. Ms. Pinzón walks towards Trey.

"Trey, who do you work for?" she asks. "I work for USMR." Trey answers. "Can you please clarify USMR?" she asks. "United States Medical Response. I have worked as an EMT for several years." he answers. "Now, you worked a call involving Mrs. Smith on the night of April 16, 2052, correct?" she asks. Trey glares at Mrs. Smith, "Correct. I reported Mrs. Smith to the CDC, for violating several parameters for prevention of HIV." Trey answers.

"I did not ask about that yet Mr. Tucca." Ms. Pinzón declares. He looks at Ms. Pinzón, "I apologize." he responds, while still glaring at Mrs. Smith. "Can you please explain, for the court, what happened on the night of April 16, 2052?" Ms. Pinzón asks him. He points at Mrs. Smith, "This woman here, bound her children to a wall in the next room. She dead bolted the door from the outside so that they could not exit." Trey begins to explain. "Hold on." Ms.

Pinzón demands. But Trey's anger overwhelms him and he continues, "She was caught having sex in the other room with a heroin junkie, upon arrival. I found needles atop their dresser." he continues to explain, raising his voice.

"Objection!" Mrs. Smith's lawyer shouts. Trey continues to look at Mrs. Smith. He stands up and points at her with an open hand, "This deplorable piece of trash took her kids over to see their father, claimed they could stay, had sex with him, and then left and called the police on him. She then goes home, locks her kids up, as is tradition in their home, and bangs a junkie in the other room!" Trey shouts. "Objection! Objection! Objection!" Mrs. Smith's lawyer shouts profusely.

The Judge looks over at Trey, "Hold your tongue or you will be put in contempt." Trey stands up and points a hand over the witness stand, "This conniving piece of trash is allowing her crimes to continue by negating valid points." he states, pointing at the lawyer. He redirects his attention at the Judge, "Then, we have you, falling for his every word." he says, staring at him. "Aiding and abetting a criminal." he says, then points at Mrs. Smith.

Trey's venom spills out again towards the Judge, "You should be punished with the same crime as her, for your disregard of the law!" he shouts. Upon this verbal barrage, the Judge screams, "Bailiff!" The bailiff opens the witness stand door and reaches in to grab Trey. But Trey responds by punching him in the face and kicking him down the stairs. He falls down and lands face down onto the tile below. He turns back to look at the Judge, "Holding me in contempt? Hold yourself in contempt of the law!" Trey yells angrily.

Trey grabs a coffee mug and smashes it over the Judge's head. The shattered ceramic falls through the Judge's hair and onto the floor below. The Judge picks up his mallet and begins swinging it at Trey.

But not a single blow lands; Trey moves back, dodging his swings, then grabs the mallet in his hands. Their fingers touch as he rips the mallet from his hand. "You don't deserve to be a judge. You have ruined this innocent man's life. You allowed him to get HIV, then you allowed his despicable baby mama to kidnap, and tie up his children!" he says, hitting the Judge with the mallet, spurting blood all over the wall. More police enter the room. Trey watches as they enter, their uniforms giving off an aura of authority.

"All your cronies here, keep you in power, so drugged up sluts can ruin a good hard-working man's life." Trey says, pointing at the police before smashing his head in again with the mallet. They quickly run over to Trey, their hands cover his body, gripping his clothes tightly. They rip him from Judge's box as he gets a few remaining kicks in on the judge. His legs dangle over the wood as they pull him out. He ignores the police and focuses on the Judge, spitting on him and yelling, "You are disgusting! Believing him just because he's good with his words! I've seen her crimes! You can't let her go free!" he yells while being dragged by the police.

His body still facing the Judge; his eyes staring into the brutally beaten and near-death Judge. The swinging doors hit his head as they pull him towards the exit.

Zaylee looks at him with a face full of pain. She mouths the question 'why?'.

Trey looks at her, "He's going to let her go free! That slut will ruin another person's life! She'll give them HIV and take their money! The courts can't stop her!" he orates loudly to Zaylee, as the police take him out of the courtroom. Zaylee looks down the exit path and sees dots of blood where they dragged Trey. His hands, covered in the Judge's blood, had dripped it everywhere when they removed him from the courtroom.

Chapter 13: Clerks II

A crowd of people sit in decadent brown chairs. Across the beautifully shining wooden floors, stands an officer, standing tall in his brown uniform. Behind him is a colossal mahogany tri-sectional partition for the Judge, witnesses, and other parties. The center is elevated with a wooden mallet placed nearby. To the left of the scene are fourteen chairs placed in two rows, for the twelve jurors and two alternates. Sitting at the edge of each chair is a human, staring in varied facial expressions at the crowd. This was the jury of peers the government had loquaciously explained in their doctrine. Their faces of boredom had turned to nervousness at all the eyes in the crowd looking at them.

The officer stands tall and faces the crowd as a door behind him opens. "All rise." he demands. The entire crowd obeys the officer. They, along with the Jury, stand. Their legs press against the edge of their seats. Zaylee stands upright near the prosecution side. Opposite to her sits the woman who brandished a knife at her manager on the street. The Judge, with his scraggly white beard, makes his way to the front of his chair behind the bench. His long flowing outfit drags behind him, covering his shoes.

Zaylee stares over at the black woman and smiles. The black woman diverts her eyes to the Judge. Her manager, who was standing next to Zaylee, also looks over. His full tuxedo and fancy lawyers beside him, strikes loss into her. The inevitable decision flashed through Ciara's eyes as she watches her own lawyer fumble his briefcase. Papers are sprawled across their table in an unorganized manner. Zaylee looks at the Judge, "I will not let the courts ruin another life," she whispers to herself.

As the Judge sits down in his chair, the rest of the crowd, jurors, plaintiff, and defendant sit down.

—

Zaylee sits in the Judge's private quarters, still dressed in her uniform, as the court case just barely ended. Her cowboy boots firmly planted on the ground, wrinkling the carpet with their pressure. Her posture is slouched forward to get closer, breaking her normal upright demeanor. A desk separates the two from each other. His black gown flows with his body as he fidgets in his seat. A picture of him and his wife on the Santa Monica pier sits diagonally on his desk. They smile at Zaylee in a fixed manner as the Judge leans back in his seat.

Before he can speak, Zaylee interrupts him: "Mack, how could you do that to her? The maximum sentence, really Mack?" she asks him in a hostile manner. Mack holds steadfast, "It is not in the description of my position to take sides or hold bias. I apply the law without any influence from outside factors." But Zaylee does not give a single cent about his words and proclaims, "You know full well that the boss' story was a load of crap. She brandished a knife to protect herself from his sexual advances. That scenario is way more likely than her simply being hysterical over a managerial decision. Don't let his fancy corporate paid lawyers convince you different." she states.

His face remains blank with no sign of emotion, "The jury decided that, not me." Mack plainly replies. Zaylee cries out, "She couldn't afford a decent lawyer. She has two kids Mack. They need their mom. The jury might have decided her fate, but you sentenced her to five years rehabilitation with absurd fines. This isn't the first time you've made a decision like this. I've heard other stories about addicts we have busted for possession. You gave them hundreds of dollars in fines when all they needed was medical help. And when they pleaded with you, you gave them an extension because they didn't have a job, showing that you have at least a fraction of a heart. But, then, when they finally get a job, you tack on thousands in late fees. Every single time. You keep making it impossible for people like her, and even criminals, to eventually rehabilitate themselves and become a functioning member of society again." Zaylee declaims with hostility.

He doesn't respond, so Zaylee continues, "The judges and politicians keep doing this over and over again. A company's CEO and executives make money off its employees breaking the law and they get away with less punishment. The lower-level employees are making barely livable wages and they are doing massive time with massive fines. Yet, if you're a top-level employee, you can get away with sexual harassment, fraud, embezzlement, stealing, and basically any crime. It's pathetic, Mack. It should be the other way around; Ciara should be facing a small sentence with a small fine and the corporate elite should be facing a large sentence and a large fine. They can afford to do the time and pay the fine. She can't." Zaylee states angrily.

Mack shakes his head, "People like her and the druggies have their chances, regardless. They are criminals. And if they wanted to change, they would." Mack responds concisely. Zaylee looks at him with disgust, "No Mack. They are forced to continue a life of crime to pay what people like you unjustly demand of them. It's why, when they get out of prison, they become criminals. They must steal to pay off their debts to the state. Otherwise, another sheriff will show up at their door, with another subpoena or arrest warrant. It's no wonder why the people are refusing to try peaceful measures. You and the politicians overpower them and abuse them. They are left with no other option." Zaylee passionately decrees.

Mack perks up, "They are given three chances before we put them down. The three-strike law. Is that what you are mad about, Trey? And how he was not given three strikes? He killed a judge you know, a friend of mine too." Mack answers. Zaylee becomes angry, "How dare you bring him up. This doesn't have to deal with him. This has to deal with Ciara. I know the law, so don't belittle me. What I'm saying is that, after the first strike, you basically force them to commit the next two felonies for not being able to pay the government. As for Trey, it wouldn't have mattered if he was only sentenced once! He knew that what he was doing meant his death." Zaylee expands upon his statement. Mack scoffs, "How else would we survive? How would we even get into office, if it wasn't for our commission with congress and the senate?" Mack asks her, greed pouring out of his eye sockets.

"Commission? You mean you get a cut from each charge?" Zaylee asks. Mack laughs, "Of course we do. And so does your station. How do you think you get such fancy drones? The government can't pay for them through simple tax rates. We use third-party companies for traffic tickets from photo-booths. We have mandatory quotas to meet for the survival of the office. The lawmakers write these bills to keep us in business." Zaylee looks at him with utter disgust, "You mean you sentenced that girl with the maximum charges so you could acquire the maximum profit for the state? It was never about the maximum punishment; it was about the maximum profit for you and your buddies?" Zaylee questions, disgusted by his pilfering.

He shakes his hands, "Well, in a way, I guess. But it's only so we can better protect the people." Mack answers. "From what!?" Zaylee cries, rivers of anger pouring from her. She stands up and stares at Mack.

"From themselves." he confirms, distinctly but quietly. "You are disgusting Mack." she affronts, beginning to label him. "Zaylee!" he shouts as she's about to walk out of the room. She turns around and looks at him, "Trillions of dollars of debt because of state pensions, ignorantly funded city and state projects for things we did not need, and worthless bonds that have not pushed society forward at all. And you spend the people's money on trying to control them. You sent all that money from here to Sacramento, never thinking about your mistakes, never trying to fix them so we don't have a homeless problem, never focusing on building a future." Zaylee yells in his face.

She walks towards the door and grips the handle. Then she turns her head around to look at him, "You did all this for what? So you can keep your fancy houses, cars, and toys? No Mack. You have only pushed our state into further debt and destruction. I hope you find the worse torture spot in hell." Zaylee articulates angrily. Mack waves his hand out at her, "You don't even believe in God." Mack responds. "Because of you, I believe in the devil." Zaylee claims. She opens the door and slams it behind her.

The hallway is full of chaos. Screams echo throughout the entire hall, signifying the disorder. A man runs down the hall and trips. His face jerks upward upon hitting the tile. Another female runs over him, her papers fall from her binder. Groups of police walk down the hall in a triangle formation. Their weapons are locked around their shoulders, with their hands grasping them tight, and the barrel pointing down at the tile. They continue to move forward, giving Zaylee a side view of them and then, finally, a view of their backside as they pass by. Their armor bulges out of their shirts on the back end, presenting the, supposed to be hidden, body armor.

Zaylee pulls out her weapon and follows behind them, holding her weapon to the side and leaning towards the wall. She moves away so she can continue walking in front of benches. Then, as she reaches the corner, she presses her back up against the wall. The bun keeps her hair tight as she looks around the corner. Images of Rayna flicker through her head as she remembers what she said to Mack; it was Rayna's words coming out of her mouth.

She remembers Rayna's youthful beauty, her delicate triangle tattoo near her eyebrow, her tattoos near her tear ducts, and her bulky hydraulic arm. Zaylee's images turn to regret; she remembers how Rayna stood in front of her, blocking her from arresting her friends. Many of them had the same tattoos near their tear ducts.

She approaches the door and pushes it open slowly. The ebony wood unlatches, removing the picturesque and claustrophobic courtroom feeling. Zaylee stares down the multitude of stairs. At the bottom is Ciara, holding a pistol up to a hostage's neck and waving an assault rifle at the police near the top. In the distance, Zaylee sees a sniper on the roof and remembers how there were advanced tactical forces parked in the lot early when she arrived. She notices that the sniper is laying down and pointing their long-barreled weapon in the direction of the now crazed Ciara.

'It's only a matter of time before they kill her.' Zaylee thinks to herself. She walks slowly down the center of the stairs. Ciara immediately recognizes Zaylee approaching but still whips her assault rifle around and points it at her. "Don't come any further!" she shouts. Zaylee looks at her calmly and raises her weapon into the air, the barrel pointing towards the air. She bends down and places her pistol on the edge of a stair, then continues to slowly approach her.

"I said stop where you are!" Ciara shouts again. She shoves the pistol into the hostage, crunching their red shirt upwards in the direction of her arm, "I will do it!" she shouts. Zaylee continues her approach, slowly. Ciara waves her weapon in the air. A few loud shots fire off in the direction of the police who are hiding behind the pillars atop the stairs, "I know you are there, back away now!" Amidst the commotion, Zaylee moves closer, closing the gap to two meters between her and Ciara. This cause Ciara to immediately raises her gun and point it at her. Zaylee can see down the barrel; its metal housing fails to strike fear into her eyes though.

Ciara cries, "Why do you stand for them? You act like you care for us, yet you let them mistreat us." Ciara shouts, tears still coming down her face, bracing the hostage's shirt below. Zaylee remains calm and utters, "Their control will slip eventually. There is power in numbers. Congress and the senate will fold if we go after them together." Zaylee reaches her hand out towards Ciara but this enrages her. Ciara points her weapon at Zaylee and says, "It won't change what's happening to me. Nothing can take back that sentence!" she screams at Zaylee, the tears flowing rapidly down her face and beginning to alter the sound of her words.

Zaylee ushers a command to Ciara to help her, "Take the sentence as it is. Go through with your rehabilitation, and pay your fines. We will do the rest and wait for your return. Your kids will await you when you come out." Zaylee states. The woman looks down at the floor and continues to cry, her words barely audible, "No, the government will take them away just like they have taken my life away." Ciara wipes away her tears and laughs, "It doesn't matter if I live or die now, my life will never be the same." she utters sullenly.

Zaylee approaches her again but this time the assault rifle goes back to Ciara's side. Zaylee opens her arms up and begins to wrap them around her. Ciara lets go of the hostage; the once captivated individual immediately runs off to the side. Zaylee and Ciara hug each other. The embrace makes them both believe that maybe it will be okay, somewhere down the road.

A loud gunshot echoes throughout the courtroom plaza. Wet liquid drips down Zaylee's uniform. She keeps her eyes closed as Ciara's limp body drops to the floor. Zaylee's face is covered in her blood, the painful warmth rings through Zaylee, piercing her soul with pain. It splashed across her entire outfit, speckling it in blood. She finally opens her eyes and looks at the scene around her.

On the floor sits Ciara's body. Her weapons, laying near her unclasped hands. The blood pools from her sideways head, coating her hair in blood. Tears flow down Zaylee's face. She looks up and sees the sniper lifting their weapon from the side of the building. The smoke had cleared from their shot.

"She had two kids!" Zaylee screams. "Why!" Zaylee says,

falling to her knees. "Why did you do this?!" she screams in agony, staring at the dead body in front of her. The blood starts to dry on her skin.

Chapter 14: Cheaters III

Zaylee and Trey are laying in a bed. White sheets cover their naked bodies. Trey runs his hand along her face, his index finger following along the cheekbone on her face. The wooden cabin makes the room feel darker, but Trey's green eyes radiate throughout the area, "I wish this moment would last for an eternity." he says, staring into Zaylee's eyes. His hand continues to move along the side of her face until it reaches her unbound honey colored hair. The fine strands fall through his fingers.

"But mortality is necessary for God's plan. I have to ask, why do you love me still?" Trey asks. Zaylee pauses and then mutters, "I've always liked people who were a tad crazy because it shows that their passion is worth more than their life. Never dated someone as crazy as you though." she declares. Trey laughs and kisses her softly on the forehead. He turns onto his back, the sheets ruffling while he moves. Zaylee places her hand over his chest and tilts sideways next to him.

He looks up at the ceiling and begins thinking of Ms. Schesis' vids, and how she has become a popular prophet. The word coryphaeus echoes within Zaylee as she watches Trey think and she remembers how Vero used that label.

Amid her thoughts, Trey begins talking: "Sex. Ms. Schesis says it's a vice like anything else. People will do anything for their addictions. Most people don't understand cheaters, but her videos have taught me the only reason for sex. Every statement, every action, and every person is ruled and defined by psychology, regardless of philosophy. Those that cheat do so because their desire for sexual stimulation and emotional gratification, is greater than the stability of shared loyalty. They seek attention, compliments, and constant support. They fail to understand their own body. How could they possibly contemplate something greater, like philosophy, if they are so weak that they succumb to such filth? Their lucky guesses and coincidences will only last for so long. Eventually stagnation will hit again, then what will we have? Only nature, which is God's and God's alone. The great truth defined by science and applied in technology, but ultimately given by God." Trey explains.

Zaylee peeks up her head, using her hand on Trey's chest to

support herself, "The Schesis Project?" Zaylee asks, emphasizing on 'schesis', since the word rhymes with thesis, giving a scientific vibe to the conversation.

Trey explains, "She articulates complex subjects, in such a way, that is makes it easier to understand. It's like I've understood it my entire life. Only God can give me such clarity and she's a prophet of God." Trey says. Zaylee derails him, "She makes valid points about society and presents a new interpretation of society but her faith in God is illogical since it is unproven. I think it is unwise to try and help everyone all at once. Too many variables; you don't know what is the best path." Zaylee claims.

The room remains quiet for a time, letting their quandaries circulate. Zaylee still propped up on his chest, opens her mouth opens and fumbles noises out, causing Trey to notice and comment on it, "What's wrong babe?" He looks at the wall and then looks back at her, "Tell me." he asks, lifting his head up and looking directly in her eyes. Zaylee reluctantly relays, "I'm thinking about resigning. The judicial government is corrupt all around. Then, the supreme court won't allow the people's propositions to stay in effect. I know prop 8 was necessary to rebuke because it is unconstitutional to not allow homosexuals to marry, but they removed the people's rights. It is just like Ms. Schesis said, the proposition itself didn't matter, it was the principle, that they removed democracy and let a panel of nine have more pull than the entire state of fifty-five million." Trey looks at her, "You're just realizing their corruption?" he ironically asks.

"I didn't know how far it went before. But every drug dealer, thief, addict, and criminal that isn't rich, powerful, popular, or their friend, is harshly sentenced and given absurd fines" she begins to explain, "All to feed cash into controlling the people, turning the U.S into something like state-controlled Russia. They are just using judges as their main power source." Zaylee claims.

Trey grabs her hand, "Zaylee, people claim darkness can't drive out darkness. But they are wrong because their perspective is skewed. They claim things as good and bad without proof. We need the proof. We need rogues of God that will send His message. We need His nature, science, and technology to advance our society. He gave us darkness to drive out darkness; there can be no other way, such is the necessity of the rogue." Trey begins to explain.

After pausing to reflect, he continues, "Who's to say that it's wrong to murder others if they stand in our way? David and many others in the scripture did it. Society does it. Our own government did it against the British. We must stabilize our society in some way. They can't be stopped because they don't want to give up their power. It's like dealing with children, and these children need punishment. And if God will not send another flood as was written in the Final Testament, we must be that flood. We must punish his disobedient children who have not learned and have had no faith in him, lest they destroy us all." Trey catechizes.

Zaylee starts to cry, "I watched them gun down a mother of two. Her blood covered my uniform. I haven't put it on since; they gave me a leave of absence. Their cruelty has no boundary." she states, a bit jaded and disgusted. He curls his lip, "Zaylee, I need you to put on that uniform again. They will not be taken down from outsiders. You must rip them apart, internally as Rayna intended. Use their tools against them." Trey says.

"I love you." she says, derailing the conversation. "I love you too Zaylee." he replies.

The sheets flicker as his foot pushes them upward, "You know they are going to sentence me to death. Killing a judge?" he asks rhetorically. "I'm done." he finishes. Zaylee pulls him close, "I want to stop it, Trey. I need you." Trey stops her and says, "Zaylee, I wrote this destiny myself. Humanity has failed to realize primordial truths. Simple things that the Romans and Greeks understood, lost in the desire for resource, lost because of their greed and lust." Trey says. Upon finishing he hugs Zaylee back.

Trey continues, "These people will not listen to peace or logic. They see people as numbers on a sheet because they do not have God. The mentality of the business has corrupted all of society and in the wrong ways. People can be seen as numbers, for statistical purposes, but we should use those statistics and numbers to help society, not drain it." Trey explains.

Zaylee remains calm but says, "I can see that now." between tears. The muffled sounds of her cries slowly rise in volume.

"Trey, I don't want to lose you. I can't." Zaylee says through her tears. He lets out a bellow of cheerfulness, hoping it will rub off, and explains, "Babe, life is short. Death comes for us all. What matters is we build towards a better future." As Trey attempts to console her, he gestures out with his hand, "Go to the Citadel. Lead them in what they lack. They will need someone like you when I'm gone." Trey claims. She looks up with a question on her face. "What?" she asks stunned.

"People like us have band together against them." Trey answers. "Like a cult?" she asks. "No. Some call us religious zealots, and maybe we are, but we are merely dispensing justice where the system fails." Trey utters, before explaining, "It's an effort to change society and force our philosophy of truth upon them. To force them to recognize our proofs of God and the universe He created." Trey finishes.

Zaylee clenches her fist, "They need to be punished for what they've done to our citizens, treating them like second rate animals at a pound, putting them down at any chance they get when they just need love and someone to care for them." she says, angry rising in her arm. She looks at Trey and cries again, "Now they are going to take my Trey." she mutters through her tears.

"You have tried everything, baby. They won't listen to you no matter how hard you try. Peaceful methods don't work and passive-aggression will just be shut down. We can't take away their money or power without going after them." Trey claims, putting his hand on Zaylee's chin. He turns her face towards him, "Where do you think Rayna learned about medicine and definitive signs of death?" he queries with eloquence.

"I taught them and showed them the body. They had the weapons but I showed them how to kill, swiftly. You might not agree with my methods but Rayna did. She reveled in the rapid pace that she could murder the public's enemies." he attests.

Eager to explain more, Trey continues, "I didn't want hard-working citizens to continue suffering. Your mentality of non-violence will never work with these people. It has never worked throughout history. If we have learned anything throughout history it's that when corruption grows rampant, it's up to the people to remove them from their office. You need a state of anarchy before democracy can return." Trey declares.

Zaylee's rage continues to build as Trey notices a scar on the nape of her neck. But Zaylee knocks his glance off with a hostile stare and asks, "Why did they do this? Was harming the rest of society to have the one percent live opulently really worth it?" she inquires, channeling her anger.

"No, in the long run it isn't, but you've seen their control seeping into society. They have militarized their police to delay their crumbling society; they will never relinquish control of their toys." Trey answers. Now agreeing with Trey, Zaylee proclaims, "Our streets are controlled by UAV drones and heavily armed police, with ballistics we use far too often. They make me so angry. And we have no choice but to abide by their destructive siphoning of our funds through judicial and food industry control. I can't handle it."

Trey injects more into Zaylee, fueling her animosity, "They don't care about us Zaylee. We are toys to control, not humans to befriend. The concept of communal animal doesn't apply to them. Most of them are fat, unhealthy, or have otherwise deviated from our naturally superior traits; they have disembarked from persistence hunting. You see these huge body builders with large upper bodies but chicken legs. They couldn't run down their prey even if they wanted to." Trey rants, his face scrunching up.

Trey laments, "Endurance and cognition are the greatest traits humans have." His mind wanders, imagining the disgusting people in power who don't take care of their bodies. "You must promise me something Zaylee." Trey insists.

"Anything." she answers. "Militarize the public."

He pauses for a second then continues, "The gangs that operate on the streets have become better than the ones that operate our government. Lead them, give them what they need, to compete against the tyrants. Raid the military stockpiles. Guide them on the prophet's path." Trey voices, eloquently pleading with her. "Why me?" Zaylee asks. Trey caresses her face, running his fingers on her cheek.

"You were in the military. You know the inner workings of our military and you know what structure is required to accomplish this feat. Give the citizens a real chance with real weaponry." Trey runs his fingers off the side of her face and back to his side, "And, once they have leverage, let them kill everyone that holds back the hard-working citizens." Trey utters rapidly, with hostility in his

117

voice and eagerness, "We must fix our country by whatever means necessary, Zaylee. Promise me you will do this." Trey asks fervently.

"I will do whatever it takes, Trey. I will rally them up and fix this country." she answers, passionately looking into his eyes, "I will remove the iniquitous from society." she claims.

He looks at her and smiles, kissing her on the lips. She leans back down onto his chest, "But for now, I just want to lay here with you and enjoy these last moments." she replies, closing her eyes. Trey pulls her closer, hugging her tightly. He closes his eyes as they both fade into a deep sleep, holding each other.

—

Zaylee sits alone in a damp, musky room. She looks through a one-way mirror. Through it she can see a lethal injection table. Just beyond that, she can see a rolling cart with a single needle and multiple vials placed upon it. She sits, shaking in her chair from the anxiety. The door on the right side of the room opens. A guard pushes Trey inside the room. His prison outfit covers the top portion of his body. The orange coloring reflects the amber lights above. Zaylee watches the guard position Trey onto the table.

His body embraces the cold metal, slowly relaxing itself. The guard straps him down, each brown strap being locked into place. He closes his eyes and starts to pray. Zaylee can hear the words through the speaker box in the corners of the viewing room, "Dear Father, please help us cleanse this world in a fire for its sins. It has denied your presence. It has run amuck. It needs to be punished." he begins.

Continuing he says, "I pray that you will gather your followers together, rallying them against the tyrants, your disobedient children, that control this world." he prays. The guard shoves him, "No more talking." he demands but Trey spew out a few last words: "In the name of Jesus Christ, Amen."

A Doctor walks into the room, making the room bustle perpetually. Zaylee shakes her head and stands up. She turns herself towards the door. An officer at the door puts his hand out at her, "You cannot leave until the execution is complete, in fear that you will attempt to stop it." he informs her.

She looks back at her seat, eventually sitting down on its

brittle plastic. Through the mirror, she can see the Doctor approaching him with a needle. Immediately, she starts to cry. "Please, no" she says, closing her eyes tightly. "Now, the insertion might hurt, but after the first drug has been delivered, you will fall asleep. It will be almost completely painless." the Doctor asserts. Zaylee stands, attempting to go to the door again.

She reaches the officer's grasp as he puts out his hand, pushing her away. "No! I can't watch this!" she shouts. "I'm sorry, I wish I could let you leave but it is our policy. If it is too debilitating to watch, why did you come?" he queries. "I-I just wanted to see him once last time." she responds. "It's almost over." he says, pointing at the mirror, "Look, he has already fallen asleep."

Zaylee turns to see Trey, his eyes closed and his body motionless. The doctor pushes the final liquid into his body. Zaylee walks a few steps to the mirror, placing her hand on it. Slowly, her hand falls, "Trey..."

—

I can't believe he is really gone, forever. Those judges will pay for taking him. He tried to save that man and his children and they had the nerve to sentence him to death. I will not stand for this any longer. If the world wishes to be cruel, I will be cruel in return. There is no God influencing me to do this. There is no Lucifer telling me to take them. I follow my own path. Trey believed in a God but that God did not save him, only we can save ourselves from these despicable people. Every human must stand up for themselves. No one will stand up to the judges and none will be on their side unless they are taught to perceive like them.

The judges refuse to listen to non-violence. They spit in our faces and take the lives of our loved ones. I will make sure they get their own. Rayna has shown the path and has rallied them up. They are ready to fight against the judges and replace them. I will stand by her, in honor of Trey. They will listen. And, with Rayna by my side, we will influence them to fight against the real and powerful enemies. We will take them down and display them to the world, so that they know the people are back. The people are in control.

I will never stop following Ms. Schesis and her videos; she is the coryphaeus of millennials as they have astutely said. Trey is my last sin that needs to be expunged. I brought him into this, I got him to believe we could stop them with non-violence. He stood up there in honor of me, trying to get me to see reason and stop them. But they cut him down so they could maintain their power, money, and control. They will pay for messing with someone like me. My eyes will burn red with fury as I smite them down for killing my last and only love.

My tears and blood will drop on your grave as a reminder that this world was never fit for you. Everything here was beneath you. The people you have helped will remember you throughout their lives. They stood at your funeral, in honor of you. I stand here, now, at your epitaph, crying, that the world lost an honest soul who knew the truth. You knew what must be done from the beginning. You saw it.

I blinded you, I killed you. I did this to you with my non-violent measures.

But I no longer believe the world can be saved through non-violence. Humanity is evil beyond comprehension. Einstein said the Universe might not be infinite but he was sure human stupidity was. But I'm convinced that his statement was misplaced; human cruelty knows no boundary. The evil within humanity is infinite but, just like the Universe, all things can be ended prematurely. You simply need to know how.

You knew the ending to all of humanities evils. I will spend the rest of my life building towards its complete purge from reality.

I am a Schesist until I die. She is my rock upon which I build my house. Now it's time to destroy the houses made on the sands of evil. I come for you, the ones I used to call friends and protectors. 'To Serve and Protect'. Bah. That is the biggest lie you ever told. I believed it and became one of you trying to live up to that standard. Now my badge will sit, forever in the mud, near Trey's grave, proving he won our battle with words before I even thought to take up the sword to protect him.

I am ready to take them on with their own tools now. This is for Ciara, Mike, and Trey. I will honor their memory by making their enemies pay.

Chapter 15: And So Cronus Crowned Atlas

The phone rings into Zaylee's ear, buzzing at a constant pace. "Hello, this is Rayna." her voice says through the phone. "Rayna, I need your help." Zaylee's voice mutters, almost cracking. Rayna senses the stress, "Well, you're calling me so you must be desperate. What do you need?" Rayna asks. Zaylee calms herself and channels her vexation, "Those that control society, the judges, the politicians, they must be stopped. They took everything from me."

Rayna replies, "I know, Vero gave me the details the other day. I am sorry to hear about it. Trey left us a note regarding you and his hopes that you would change; we didn't know what you would do. But, do you finally see it our way? Or do you still believe these wicked individuals will change through word alone?" Rayna asks.

Zaylee looks at the dash of her car, its black and white striped interior beautifully concomitant and looking back at her. Zaylee punches her dash, lifting some dust like Rayna did over six months ago when they were partners, and collects her thoughts, "I'm not sure if I see it your way, but I'm ready to kill all of them for the plague they wrought on society." Zaylee's anger flows through the phone and into Rayna's ear.

She remains quiet, not responding and waiting for Zaylee. Eventually, Zaylee states, "I want to command again, give back to the people using my skills as a general. I just need forces." There is another long pause, Vero's voice is incomprehensible, but making noise on the opposite end. Rayna begins conversing with him.

Finally, Rayna picks back up the phone, "Vero and I can help, but I'm not sure we have military forces." Rayna relays on behalf of both of them. "I can train them. Who are they?" Zaylee asks curiously but calmly.

Rayna gathers her courage and says, "The ruthless cyberpunk squads that rule Koreatown was restructured some time ago for the Schesis cause. They are loyal and religious, but destructive and unforgiving. Some of whom you have arrested already. But we busted them out before the system took control of their lives. Cause they couldn't pay those fines, you know?" Rayna replies, a sense of worry in her voice regarding Zaylee's opinion.

Zaylee calmly queries, "Ah. And you were part of this

gang?" she asks. Rayna's tone oscillates into slight annoyance, "I grew up on the streets Zaylee, I had no choice. Vero and I run the Hydraulic Squad. Our choice of cybernetic nectar is pneumatic modifications. We use air pressure and cyber muscle modifications to give us colossal strength, similar to how an ant or spider uses fluid to lift tremendous weight, we do the same." Rayna explains. After a brief pause, she continues, "The others use Mantis-blades and electric based weapons, with a heavy Tesla influence, coils and stuff. You know?" she says, asking if Zaylee understands.

Zaylee remembers her discussion about using acetylene over propane for their blades, "I can amplify their potential, give them the resources they need, expand upon their technology. Let me command them." Zaylee pleads. Rayna pauses for a second to think before saying, "I will let you take my place as commander, but Vero must remain the voice of the cyberpunk squad. He is the glue that holds all the gangs together." she explains before adding, "He has gathered them for a meeting later today, regarding the caustic corruption video Ms. Schesis just released."

Zaylee thinks back on how she arrested some of them, "Are you sure they will follow me? Some of them probably want revenge for what I did to them." Zaylee asks.

Rayna doesn't hesitate, "Vero will rally them for you, before you arrive. They will listen to him and they respect your ability cause I've already told them about you and not to mess with you. But we will have to do formal introductions later. We are in a time crunch and need you to train us, develop a plan, and lead us on our first mission against the wicked as soon as possible. If you can prove yourself worthy, technologically and logically, they will follow you to their graves. This is all they care about, since logic is of God and those with the best logic are his greatest servants." Rayna replies, initiating another silence, causing Rayna to fill in the gap, "Anyway, Ms. Schesis has taught us that those who make the current ideology obsolete should be our leader. We all believe it, you just need to prove that and we will follow." she says, finishing her statement.

"Trust me, I can do that, and more. Just you wait Rayna." Rayna pauses and nods, "You're old so you probably remember texting back in the day and reason for the letters beneath the numbers on a phone. The code for our base is 7243747. Punch it in and our command center will let you in."

The Pantheon Forms

Zaylee's magnificent white supercar roars down Wilshire Boulevard. Its police lightbar fashioned to the top, ready to light up at any moment. The grill, clinging to the front, looks sturdy and powerful, adding a new vibe to the car. Zaylee uses the vehicle to briskly maneuver in between traffic. She drives close to the vehicles in front of her and pulls around them, repeating this process down the boulevard. It roars brilliantly as she pulls around each driver. To the left she sees the Warehouse, which by her definition, was painted a putrid green. She looks back at the black asphalt in front of her, and continues to speed down the boulevard. Upon reaching Oxford Avenue, she begins to slow down and veer into the left-most lane. When the light turns green, she steers the car diagonally towards the sidewalk.

In front of her is a tall, white building with a flat awning awaiting her. She slows her vehicle and pulls onto the curb, near some palm trees. White arches line the building to her left. She drives slowly towards the center. Her eyes gravitate to the ceiling above. The buildings make an open-ended circle. Her eyes follow the circle down to its center. Dead center below the buildings is a small width plaque, barely noticeable unless she pays close attention.

The words 'Schesis Revolution: The Lord's Will Be Done' have been etched into it. Encapsulating the plaque is a plethora of fountains, shooting water into the air. Just beyond the fountains are picturesque green hedges in a horseshoe shape. The pattern continues with another circle of fountains and beautiful green trees just beyond them.

The car comes to a stop. The driver grabs the black and white striped gear shift, placing the vehicle in park. She turns the key towards her, turning off the vehicle. The engine stops its tantalizing purr. Zaylee unlatches the car door, swinging it open. She plants her cowboy boots atop the concrete, their white and black coloring matches her vehicle. The words 'Police' written on the door swing with it. The glossy white paint stays stagnant in the shade,

123

while the shade simultaneously extenuates the black stripes along the vehicle. She makes her way out of the vehicle and pushes the door closed behind her, continuing to look forward.

A noise echoes through the plaza; the trunk opens. Tommy flies up into the air, its mostly black paint job lined with white stripes matches Zaylee's vehicle, denoting that it has recently been modified. It pushes the air around it and flies slowly behind Zaylee, following her down the plaza. Suddenly, in front of the plaque, a metal covering slides slowly over, scratching the concrete. Upon opening completely, an ancient black telephone box rises from the clearing. The door of its booth swings open, inviting Zaylee inside. Zaylee keeps moving forward at a confident, yet hasty, pace. She finally reaches the booth and enters inside its metal exterior. Tommy buzzes, following her in.

The door closes and she pushes on the numbers, typing in 7243747 in the correct order. As the final seven is pushed, she looks at the tiny camera in the corner and the phone booth lowers down. A metal covering slides over the top of the phone booth slowly removing the outside light from entering the chasm below. Chains lower the booth slowly, rattling as they compensate for gravity. Zaylee looks below and sees Vero standing on a platform, a multitude stands in front of him, leaning on his every word. She watches while he points at the crowd, the exertion of each word propels his head forward with great ferocity.

The speakers crackle with his voice as spittle flies out in his emotional speech, "Cyberpunk gangs of Los Angeles, it's time to fight together, despite our differences. Those can be left in the past as petty squabbles, compared to the problems we are facing now." he says, pausing, as if waiting to say something serious, "The rich elite have taken our land! Violated it with greed and things we do not need, in attempt to saturate their insatiable lust for decadence. Our society stagnates technologically because of their frivolous spending, all while our debt increases and their sins mount up, piling up and damning them." Vero shouts at the crowd. His black combat boots stomp as a red LED light flickers onto the floor beneath them. His cut up black trench coat is lined in the same red LED's, which are also glowing.

He beckons again, "Politicians stand on the pyre of

California, holding a match from Sacramento. They think they stand high above us, at the peak of Mount Whitney, but we have learned from the ancient cultures before us, the ones that gave us the Final Testament of Jesus. And like Atlas of old, we can move mountains, and we hold the burden of this nation on our shoulders. Without us, the sky would fall. So let us throw down their sky, and shatter their world from beneath them. Sending them a message that we are the ones that keep society afloat." Vero exclaims, pointing outward at Zaylee, looking at her in the eyes.

The phone booth door opens, just outside the door are stairs, greeting her and pleading with her to head down.

Tommy flies above her, she looks up and smiles at it. The multitude of people open a path to the stage. As she walks through, they each stare at her, remembering how she arrested some of them but they keep to themselves.

Their attire is similar in aesthetic to Vero's. Black metal clasps are bound to their limbs and hair. Electricity protrudes from various arms of a group. Another selection of people's hydraulics push air out at random intervals.

A final group stands in front, their face is different in the way that it is covered in the same tattoos that grace Rayna's face, except their tear duct tattoos are covered in varying degrees of red and black. Each of them also carries different cyberware. The more advanced the hardware, the higher the rank, Zaylee presumes. She looks over some of their tattoos that denote that these are the leaders of the various gangs that have come today to meet her. At the front of the stage, Rayna stands, her arms folded, and her tear ducts, completely black, symbolizing her leadership over those with red tear duct tattoos.

Upon spotting her, Tommy instantly flies over to Rayna. She pets its top plate, covering the white lettered words 'Police' on its mostly black exterior with her fingers. Zaylee pushes through, her hair wrapped in a bun and staying solidly still on her head. Rayna leans forward and hugs her, "I'm glad you are here." she whispers into her ear, indistinctly muffled to the crowd beyond. Vero leans towards the microphone, "Give a warm welcome for our Atlas." he asks of the audience, pointing at Zaylee. They clap, making a boisterous sound but no audible noise comes out of their vocal cords. Zaylee walks towards the microphone. She looks at the crowd, each face eager to hear from her. The nervousness never reaches her mind but a slight twitch pulsates through her hand.

Zaylee thinks up something to say on the spot, "Under these banks we meet, waiting to move out and strike down our enemies. It's symbolism for what we are about to do. These next few days are going to build up to a swift twenty-four hours of attacks. It will be strenuous and difficult for all of us but it is a necessity and we cannot let up. We only have one chance at this because as soon as they find me out, our illusion fades and they will try to dwindle our resources. We must break their sky in one night, so that they cannot recuperate. This is a total war." Zaylee speaks to the crowd, the twitch in her arm fades out. She raises her arm at the crowd.

Zaylee's voice increases in decibel, "They have taken what we were promised! Killed our family, our children, and taken all our money, land, food, and water. All for themselves. To become rich and abuse us with their falsehoods and their manipulation of culture. We will show them that our minds are more powerful than their false beauty, power, and their material goods!" she yells, with anger in her voice. "This is our battle of the Gods, just as the Greek Gods fought, because we know we can rule better than them. We have the interest of the people in our hearts. We know what they need and how they can help us grow as a society." Zaylee says, placing her arm on her chest. She puts her hand back down to her side and steps closer to the microphone.

"The poor know more than the rich. A statement said by a dear friend of mine. He lived the struggles of reality, just as the rest of the poor do. Nature is something they are forced to understand and abide by, or they will perish. When the rich and first world begin to tell the poor and less fortunate that they know their problems, that's when the virus starts. That's when the people begin to look for a cure." she proclaims. The audience looks at her, waiting on her every word.

"Ms. Schesis is the cure. She has a new philosophy, a new perspective, a new gospel given by God, and a new, unstoppable, mentality. For she sees not culture, but only logic and has changed our views. And she sees our problems, even from a distance, and her new vid regarding our corrupt politicians shows us we have much work ahead of us. Those that stand in their white tower of Los Angeles, their supposed place to help the people, remain untouched by the plagues they have wrought upon the streets below. No different than the Egyptian Pharoah's that used people as slaves. They use the poor as slaves, giving them a pittance to live off. In fact, some of the poor make less than slaves and cannot afford housing and food." Zaylee says passionately.

Collecting her voice again she continues, "To protect this people of this city we must rip it apart from within. I have devised the plan accordingly, then we can attack the fools that stand in Sacramento. Their buildings and corruption are no different than what stands in the center of Los Angeles." Zaylee explains. The crowd looks at her with determined eyes. "Today is our day!" Zaylee shouts, Vero pulls up a giant LED sign, its black and red LED's shine brightly at the crowd. The word 'Cyberpunk' is written diagonally in the lights, followed by 'Squad!' written horizontally. Just beneath that, in the corner, is an image of Ms. Schesis triangular mask.

The crowd squeezes their various custom-made cybernetic parts. Electricity and pressurized air emanate through the environment at varying levels of intensity. The tear duct tattooed individuals in front turn and face the crowd. Their jackets transfixed into the air. Its straight collar appearance jutting upward. The black leather shimmering and accentuating their clasps. The various gangs group up to their specific leader, wearing similarly fashioned gear. The one aesthetic they all share is a cross. Some wear it on their skin via tattoo and others are wearing golden cross necklaces.

Off in the crowd, deep within the sea of cyberpunk gang members, Zaylee sees the electrical squad with their voltaic supercharged leader standing in front of them, screaming violently, building up hype. Their leader's spark filled device flickers, constantly lighting up her jacket. The various members bump each other with their chests, similarly launching blue and white sparks off onto the ground. She notices a red spiky haired individual standing beside the leader, with his arms folded.

The hydraulic powered members stand beside their hydraulic head, Rayna, in the center of all the gangs, with the most members out of any of the gangs. She watches as they bump fists with each other, testing each other's muscles. But Rayna calms them down, telling them that they need strategize and remain logical rather than emotional.

The mantis-like blade wielders stand in front of their leader, whose shield, held high up in the air, can still be seen by Zaylee. He smacks it back down and cracks the floor below. Their metal Mantis-blade weapons, of numerous sizes, are sharpened to a brim with red and green LED's shining through different parts of them. A few of them have gauntlets, while the rest have metal blades embedded to their index and middle finger, but all are filled with intense heat that has raised the temperature of the room at least a few degrees.

Zaylee looks at the various groups, "First we need to add to your arsenals." she looks across the stage. "Vero." she states, as if giving a command. He places his hands into the air, palms facing away from the crowd, and tilts his head down. The gesture releases a mechanism, pulling the front part of the stage backward. Lights shine through the air, through the foggy air that was release prior by the hydraulic gangsters. He presents three boxes to the crowd, which slowly open as their hinge stretches.

After looking at the groups, Zaylee relays her heuristic analysis, "I know cyberpunk is all about fashioning your own tools, modifications, and weapons. Your hydraulic hardware and clever phone booth dumbwaiter are spectacular, but nothing beats ballistic gear." Zaylee says, as they stare at the gear inside the boxes. "I contacted every colleague from the military I could. Each of them supplied weapons, grenades, and military equipment for us to use – risking their life by giving us this gear." she explains to them.

She points to the boxes, "From assault rifles, bullet proof vests, to grenades, it's all there, in the boxes." The head of each group reaches into the box and grabs an assault rifle and bullet proof vest, passing them around to each person. A man with a large electric barrier-based shield approaches and grabs Steyr AUG rifles; its bullpup design coated in a beautiful matte gray to match their mantis-like blades, and hands them to the members of his group.

The electric group leader picks up several single six barreled gatling gun, one at a time, and hands them to each member of her group until all of them are carrying these modified gatling guns that have been adapted for handheld use.

Zaylee notices that they all have one and instructs them, "Hook them to your power packs. They are electrically driven like your pistols." They look for an open connection on their packs and pull a red wire down. Upon hooking the red wire into their weapons, the gatling guns hum. Zaylee notices that a few are struggling to pick them up, due to their weight, and says, "For those of you that cannot hold the weapons up, you can work with the Hydraulic Squad. They should have sufficient air pressure to keep the gatling gun level. And if you need help writing the code, let me know, I'll apply the calculations to keep the weapon steady into some software that will control the pneumatic devices." she offers to the electrical team.

Zaylee then talks to the Electric Squad directly, "You, Electric Squad, will run the first mission." she says, pointing at their beefy female leader.

Then she looks at the Mantis Squad, their weapons dangling down, curious about their cyberware. Rayna notices and grabs her attention, "The Mantis Squads are unique. They have varying degrees of swordsmanship. The lower tier members are only allowed blades less than fifteen centimeters. The most experienced members have gauntlet styled blades that start out small but can extend to two meters. Regardless all of the blades are deadly and precise. Their anger might get in the way with this mission, but my Hydraulic Squad will add support to taper their rage, stopping it from getting too out of hand." she explains.

Zaylee digests the information, "Good." Zaylee replies before looking at the group collectively, "The rest of our forces will help build the Citadel up, for our next missions." Zaylee says confidently.

Rayna pulls several different weapons from her case. She hands out M4A1's to the majority of the soldiers, their black exteriors made from the finest material available. Near the bottom, she finally picks up AX50 rifles, capable of launching fifty caliber rounds on a consistent and reliable basis. They looked and felt like military grade equipment. Then, at the bottom, Rayna finds cases of depleted uranium rounds. Rayna looks at them with astonishment before looking up at Zaylee, "How did you get tank buster bullets?"

Zaylee smirks and bends down.

"When martial law is declared, they will send tanks. If my friends had stolen those tanks, the government would have called their forces out to recover their gear and we'd be at a disadvantage. However, we will still need to circumvent them and act quickly, as their power is still beyond ours. Meaning, when martial law is declared, our objective will become much more difficult to complete. But, when they do come for us, we will have some tools to stave them off. We will also have something even new, untested, but my source has proven to be quite capable, even with his prototypes." Zaylee says as her smirk grows even larger. She bends down into the container and looks around.

She picks up a case of bullets, the word 'EXACTO' followed by '5.0', is written on its face. She pulls out a long bullet with a unique metal backing on it. The metal flows through in a spiral manner, forming fins that flow down to the tip of the bullet. Zaylee pets Tommy, "The real treat comes once we liberate the rest of the drones." she says. Tommy flies down to her level. She opens a cavity on its underside, and grabs a clip of the rounds. She shoves it into Tommy's underside. It clicks and Tommy flies back up into the air.

Zaylee points out to a spot in the distance, "Look at the marking on the wall." She then looks at Tommy and commands, "Tommy, shoot it like we practiced." Its protocols load up, it turns its barrel one hundred and eighty degrees from the target, becoming unaligned with it. "Fire." she demands. A round fires off, and another, and consistent small explosions come from its barrel. It propels back from the discharge but each bullet hits the marking causing it to be destroyed by Tommy's bullets. Zaylee explains, "The bullet curved using its electromagnetically actuated fins."

Tommy clamors with joy and hovers down to Zaylee, "Good boy." she says pithily. "Wow!" Rayna exclaims. Tommy flies over to Rayna upon hearing her ecstatic voice, "That's a good boy, Tommy." she says, petting him. Rayna squeaks happily, "I'm glad we have you two back." Rayna says, looking at Tommy and saying "My drone baby" and then she glances over at Zaylee, "And my Commander, a legendary blue glass hacker." Rayna ponders for a bit then asks, "I've always wondered, why do some people call you a grey hat?

Aren't you a white hat hacker?"

Zaylee pauses, "I was a grey hat hacker because I was with the military. Sometimes we had to act in ways that are considered evil, unfortunately. I was meaning to ask you, do you want me to hack for you when the time is necessary? You know, equitize the rich and poor and so forth by messing with their stocks and bank accounts? Or what exactly are we planning?" she asks.

Rayna looks over some of the weaponry and smiles, "Oh, no hun, I've told you before, the rich are part of the problem. Making more people richer is not our goal. We want to send a message. We want to change the culture, get the people to listen to us, and force the government to listen to us. It is no different than when our founding fathers wanted to send a message to the British to stop the egregious taxation. We want them to know that, if they don't listen to us, it's going to be all-out war. And, if things don't change, we'll break off from their evil country and create our own." Rayna declares.

Zaylee nods her head, "I will do what I can to make that happen."

Chapter 16: Fiat Justita Ruat Caelum

Perceived Sebastomania

Zaylee drives her vehicle down the street. Behind her, three large sport utility vehicles, in all black, follow her. The tint on them is a visible light transmission of under five percent, making bystanders incapable of looking in. Each squad has a different car, four members of that squad stand on the outside of the vehicle, dressed in black SWAT attire, their weapons matching that of SWAT personnel. They push down the street, palm trees on both sides, their weapons clutched diagonally in their arms, their fingers near the trigger.

They continue down the street; a line of palm trees stretches down into the distance. As far as the eye can see, out beyond the palm trees, is a large bank building, piercing the sky. Zaylee continues down the street, her low supercar gripping the pavement. She pulls to the left, into a driveway, and slows her car to a stop in front of a gate. The vehicle recognition software scans Zaylee's vehicle, a green-light flickers and the gate opens. She pulls forward and turns right immediately. The jet-black vehicles follow her inside. They look forward and see a parking lot full of police cars.

In the center of the parking is a red and white tower. It slowly disappears as they turn right and head down under the police station. The ambient lights, transfixed to the ceiling by metal bars, shoved into the ceiling. Their vehicles head towards a pair of doors on the opposite end of the lot. Officers continually pour out of the doors, their arms stretched out perfectly horizontal, their small pistols pointing towards the approaching vehicles. Zaylee parks her car diagonally in front of them, the cars behind her stop, their riding mates dropping off onto the ground.

"Zaylee!" one of the police women yells. Zaylee looks over and sees Jessica and Dekima pointing their weapons at them. Zaylee spits out, "Stand down" to the soldiers behind her. Dekima inches forward, pistol still pointing at her, "What do you think you're doing?" Dekima asks. Zaylee walks forward, her spurs jingling, "My friends, this world has a new philosophy. A better one than what was shoved down our throats by those that control this nation.

One claim to be given by God. These forces honor our people, desiring to protect them from the evil that harms them. We have come to ask you to join our ranks and help us take them down." Zaylee claims.

Dekima scoffs, "Protect them?" Her face scrunches up in disbelief as she finishes speaking, "Protect them, by attacking a police station?" Zaylee raises her hands, "I will speak plainly. Too many times have people wasted time with long speeches." She opens her arms towards them and then looks at the soldiers behind her, "I want you to join my new army. Together we will give this world back to the people. I am not entirely supportive of the God aspects but this new ideology will help us grow."

Jessica lowers her weapon and begins to walk forward. "Jessica!" Dekima shouts, calling her back. "What? Do you really want to continue living in a nation where workers, like the police, can't afford a home because of property prices constantly inflating?" Jessica asks. "Well, no." Dekima replies. "Then join, and together we can take back this nation from those that stole it from us, those who mutilate it. They caused our downfall; the people are innocent!" Jessica continues.

"No." Dekima answers, precisely. Not satisfied with the answer, Zaylee's face scolds Dekima, causing Dekima to explain, "I will not join you, the United States, and, maybe the entire world, might be a messed-up place, controlled by the unintelligent, but that's no excuse. We are the citizens of this nation; we should have stepped in and solved the issue diplomatically." Dekima says, lowering her weapon. She steps forward and attempts to reason on their level, "Then said Jesus unto him, put up again thy sword into its place: for all they that take the sword shall perish with the sword." Dekima enunciates from memory.

Zaylee retorts back, "Christ also said he could call twelve legions of angels, but that he didn't, and he isn't sending them now." Zaylee says to Dekima.

"Show us your legion of angels that will save the people." Zaylee demands. Dekima sighs, "It doesn't work like that, nor do I believe in any God, but I've seen your kind of violence before, many times throughout history."

Zaylee lurches forward, "I am like you, weary of God

because I have no need for someone who lets evil happen, but how dare you compare these people to the religious zealot conquerors of long past. Those zealots had no proof; Ms. Schesis has shown the world the texts containing the lost years of Jesus."

Zaylee takes a breath, "I am not like them, but I share the same mission. I want to stop the iniquities done by those in positions of power. Judges and politicians take away our rights while they sit in air-conditioned rooms. And corporations enact a slow death by paying us too little, taking all that we have, threatening our livelihoods, and stomping out our voice. While controlling the culture with their money and power. What do you have to say about that?"

A soldier steps forward, "In both cases, we kill only to protect our people. With or without God, the mission is the same: protect our people from those in charge that have let us suffer under their grip. Zaylee leads us because our mission is the same. And, for those of you that call us sinners, I say to you only this: Let justice be done though the heavens fall."

Dekima looks at Zaylee, eyes filled with tears, "My father wrought the same terrible destruction, proving that humans were capable of true cruelty. He viewed them as weak, miserable creatures, who couldn't even kill someone properly, so he would do it for them, since they were weak and needed to be cleansed. He needed no God and neither do you to be as evil as you are." Jessica turns her head to look at her.

While staring at Jessica, Dekima pours her heart out, "I watched as he took out the central community police station. He started a fire inside the station, rigging the coffee machine. Then he lopped off the heads of several compressed natural gas tanks he had stolen from the bus yard. The pressure launched them into the building, once they heat hit them, they exploded, taking the entire structure with them." Dekima begins to explain.

"Fuego." Jessica says. Dekima nods, "Yes, Fuego was my father. Like many children of Los Angeles, my sister and I were orphaned. I had to build my way up with my sister Lacio. You know her as Lacy. We went to UCLA when we were very young. Then, my adoptive-father returned. His children are spread throughout the states, like franchises he setup, and my sister and I were his latest tools in his desire for power." Dekima says, looking at Jessica. The officers around her look puzzled, "She's a psycho twin?" someone says. Jessica ignores their comment, "Why didn't you say something before?" Jessica asks.

"I was afraid. As you know, I followed my father for a time. Before the police station, when my father was under investigation, my sister and I posed as technicians for the FBI. We were the ones that burned their building to the ground. My father altered their piping system and the fire prevention system, replacing all the water with acetone. We rigged their computer power supplies to blow at a coordinated time. Then, once they blew, the sprinklers turned on and the acetone lit up, blowing up all the pipes in the entire building simultaneously. But know that I'm not proud of what I've done." The tears slowly falling down her face and onto the concrete below.

Zaylee reflects on the situation, "The Lord forgives, and those who don't believe can forgive too. Life is a learning experience so join us and enact real justice this time around." Zaylee replies. Dekima looks at her, "It's not that simple, I don't believe in God because, it as you believe, if there was someone who takes care of his servants, then he would stop the cruelty, but he doesn't, he lets us suffer and wallow in misery. You use the name of God to justify your killings, just as the crusaders did."

Zaylee laughs, "The crusaders were led by Kings who knew nothing of God, and just wanted power. We justify our acts because we know it is necessary to protect the people, with or without God. We are not like Fuego either." Dekima derisively looks at Zaylee, "Fuego was the epitome of humanity; his philosophy was that if the world was cruel, he would be the cruelest of them all. He would teach them that it doesn't matter how willing they are, cruelty will rule over them. This would allow him to destroy them and take control. You are but a pittance compared to him." Dekima explains, the tears slowly stopping.

Dekima shakes her head, "But I am not my father. He is a weak-minded man no matter how capable he is. If you believe in God, you should know that those that sin the crime of murder are not forgiven, but lose more than just their humanity, but their soul as well. Even your dear Ms. Schesis' translations and the Final Testament corroborate what I say. The Lord said in the Final

Testament that he would not kill his children anymore and that that time had passed." Dekima answers. Zaylee's eyes project vexation back at her, "And your father, was his soul not evil? Why has God let him live?" Zaylee asks.

The question lingers in the air, the dark lot filled with rumblings of the individuals on both sides. While her and Dekima converse, she hears the other soldiers muttering beside them. And, on the side with the cops, she hears them talking amongst themselves. She looks at them, their guns attached to their sides, and their badges pinned to their chest.

Their faces contemplate the situation at hand, soaking and basking in the words of their peers.

"My father has no soul. He is no son of the father and believes in no God and, while I do not believe in God, I do believe in peace and I believe that the testaments attest to that fact and want everyone to live in happiness with each other." Dekima answers. Another police officer points his weapon at Dekima, "You son of the devil! Stop your ignorance!" he shouts, pulling the metal trigger.

The bullet flies through Dekima's skull. The blood pours from her head and onto the concrete below, while her body abruptly falls to the ground.

The sound of the gunshot reverberates through the structure, and all of the chatter ceases, causing everyone to focus on the individual that just fired the shot. As they look around, they see Dekima's limp body twitch on the floor. The room changes abruptly and silence permeates throughout.

Jessica looks at him, and breaks the silence, "WHY?!" she screams, looking at Dekima's body on the floor.

"She does not believe in God, and people like her, without faith, are the reason why we suffer!" he yells back. Jessica's angry demeanor changes the aura of the scene. She gets into his face but his words bellow out fast, cutting Jessica off, "Those psycho twins and Fuego killed my family. They were working at the Bureau building on Wilshire when they burned it down. People like him are the reason this world is controlled by the crazy and atheistic who do not believe in God. And his child posed as a police officer? One of us? One of us who helps people every day by putting the bad guys away? No. She deserved to die and the entire police force deserves to perish for allowing a non-believing heathen to work among us. There is no telling what she has done as a member of the force. But there is still hope. We can still try to remove the cruel ones that are truly in control; politicians and Judges are the reason why the Bureau and officers of the law get blamed. This is their fault. They allowed her to work with us. They're all disgusting." he says pushing Jessica out of the way.

He heads towards Zaylee, nearly all of the officers follow him, smirking and giving dirty looks at Dekima's body. A few cops stay with Jessica, and begin surrounding the body of their deceased comrade. The tears pour down Jessica's face as she clutches Dekima's lifeless body in her arms.

Zaylee looks at the new officers joining their fold, "Procure all the drones. Use my software, I coded it with Haskell, after looking over that virus that Ms. Schesis used to deliver her vids to everyone online. It should instantly override their software with our new protocols." she says to the police officers, they nod their heads at different intervals and start to head off, but Zaylee opens her mouth and begins speaking again: "Since all of you have experience with the drones, you will stay at the citadel and control them from there." she says, stopping and looking back at the squad members behind her.

"We will go after city hall, room 300. To rally our new police officers to our cause permanently, we will kill the Cartel's consultant and ensure that the Cartel perishes. It is as Rayna said, these people only care about money and it's how the Cartel controls them. Ms. Schesis has confirmed they will never leave office, so we will remove them all from office and make sure that the Cartel never returns to bribe our government officials ever again."

City Hall: Rewards of Preparation

Zaylee sits in her car at the end of a street that has been grid-locked from the rest of the town. SWAT cars race by, the force of their ascension down the street blowing her vehicle slightly in the opposite direction. She pulls up her tablet and the image of a drone appears on the screen. The aerial view gives a glimpse of a white building below. Its arch flowing over the street below, connecting it

137

to its sister building. Beneath the drone are fifteen members of the Electric Squad. Inside the building the drone can see six SWAT members waiting in the lobby between two marble pillars. Its sirens spin, alerting the Electric Squad below of the SWAT presence. Their leader, wielding two gatling guns, busts through the door, her bulking thigh muscles rip the door off its hinges with a single kick.

The hydraulics and electrical work lining her body, spanning from her thumb to her shoulder blade, light up in an orange red color. The gatling guns start to spin, their bullet casings falling onto the floor. The hydraulics keep the weapon level while she begins firing rounds into the SWAT members. Drywall flies across the room as it's torn off the walls, mixing with the SWAT member's blood. They turn as bullets penetrate their armor and pierce into their skin. She gets a glimpse of their faces before her gatling guns tear them apart.

She runs to the center of the room, her gatling guns swinging beside her. She throws out three battery boxes, forming a triangle as she does. One goes north, one east, and the last one goes west. They land on the floor and immediately start blasting lasers into the air. The voltage of the lasers ionizes the air, causing the hair on her dark skin to perk up. She hastily runs back towards the entryway, where the members of her squad waiting to enter.

"Bring it! Quick!" she shouts at a member with a black duffel bag strapped over her shoulder. The girl moves forward into the building and pulls out a sapphire crystal ball, the size of a bowling ball. Lightning bolts surround an etched writing of 'Tesla Grenade' upon its face. The leader walks back out of the entryway, where there's a burly man with a large shield. Two large Tesla coil wrapped gloves with large capacitors sit on his hands, humming with electricity. A red wire runs from along his chest, to both gloves, and then back to the electric barrier shield in his right arm.

"Help her." she commands him. He nods, picks up his shield, grips it with his massive gloved arms, and rushes in. He runs until he is in front of the woman. He grunts loudly, throwing his shield upward, before slamming it into the ground, planting it. The protective device in front of him clicks, magnetically locking it to the ground, as it energizes from his connecting wire.

Ten more SWAT members pour from each hallway of the

building, making a total of forty. They stand in the center, looking at the shielded woman. They fire their weapons; bullets begin ricocheting off into the nearby walls.

The woman grabs the sapphire crystal and throws it up into the center of the room; it flies through the air, separating itself into four pieces with a singular shiny silver ball in the middle.

The four sapphire crystal pieces each have a Tesla coil protruding from them. They magnetically align with the shiny silver ball, and begin sparking with electricity, channeling through the previously ionized air particles. The SWAT members stare at the floating pieces.

Electricity channels through the air in a circle. It zaps every SWAT member inside its capsule. They scream in agony from the electrified air, clenching their chests, until it terminates their pules and kills them.

They all fall, simultaneously, dead onto the ground. The magnetic connections fade, and the pieces fall next to the bodies. Her guardian lifts his shield up, disconnecting the grounded portion that protected them. Their leader enters the hallway again, staring at the girl, still holding her duffel bag. She looks back at the remaining soldiers waiting outside.

"Go! Go! GO!" she yells at them. They march through, holding their gatling guns at their side. One of them brushes up against her while they pass her by. Zaylee commands a second drone to fly on ahead. It passes by the Electric Squad invaders that are heading through the building. She pushes a button, commanding the drone to head left.

It pushes through the office building. Zaylee looks at the screen, several more SWAT members stand prepared in the hallway, pointing their weapons at the entrance.

Pressing another button on the tablet activates the drone's sirens. The Electric Squad members look wearily at the door. One of them takes initiative, creeping slowly towards the door. He peeks through the glass and the SWAT members notice him immediately. Three consecutive shots fire through the window, breaking it and passing through his body. He steps back, crunching the glass. A small red circle of blood seeps through his shirt and starts to expand. As it becomes a gargantuan puddle soaking his shirt, he looks down and touches the circle with his hand, blood sticking to his fingers as he does so. He looks up at the other members of the squad, then falls over.

Two Electric Squad members rush the door, starting up their gatling guns. A stream of bullets flies down the hallway, killing the SWAT members. However, simultaneously, a SWAT member licked off a few assault rounds into one of the gatling wielders, causing her to fall to the ground, splattering blood along the wall. Her partner looks back at the remaining members, "Well, let's move!" he commands the rest of them. The drone pushes on ahead. The rooms to the side now have numbers placed on them, starting with 100, the drone pauses in front of a pair of doors.

The Electric Squad members catch up to it, the drone buzzes, tilting itself back with the doors in its sights. One of the members in the back walks forward and opens the door. Its open state allows the drone to fly up the stairs. Diagonally on the wall is '200' with an arrow pointing up. Soldiers walk up the stairs in a rush but their bulky gatling guns prevent them from reaching their maximum speed as the weaponry bounces on their knees.

Zaylee watches the drone's video feed, multiple SWAT members run down the stairs in single file. She presses a button on the drone and its weapon drops out of its carriage.

Its targeting protocols activate, creating a red crosshair around the first SWAT member. It fires, pushing itself back, as the bullet reorientates its trajectory and lands in her head. The drone flies over to the center of the stairwell, tilting vertically, presenting its weapon to the ceiling high above. It fires five rounds into the air. A few SWAT members, who were close to the center of the stairway and were tagged by a drone who saw them through the window, fall down with a loud thump as the tracer rounds kill them. One of the SWAT members lands with their body on the edge. It slowly slips off the concrete side and onto the floor below.

Blood splatters all over the bottom of the stairwell. A battery warning appears on Zaylee's tablet, denoting that one of the drone's is running low on power. She commands the drone to approach a nearby soldier. "RECHARGE." the drone demands in a monotone computer voice. She looks up at the drone then back down to her waist, where the end of a red wire protrudes out. She pulls the wire out and connects it to the drone. A meter gauge audibly rings on her belt, showing how much is left to charge.

The rest of the squad continues to move upward. They wait as a group by the door, before they enter the floor with room 300. Once they all have arrived, one of them pushes through the door. The floor is covered in SWAT members, who instantly kill him before his gatling gun can begin to spin up. His screams fade with the gunfire. The girl with the duffel bag approaches the door, her shielded partner to her right. He puts the shield in front of him, walks through the door, and the girl follows behind him. She sits behind him and pulls a grenade out; she quickly throws it down the hall. It explodes, creating a smokescreen in the hall.

She looks into her duffel bag and grabs another sapphire crystal ball out of the bag, holding it in her hands. Her partner grounds his shield, magnetically stabilizing it. She holds the ball tight and rolls it down the hall. In the midst of the smokescreen the ball rolls, unseen. Upon reaching the end, the ball opens like a flower, its sides laying out. Lasers shoot into the air, ionizing it. The shielded soldier places a shiny silver ball on the slot at the top of his protective device.

The Tesla coils activate, attempting to channel their electricity through the hallway towards the metal ball. Its path is blocked by the SWAT members, but it quickly annihilates them to make room; the electricity pours through every sliver of their body, vibrating them erratically, until they collapse onto the floor, similarly stopping their hearts via electricity. Their bodies continue to electrify in the hallway, until the electricity finally reaches the silver ball. After the connections cease, the electricity stops.

Slowly the smoke begins to fade, revealing a hallway full of SWAT bodies from the electric wake. Their leader looks into the hallway and notices the dead bodies and mutters, "We send these people, who ignorantly protected sinners, to you God, that you might help them learn." Then she does the sign of the cross and says, "In the name of the Father, and the Son, and the Holy Spirit, Amen." After finishing, she pulls up her radio, "Commander Zaylee, the building is clear." she confirms into the radio. Zaylee moves the drone controller, and it moves through the hallway.

The Electric Squad leader follows the drone, her soldiers

follow behind her. They reach a door labeled '300'. Their squad leader opens the door, without peeking into the room, allowing the mechanical drone to take the risk of entering. The drone enters to find a mostly empty room, with only the mayor hiding under his desk. Zaylee turns on her microphone, connecting it to the tablet, and commands the drone to replay her words: "Mayor Antonio, you are hereby sentenced to death by hanging for your crimes against the people, any last words?" The drone stares down at the mayor with its red lens. His fat body showing on the camera; on his desk, she notices multiple bags of candy.

"I didn't do anything!" he begins to supplicate. "Please, the caustic corruption vid was wrong. I never accepted any bribes! I swear! I have never worked with the Cartel! Her videos are lies!" he shouts. Zaylee watches on her tablet and speaks through drone again, "Your lies are like your heart, black and weak. Your judicial system took our families, our lovers, and our friends. All, so you could get rich and fat." the drone says, replicating her voice. The mayor pleads, "Then go to the courthouse! Take the district attorney, the judges, anyone else but me! I am a servant of the people!" he shouts, his fat wobbling in his fear.

"Don't worry, we will. You and your city council were the first to go. I just heard that the other squad has killed them and have moved on to the courthouse. But right now, it's your turn." she says through the drone. He squeals in fear, "No, please!" he begs. The drone turns towards the Electric Squad leader. "Hang him now." Zaylee instructs.

The tall toweringly leader drops her gatling guns and pulls out an already tied noose. He begins to squirm away, hiding under his desk and gripping the leg tightly. "Get him!" she orders her soldiers. A few soldiers likewise drop their guns and walk towards the mayor's desk, grab him, and attempt to pull him out, but he resists so a female soldier activates her electric arm and zaps him. "AHH!" he screams in pain, before falling to the ground limp.

The Electric Squad soldiers pull him towards their leader. The squad leader locks the noose around his neck, tightening it. She grips its wiry texture, sliding her fingers until she reaches the end. She grabs the end with one hand and lifts her leg up to smash into the dry wall. She kicks most of the drywall out, finding a steel girder support. Hastily, she ties the rope around the beam.

"Throw him!" she commands. Her soldiers pick him up and throw him out the window. They likewise do the sign of the cross as his body flies out into the humid air, the glass shards shooting out of the building along with his body. He flies outward until gravity takes effect and pulls him down. The weight presses him down, the rope snaps tight, breaking his neck. His body dangles over the side, for all of Los Angeles to see. The squad leader walks to the broken window and takes a peek out.

She is greeted by the cheering of the citizens below, who begin chanting "Hallelujah!"

Chapter 17: Blackstorm Mission

"Lieutenant Rayna, what is the situation? Have you finished the prep work for Mission Blackstorm?" Zaylee inquires, looking at Rayna.

Rayna addresses Zaylee immediately, "Commander Zaylee, we are addressing the wounds of the infantry. Mission priority has changed to prevent the death of our soldiers and civilians. Two judges, Supreme Justice O'Conner and Supreme Justice Yangsu have been terminated. But the government was well prepared. After the termination of the mayor and the city council, they called in the National Guard, SWAT, and FBI. All of them are protecting every political official. The prep work has been completed for two other targets, while the final target is still in the preparatory phase. My mission will be resumed when transfer of care is complete, but I do suggest we cancel our mission. We cannot handle our adversary." she says in reply.

Zaylee retorts, "Negative. The mission continues. Leave the soldiers here, we will take care of them. Finish your mission before more forces arrive." Zaylee commands. Rayna doubles down and fights Zaylee's command again, "The police are still looking for us. The FBI and military are no doubt shortly behind them. This delay of time is doubly effective for us." she says.

"Negative. Fend off the police. Do not lose to them. You have the advantage. The police force is ineffective. We must finish this mission quickly or we will never be able to complete it – the military will surely thwart us. We must make Trey, Mike, and Ciara proud."

Rayna stands firm again, "Zaylee, my priority is my friends. I will not leave them." she repeats, insubordinately.

"Mutiny will not be tolerated. I will finish your mission and deal with the repercussions of your insubordination later. Continue addressing their wounds, when transfer of care is complete notify me. Dismissed." Zaylee commands her, using her hands to gesture for her to leave for her mission. Zaylee clasps her hands behind her back, cracking her knuckles as she does, and begins pacing back and forth. She looks at a soldier sitting at a computer, watching the drones fly back and forth on his screen.

She walks closer to him and their eyes meet. He immediately stands up and places his hand laterally upon his forehead, "Sir!" he shouts, while tightening his stance. "At ease soldier." Zaylee orders him, allowing him to separate his legs, and put his arms behind his back in a locked position.

She peers at his computer, looking at a drone's camera view of the situation below, "Which drone are you currently on?" she asks, looking at the screen. He turns and looks at the screen, maintaining his relaxed position, "Sir, drone sixteen just made its way to judge five's house for a preliminary search." he responds. Zaylee can see the interior of his house through the camera feed, fancy leather couches are in the center of the living room with an exorbitantly expensive television on the wall.

Zaylee looks back at the mission tasks, "Pull up the logistics surveyed by drones one through fifteen." she asks nicely, handing him a tablet to connect to them. "Yes sir." he responds, dragging his finger across the screen to bring up multiple graphs of each drone's geographic information quarantined into boxes around them. Half of the drone's boxes flash with red 'X's striped through them, symbolizing their destruction. He holds the tablet out for Zaylee to grab, "Here you go, sir. Drones one through seven have been destroyed. Drones eight through twelve are in position for judges three and four. We will be releasing drones thirteen and fourteen for judge five momentarily. They will survey the area while the technicians complete the prep work, most likely within the hour. The other squads, Alpha and Gamma, are ready to move on judges three and four, they are simply awaiting your command." he says, sliding through each drone on the tablet to show her their status.

Zaylee nods, "Everything seems like it's in order. I will accompany Alpha squad and take judge five. I want you to commandeer Gamma squad for judge three. We will act in quick succession. As soon as you have dealt with judge three, move onto to judge five, provided the prep work is complete." she says, grabbing the tablet from his hand.

She stares at the drone's cameras viewing multiple areas of where they will strike, "Once again, use the drones first and take out any hostiles before you arrive. And make sure not kill the judge prematurely as their sins must be televised. This is an important mission; do not screw it up." Zaylee tells him, her eyes burning into his soul.

"Yes sir!" he replies, hurrying over to the other side of the citadel. He gestures to the Electric Squad members recuperating from their injuries. Some of them are still mobile and begin to follow him towards the central computer of the citadel. Zaylee looks over and sees the Mantis-blade wielding squad waiting for her. They stand uniform and straight, waiting for her command.

"Atten-hut!" she says, the five Mantis-blade soldiers tighten their stance with a single jolt. "MARK TIME!" she yells, the soldiers begin marching in place. Their feet stomp on the ground below. "RIGHT FLANK, MARCH!" she yells. They turn ninety degrees to the right and begin to march forward, she follows behind them at their slow pace. Her face turns to vexation, she jogs to the side of them, "DOUBLE TIME!" she commands. Their stomps become more frequent as they begin to jog due to the command.

In the distance, Zaylee sees their vehicle parked on the opposite side of the street. She quickly jogs over with them and slides her key into the metal slot. It turns and unlocks the vehicle. She opens the door of the vehicle, "IN, IN, IN!" she shouts and they quickly enter in the vehicle. She stops the last soldier, placing her hand on his collar bone. She notices he was a fellow cop from the station, whom she worked with at one point. He backs up and her hand quickly removes from his chest. She points at him, "You, soldier. Drive." she commands the resigned officer pithily. He hops into the driver seat and Zaylee hops into the passenger seat before tossing the keys at him.

She looks at him and then back at the road, "Drive to Grand Avenue," she tells him. He looks at her, then back at the road in front of him, "Yes sir!" he replies, pushing down on the gas and launching the vehicle forwards. The four soldier's guns are pointing upward toward the top of the vehicle, while their other hands, wrapped in a silver Mantis-blade, point down at the floor. Zaylee looks back at their assault rifles and nods. They gather confidence from her nod.

"Soldier, next exit," she instructs. He pulls over and exits the freeway, the vehicle continues down the street and turns onto Temple Street before immediately turning left onto Hill Street. They continue until they see a large white building to the right. Zaylee points outward, "Pull to the side of the road. The Supreme Justice will be leaving the courthouse soon. We will wait until he comes out." Zaylee commands him. "Yes sir!" he replies again, pulling the vehicle onto the concrete just past a subway station.

She looks at the soldiers in the back of the vehicle, "You hear that, soldiers? Remain alert." she tells them. "Yes sir!" they reply in unison.

After reaching into her bag, she pulls out her tablet and watches their drone flying near the courthouse. It spools a vid to her tablet, giving her a wide view of the area. She spots a few sheriffs by the exit, guarding the door. They just sit, motionless staring out into the street. Zaylee looks over and sees a plethora of stores, "Park in the shopping lot over there." Zaylee orders the driver. He exclaims, "Yes sir!" as he pulls the vehicle forward and into the lot. Zaylee gestures to the subway station, and so he heads over and parks near it. From here they have a clear view of the building.

The time on the tablet reads 17:53. She watches as it clicks to 17:54. The drone gives her a video of the judge exiting the courthouse, from the wrong door. He walks over and enters the parking lot, the sheriffs escorting him. She looks at the drive at commands him, "Soldier, block the gate." Without thinking he replies "Yes sir." The vehicle moves forward and blocks the parking lot exit. She looks back at the soldiers sitting in the back, "You two take the rear." she directs. They immediately open the door, exit, and head towards the back of the building. Zaylee looks at the remaining soldiers, "The rest stays for the frontal assault."

She looks at the soldiers heading towards the rear of the building and yells, "Do not hurt the judge! We need him alive if we are to set an example!" she commands them, looking at all the soldiers individually. They nod their head, "Yes sir." they reply in unison. The drones circle above the sheriffs, their illusion fades as their lights turn on. They pull back and put three rounds into each sheriff, causing them to instantly go down. The judge hears the commotion and frantically starts running, trying to get back into the building, but Zaylee swipes the controls on the tablet and the drones block the door. She selects 'warning shots' on the tablet and the drones spew out three shots near his feet.

147

His briefcase swings as he rotates 180-degrees to look at the drone; his shoes press into the gravel as he rotates. Zaylee hops out of the vehicle and begins approaching him. As he gets into her line of sight, she points her pistol at him and aims it at him carefully. The two other soldiers stand behind her, also pointing their weapons at him. He looks at them, raises his hands into the air, and drops his briefcase.

Zaylee glances at the soldier on her left, "Soldier, pick that up." Zaylee commands him. He walks forward and picks the briefcase up, moving the gravel around it as he lifts it up. Zaylee walks forward, and points her weapon at his torso. "Turn back around for me Supreme Justice Rosalez, and grasp your hands behind your head." she instructs him while opening a velcro slot on her cargo pants. He obeys as she reaches in her pocket for a cable tie and loops it around his hands, pulling it as tightly as she can.

She looks over at the soldier on her right, the one without the briefcase, "Soldier, take the Justice to the car." she commands. The soldier puts one hand on the back of the Justices' head and the other on his tied arms. He drags him through the lot, towards their car, near the gate. Suddenly, a door opens nearby, out of view. Multiple sheriffs dressed in brown pour out of the building. They fire rounds into the drones, the noise echoing and penetrating into Zaylee's ears, almost hurting her. She watches as one of the drones goes down, failing to activate its offensive protocols.

The remaining drones rotate and fly behind the building, out of sight. The sheriffs' attention transfers to the soldiers near the car. The drones' patter with excitement upon seeing the two other soldiers, who took the rear, are behind the wall. The soldiers peak up and fire at the sheriffs with their assault rifles. The drones fly up and fire a round into a sheriff, killing her. A soldier from behind the wall makes his way over to the parking lot, hiding behind some cars. He creeps behind a sheriff and activates his gauntlet Mantis-blade, it glows dark green and then begins to burn white with its new acetylene tank.

He extends his blade and lunges forward, thrusting his blade into the sheriff, tearing him in half, easily. The body falls to the floor, he looks over and sees another sheriff peering over the top of a vehicle, licking off shots in his direction. The sheriff pauses, scared of the bladed individual, and ducks down, using the vehicle as cover. This gives the Mantis Squad member time to look at the corpse, do a sign of the cross, say, "I send you to God that he might cleanse you of your sin." and rush forward. Then, as the Mantis Squad soldier jumps through the air, he slices the vehicle completely in half. Upon landing, he ducks his head down from the impact. The sheriff's face changes to moderately afraid to terrified within seconds as the soldier shoves his Mantis-blade through him. He yanks it out and looks at the body and does a sign of the cross while saying "Jesus, forgive me of my sins. I say this in the name of the Father, and the Son, and the Holy Spirit."

On the other side of the battle, Zaylee runs with the two soldiers she attacked the judge with. They try their best to make it to their vehicle. The bullets keep flying and the soldier next to Zaylee takes a bullet in her leg. She falls to the ground, causing them to redirect their path to avoid the gunfire. They move out into the street as Zaylee hears another screech of a blade and cringes; the other soldier had torn apart yet another Sheriff. Even at her lengthy distance, she spotted the blood spraying across the wall out of the corner of her eye. They enter their secondary get-away vehicle, the soldier with the Judge throws him into the back seat.

Zaylee grabs her radio, "Come back, no more killing! Throw the chlorine bombs and get over here." she says into the radio. She looks over the wall and sees a yellow-green cloud pouring over the wall. "Where are you?" a voice asks through the radio. Zaylee notices the confusion in their voice and replies, "Secondary vehicle parked on the street. Hurry." Zaylee relays. She turns on the vehicle, it begins to hum. The two soldiers who took the rear run across the street and hop into the back of the vehicle.

A male soldier looks at Zaylee, "We dragged three sheriffs, that passed out from the chlorine bombs, away from the gas." he says. The female perks up, "Don't you think it's a little ridiculous that we were saving them after we were just firing at them with guns and tearing them apart?" she asks. Zaylee pushes down on the pedal and the car moves forward down the street, "No, we are not here to torture and kill them, we are here to torture and kill the judges. We only kill those that get in our way. After the massacre of those SWAT teams, I realized that innocent people, just doing their jobs,

149

were getting killed and we could be more efficient by merely focusing on the mission at hand, such as repelling into the mayor's office from the beginning and avoiding the whole confrontation in the halls." she responds, looking at the judge in the back seat.

Zaylee's face cringes as the male soldier, with a short Mantis-blade attached to his fingers, peels off the skin on the judge's hand. The Mantis-blade digs into his skin, peeling it off, allowing him to cauterize it to a AX50 sniper rifle. The judge begins to scream, but they quickly put tape over his mouth. They then put on a custom court dress they fashioned to a straight-jacket and place it on him. Only his hands are showing now and there is no sign of him being skinned, although the sniper rifle remains permanently attached to his hand. Zaylee looks at him, bound and unable to speak, "How does it feel to be unable to move, just like Trey, before you had him executed." Zaylee asks. The judge muffles through the tape, but she can't make out any words. The soldiers then peel his other hand and cauterize an unbalanced Lady Justice scale to his right hand. His muffled screams of pain go unnoticed.

The wound smells horrid and fills the car with its stench. Zaylee grabs a napkin and puts it up to her nose, in an attempt to stop the particles from reaching her.

As she lowers the napkin, Zaylee looks out at a park, lined with palm trees and water. In the center of it all is a pile of brush. She parks the vehicle and they exit, dragging the judge's feet over the curb. Zaylee leads the way as they walk through the park. The judge's sniper rifle and scale hold tightly on his chest with little movement. Zaylee picks up a wooden cross, "I will help you strap him to the cross. You get the other side." The soldier, obsequious to Zaylee's orders, instantly grabs the other side of the cross.

They stand the judge up and tie his wrists to each side of the cross. They rope his feet around the bottom, binding him completely to it. Then they place the cross in the center of the brush and begin to pour gasoline over it, including on the Justice himself. His skin is now wet with gas.

Zaylee looks at the male soldier that helped her so valiantly, "You can do the honors, soldier." she says to him. "Thank you, sir." he replies, pulling out a camouflage painted lighter from his pocket. He flips it open and uses his small Mantis-blade, that designates him as an inexperienced Mantis, to spin it.

The flame ignites as a crowd of people gather behind them at the park, their phones out as they start to record the scene.

The soldier throws the lighter into the brush and it instantly lights up. Zaylee turns and looks at the crowd who are now doing doing the sign of the cross. They circle around as the brush lights up

She looks at the soldiers, "The world shall judge him now. Let's go, there is much work to be done."

Chapter 18: Shock Therapy

Vero stands on an elevated platform; an audience stands in front of him. Their clothes are withered and old, and have restaurant logos on them. Zaylee stands behind him, her hands crossed in front of her. The brown police outfit strapped to her body, all the way down to her boots. A gun sits in its holster upon her hip, matte black, but scary nonetheless. Vero pulls out a crimson red LED megaphone. He flips the red switch on and presses the button, like one would press down on the trigger of a gun.

"People of Los Angeles, cooks and clerks alike, we have called you here and asked you to wear your old uniforms as a statement to what will happen next, for we are going to avenge you and take out the robots that took your job. This message is from the great prophet herself. She claims, with proof, that our society can survive like the tribes of old. The corporations have spread their caustic mentality, siphoning our money for themselves. We can survive without them!" he shouts. Most of the crowd just listens, but a few cheers bellow out of some vocal cords. He turns back and looks at Zaylee, who has pulled out a tablet. The protocols for a food service robot read out on its screen. At the top there is a label, defining this robot as Salt version 18.1024. There are arrows in the corner, allowing complete control of the robot.

Zaylee uses the arrows, nostalgia rushing through her. The tablet controls remind her of the handheld video game players from her childhood. Filled with emotion and giddiness at playing with technology, she flicks some buttons that are labeled as an arrow. A one-meter-tall robot walks onto the stage and stands beside Vero, moving in an artificial fashion. He looks at the screen on its chest, loading through its bios. 'MiT Artificial Intelligence' pops up in mostly black letters, only the bottom portion of the 'i' is red.

The bios begins to flash, red and black words flash along the screen. 'Haskell Hack' and 'Property of The Cyberpunk Squad' flash until it finally loads completely, hitting the splash screen for the operating system. Vero proclaims, "We have successfully hacked their robots; they listen to us now." The operating system finishes loading and the robot sits with the desktop on its screen. Zaylee pushes on the controls; her commands begin to duplicate on its screen. Pneumatic controls fire off while the robot raises its mechanical arm into the air. A new Mantis blade is strapped to its arm, glowing whitish-orange as it heats up.

Rayna quickly brings over a two-meter block of drywall on a cart, the wheels shaking while it's pushed to the center of the stage. The robot's light illuminates green, signifying the heating process is complete. It drops the arm down, slicing the drywall diagonally in half.

The drywall slides down onto the floor, crumbling upon hitting the stage. A smile spreads across Zaylee's face. Vero turns back to the audience, "These robots took your jobs, prevented you from paying your mortgage, stopped you from getting your children what they wanted for Christmas, but now they are the peoples once again."

Vero continues, "May the floating farms Ms. Schesis speaks of rise up. May the people once again keep the money for their work, no longer feeding into an unnecessary corporate sponsored dependence. May the people take their country back from those that seek to abuse us, control us, and take our money!" Vero shouts at the crowd, holding the megaphone in a tilted position, "Citizens of Los Angeles, we fight for you!" he yells before pausing. As he paces back and forth on the stage, he holds the megaphone towards the floor.

He puts the megaphone mesh near his mouth, "People believe that you need groups, riots, and protests to solve your issues. We have proved that to make some noise and solve your problems, you only need to kill a select evil few who deserve it. Instead of rioting, go after your enemy directly. The politicians that sit on their throne in Sacramento were destroyed by a group of less than fifty people. We raided their courts, killing those that fought against us and balked God's righteous children. We placed their bodies on crosses and we put them on a pyre, killing them in Echo Park and the International World Peace Rose Garden for the world to see. They burned like witches at the stake, as a subtle irony for the silent death they brought upon us; for the voting rights they took away from us, we burned them at a place that represented peace."

Vero points to the robot, drawing their attention to it. The screen on the robot plays a video of Electric Squad members lifting up a metal cross with two Supreme Justices strapped to it, their faces have been locked into a kissing position. The two male Justices remain strapped to the cross, squirming in the center of the garden, inside a fountain.

They cannot escape and they cannot unlock their lips. A soldier drops a bag of sand into the fountain, pouring the remainder of the bag onto their wet bodies. Their squad leader then drops her Tesla coiled arm into the water, electrifying it with high amperage. Their squirms fade as the life leaves their bodies.

They all do a sign of the cross and run back into their vehicle as the vid ends.

—

"Chief executive officer and employees of MacNeils, you are sentenced to death for your crimes against the people." Zaylee utters into a microphone. Every speaker in the corporate office repeats her statement as she continues, "The MacNeil founding brothers and their relatives will be burnt to a crisp for their crimes. There is no denying what you have done. Being Irish, you know what it is like to suffer. And you have done the same to the people, creating a long-lasting cruelty. None of you are innocent, only your working employees are, since you treated them worse than slaves. You, and the rest of the fast-food industry, have violated markets from the U.S, to Europe, to the AUE, to the Middle East. None were exempt from your vandalization of the various world markets."

An army of robots stand in front of her, with drones flying above them.

She nods to the police officers next to her. They pull out their tablets and click ono the screen, activating it. Then they use the touchscreen controls to begin controlling all of the robots, making them rush towards the offices, banging on doors, until the wood crumbles and they can roll in. Drones fly in over the robots and into the hallway. Zaylee looks at the building and puts on a hydraulic arm, crimping the end and shoving it into her skin. Blood drips down her forearm as the device locks into place. Rayna opens a van door and drops out from the vehicle with a long coat on her back flowing as she drops.

People continue to exit the vehicle until all of them stand

behind Zaylee. Rayna looks at Zaylee, "Our video feed has been updated and all streams are being uploaded live online. Electric and Mantis Squad have destroyed every MacNeils, Cutters Jr, Frankfurters, Taco Chime, John's In Boxes, IceCream Hut's, and Sundollar along Sunset Boulevard. They have also burned down a few hundred homes on Coldwater Canyon Avenue, and its surrounding streets in Beverly Hills." Rayna claims.

Zaylee exclaims, "Spectacular. Mike would be proud to see those houses burn. And I'm sure that the many people that have suffered under the rule of those oligopolies will be happy that they got their retribution."

She pauses for a second to collect her thoughts, "Is the video playing through every television inside?" Zaylee queries, pointing at the corporate building. "Yes, it is." Rayna replies.

The inside is flooded with robots, wielding Mantis weapons on their arms. They slice through the doors of offices, approach the workers, and carve up their desks. Eventually they reach them, cutting the employees in half. Blood splashes along the walls from their torn apart bodies. Their organs lay out along the floor below. Another robot chases down a runaway employee, her face looking back at the robot with fear. It finally catches up and thrusts its blade into the right upper quadrant of her body. She screams in pain and, as the robot relinquishes it blade, her body falls to the floor, bleeding out severely as the stages of hemorrhagic shock take place.

Televisions on the wall show Electric and Mantis Squads running into restaurants. Their leaders' gesture with their hands, motioning for them to enter. Mantis Squad members eventually exit, dragging out a tuxedo dressed female. It zooms in, and the viewers can see a placard pinned to her chest, designating her as the manager of the store. All the employees walk away from the building, while a Salt robot enters and stands in the center of the restaurant. Promptly, it explodes.

The flames pour out of the building, blowing the doors off their hinges and into the street, where the Mantis Squad leader is standing near the manager. He ducks down, onto his knees, while the soldiers hold her by the arms, her feet dragging beneath her. "You are one of us. We are freeing you from the chains of corporations." The camera catches his words as he continues to free her, "Ms. Schesis has freed us from their control with philosophy and proof of a better life alongside God. Help us build that better life." he says, as they lift her onto her feet.

Now, every television playing the video transitions, showing magnificent houses on Coldwater Canyon. Four soldiers exit from a Japanese sedan styled race car. On its hood is the logo of the Mantis Squad with various lightning bolts spread around the hood, similar to the Electric Squad vehicles, denoting that the cyberpunk squads are clearly corroborating and sharing technology now.

Two of the four soldiers are holding assault rifles in one hand and Mantis-blade gauntlets in the other. The remaining two soldiers are carrying enormous gas cans. A soldier walks towards the house, pointing at it while looking at the camera, "Finally, we can attack the rich members of society. They claim to have helped the poor, but if you've seen houses like this, you know that's a lie."

He points down at a beautiful barrage of roses and fountains on the lawn, "Just look at this. Pure rapacity." The soldiers continue to walk towards the house. When the two soldiers, with the gas cans, arrive near the side, they begin pouring gasoline all over it. Then, after pouring all the gas, the two Mantis-blade gauntlet wielding soldiers, extend their blades, allow them to heat up, and touch the side of the building. A small flame begins to accrue, but it hastily spreads itself up the wall as the gasoline catches fire.

After a few seconds, the fire spreads over the entire structure. All four soldiers walk out, and the video speeds up. The soldiers enter into their vehicle and drive down the street. Behind their car, in the background, are massive fires reaching into the sky. Billows of black smoke block out the sun. Six more vehicles are behind them; some vehicles are parked and others are trailing behind them. The ones trailing behind them are also filled with Mantis warriors. Nearly every house behind them is on fire, adding more black smoke to the sky. Ash begins to fall around them as the houses continue to burn.

Beneath the televisions video stream, commotion continues to occur. A robot rushes down the hall, past the televisions, towards an office at the end of the hall. It slices the door in half. An older gentleman stands behind a desk, he gets up and shoves his chair, before clutching his chest. He falls to the floor, wriggling in pain.

The robot exits the room, looking towards the left, leaving the man to die, and go through the phases of cardiogenic shock. The robot punches into the wall, finding the main air unit, it crimps the metal line with its hand, stopping the air from flowing.

The robot continues its descent down the hall, with a group of other robots following it. The bots push a button and the elevator doors open. All of them enter the elevator and as the doors close, the cameras slowly lose sight of the sea of dead bodies on the floor.

Water systems activate, stopping the elevator at the next floor. The door opens though, allowing the robots to exit. They position themselves at various places on the floor and drop around a hundred canisters labeled 'carbon monoxide' onto the floor as they roll to the other side of the building where another elevator is. A slow audible hiss pours through the floor. Corporate workers open the doors to their office. Some of them vomit, others grab their forehead, and a few grab their throats. They fall to the floor at different intervals from varying degrees of respiratory shock. The robots enter the other elevator, opposite to the one they initially exited from. And the robot's camera captures the employee's deaths as the elevator door shuts.

Zaylee and Rayna push a button on the first level, commanding the elevator to meet them. The robots slowly descend to the first level, the doors open, allowing them to enter the robot filled elevator. Zaylee clicks her hydraulic weapon to 8/10th full power, green to yellow to red lights activate on a scale with the LED screen beneath it. Rayna does the same, activating her hydraulics to 8/10th full power, allowing the lights to sit on the first red light. The device bulges from under the skin on her arm, while Zaylee's black hydraulic sits on the outside, easily visible to everyone, but her forearm has stopped bleeding from the insertion.

The elevator makes it to the top floor, opening its door to the massive marble floor. Security forces wait on all sides of the room, pointing their guns at them, "Freeze!" one of them shouts. Rayna looks at him and chuckles, "The derisory wages you are paid can barely sustain your life. Why do you defend those that care so little for your services?" Rayna inquires madly, the security forces look at each other, "Well, at least we have a job!" another one shouts.

Zaylee scolds them, "You have a job where you are forced to

risk your life for only slightly above minimum wage. Security and emergency personnel are the most underpaid services. You wish to die in order to protect those that enforce this heinous siphoning of your money?" Zaylee asks. They look at each other and a few of them lower their weapons, "She's getting into your head!" the lead security guard screams.

Zaylee chuckles as Rayna steps forward, "The corporations have gotten into your head, like a virus that's turned this nation septic." Rayna says to them. Zaylee continues for her, "And do you know what happens during septic shock?" Zaylee asks, they shrug. "Poisonous substances accumulate in the bloodstream and blood pressure decreases, impairing blood flow to cells, tissues, and every organ in the body. Thus, the entire system eventually dies." Zaylee answers.

Rayna declares to them, "We are here to stop the murder of this nation and its people. Stand aside or die." The security personnel immediately step aside, allowing Zaylee, Rayna, and the robots to make their way to the three offices at the end of the room. Zaylee looks at Rayna, motioning for her to enter the room all the way to the right.

Zaylee grabs a door handle and enters the room all the way to the left. A man in an expensive suit sits behind his desk, littered with calculators and papers covered in numbers. On the wall by the door is a television, playing the videos of Mantis Squad taking down a Cutters Jr, dosing the manager in the fryer after he refuses to cooperate. A soldier in the vid says, "I wish we didn't have to do that. You should have cooperated like the others or, at least, allowed us to drag you out." They pull his head out, covered in burns, and let him drop to the floor. They exit and a robot enters the building, exploding in the center, and destroying it, much the same as the other buildings they had destroyed.

The man stands as Zaylee enters. She looks at him, "Robert Pouts, CFO of MacNeils, you are hereby sentenced to death." Zaylee states, flexing her hydraulics at him. Robert frantically screams at her, "Your polemic videos weren't enough, were they? You just had to go and muck up society!" Zaylee pauses, pulling her hand back as he continues to speak, "We helped those that are stupid and incapable. We gave them money even though they constantly destroyed our equipment. But that wasn't enough, was it?" he asks.

She walks closer to him; their faces are now close. Fearing for his life as she pulls her hydraulic fist back, he yells, "Caustic corruption, how pathetic. Society depends on us!" Zaylee thrusts her hand forward and punches him in the spine. A loud crack echoes through the floor. He falls to the floor, motionless as Zaylee looks over his body, "Your services are no longer necessary. The people will have their farms and they will keep all their food and profit. Your financial strain on society will be purged." Zaylee utters, his body going through the phases of neurogenic shock. Upon further inspection, Zaylee notices a clear liquid dripping out of his ear and a change in his pelvic region. She grimaces and walks out of the room, breaking visual contact with his body. Rayna is in the hallway, waiting for her.

They look at each other and meet at the center of the room, staring at the final victim. In big letters they read the acronym 'CEO'. Both of them look at each other and nod before walking towards the door. Rayna opens the door, giving Zaylee a clear view of the female standing behind her desk. She walks in towards her, Rayna closing the door behind her. Zaylee stares down the woman in the office, "April MacNeil, for your blatant disregard of the people's plight, you are sentenced to death." Zaylee declares, pulling out a syringe and placing it on her desk. "You have no idea what you're doing, you're just ruining more lives!" April yells at her. "Is my life not valuable?" April asks, afraid.

Zaylee confirms, "We are ruining only a few, so that the rest, the majority, can flourish, not just you and your precious one-percent." Rayna looks at her with disgust, folding her arms, "You failed to realize the plight of immigrants, the very same that your Irish ancestors faced. You have taken my fellow Latin Americans, abused them, and paid them unsatisfactory wages. Instead of learning from the mistakes of the past, you have continued them. We need immigrants, simply pay them a decent wage, tax them, and our nation will progress forward." Rayna explains to her.

"But I-" April begins. "Enough!" Zaylee shouts, looking at Rayna and following up with, "Do not let her believe that she can change her ways and walk out with her life; all she will tell you is lies, because all she cares about is keeping her life and her money."

159

Rayna nods and grabs April's arms, pulling her tightly to the chair and restraining her. Zaylee picks up the needle, flicking the liquid with her index finger. She inserts the needle into April, dispensing the liquid into her arm. "What did you do to me?!" she asks, her body begins to shake, upon Rayna's release of her arms.

She falls to the floor and twitches. "It's insulin. Thus, you will die a death that many of your customers have died. It's called irony." Zaylee states, walking out of the room. April shakes violently on the floor, proceeding through the stages of hypoglycemic shock until she, inevitably, dies.

Chapter 19: Nettle Corporation

Zaylee looks at the Nettle corporation building on her tablet and mutters, "This is for you Ciara." Then she looks at the mission currently taking place, "Alpha squad, give me your report." Zaylee says while speaking into the radio. "Alpha squad reporting in. Bomb has been planted. Five minutes until detonation. We are still evacuating the premises, sir." their reply comes through the radio. The bomb did not beep through the speaker as a soldier beside Zaylee thought it would; Zaylee listened close and could hear it ticking away, almost vibrating. It was in a bathroom on the sixth floor of a twelve-story building. It was at office level, but the bomb was tucked away, hidden in the false ceiling. Zaylee looked at the cyclopean building in the distance, vaingloriously smiling at it.

"Have you started the repelled descent?" she asks, into the radio. "Yes sir." a reply comes from the radio. The soldiers push off the side of the side of the building, repelling downward. "This is stupid." one of them says, "Won't they see us?" he asks. "Yeah, we should have taken the elevator. But the commander has her reasons." another replies, as they all continue to descend down the building. They slowly reach the bottom, when they come within a few meters from the ground two of them slice their rope and stab their Mantis blade into the building, grinding down the wall to slow their descent to the floor. Their feet hit the floor, they stare off, noticing a car in the distance waiting for them. Its doors are wide open with weapons waiting for them to grab.

Zaylee switches the channel for her radio to channel two and gives commands to another squad: "Bravo squad, destroy the electric motor for the elevators. After you have done so, leave the building immediately. Rally with Zeta squad." she commands them through the radio, letting go of the button.

She then switches the frequency, turning the dial at the top of her radio, in attempt to talk to the final squad, "Gamma squad, Zeta squad, are you properly positioned?" she says through the radio. "Yes sir." Gamma squad leaders replies. "Yes sir." Zeta squad quickly follows up after Gamma squad frees up the frequency. Zaylee stares through her binoculars at the side of the gargantuan glass building buzzing with activity at the bottom. The members of

161

Zeta squad are picking up assault rifles out of the van, and the members of Gamma squad are collecting their gatling guns, attaching their red wires to them.

Zaylee bellows through the radio, "Remember, unlike the police, none of these people are not innocent. This is their headquarters, everyone inside is an enemy of the people. Leave none of them alive. Mitigate all other causalities though. Make sure the other buildings are empty before the Nettle corporation is destroyed." she says, as the radio clicks over to another station, ready to receive incoming messages.

She looks out of binoculars again and sees the large Nettle logo spanning over the top. Through the lens are people on nearly every level of the building and, at the bottom, the squads are converging on the exits. The tablet flickers, alerting Zaylee, so she taps on the notification that appears in the corner. It is from a squad at the docks that they have completed their mission in sabotaging much of the port.

She reviews the details of the attack and notices that they destroyed all of the containers and associated ships, completing their mission of completing hampering the economic structure of the oligopolies on her list.

A soldier taps Zaylee on the shoulder as she continues to read over the details, "Commander Zaylee, Alpha squad has been noticed by their private security. They are activating their defensive protocols. Most of the other nearby buildings have been evacuated but they have also alerted the police. Furthermore, the Nettle building will be on full lock-down within seconds. We will face heavy resistance." Zaylee keeps looking at the building, people of every age are freaking out, throwing their hands in the air, knocking things out of their way, and rushing towards the exit.

"I will redirect the dispatch signals and send the police off elsewhere." Zaylee nods and finishes, "Thank you. Back to your post. Notify me if anything unusual develops on the drone cams." Zaylee tells the soldier. He hands her his police scanner and walks away.

She scans with her binoculars, searching the lower levels. The building's security stands up, holding their weapons out. They point them towards Alpha squad, as Alpha squad begins setting up their shield.

A private security officer picks up a phone, dials down on the pad with a worried face. Zaylee puts her binoculars down and picks up the police scanner that the soldier handed her. The dispatcher says, "Glendale police, how may I help you?" The caller replies with, "We have hostiles repelling down off the side of our building, explosions on level one and twelve. Both elevators are inoperable. Need assistance immediately."

Zaylee clicks on her software and imprints on the police dispatch system, cause the program to run and alter the data. She puts the software down and watches as security finishes their preparations for the building lock-down. The head guard picks up a radio, giving a building wide announcement to his personnel, "This is security, protocols must be followed, but help the people exit anyway you can."

Zaylee watches the security members rush up the stairs to every level so they can help people exit. She moves the binoculars back over to the guard station, where the Electric Squad has finally set up their shield. The head guard hits a button on his desk, it is massive and red in color, and activates a voice protocol. It initiates the buildings speakers and warning system. A girl behind their electric shield throws out a ball into the air. From the inertia, it separates into four pieces, sending out electricity, shocking everyone at the guard station, killing them by heart attack.

Security breach. Please evacuate the building the automated voice echoes throughout the building. Zaylee looks through her binoculars at the people on every floor. They are all dressed in skirts, suits, tuxedos, ties, slacks, and typical professional attire. Everyone on every floor begins to run towards the elevator; the alarm has put them all into a state of panic. They mash the button.

Nothing happens.

They continue to mash the button. Finally, one guy takes initiative, "We can take the stairs down. Let's go!" he says, standing still and pushing others towards the stairwell. Zaylee watches as his arms continue to wave, pointing his co-workers towards the stairway. "Hurry!" he screams. As the last person heads to the stairwell, he presses a button to notify security that the elevator is not working. But there is no response. Zaylee perceives a look of worry on his face, but watches him make his way back to the rest of the group.

He finally makes his way to the stairwell and out of Zaylee's view. Zeta squad stands at the first floor exits and target each worker as they attempt to exit. They shoot round after round into them. A few of them run out of ammo so they pull out their Mantis-blade's and begin slicing up the workers. The heat emanating from their blades heats up the entryway, as they continue to cut down worker after worker, splashing their blood in every direction. The violence is seen by most of the employees, horrifying them, and making them rush back to the office portion of the floor.

Zaylee watches, as they return to their office floors and cower under their desks in fear. She pulls out her radio, "Zeta squad, exit the building, lend support to Gamma squad." she commands. "Affirmative." a voice replies. She uses her binoculars and looks at the bottom level, Gamma squad is ready with their gatling guns pointing at the front door. After some waiting, more people try to leave through the front doors, their skirts and ties flowing as they run for the door.

Gamma squad's leader stands dead center, wielding a gatling gun towards the door. It clicks on, beginning to spin, bullets fly through the front doors, breaking the glass. Blood mixes in with the glass, while the employees fall to the ground, bullets penetrating them at every angle. Their bodies flop wildly until they settle on the floor, in a pool of mixed blood. After the barrage ends, Gamma squad leader kisses a golden cross and does a small prayer, asking for forgiveness.

Zaylee scans the area, noticing multiple police cars approaching behind them. Upon parking, they exit their cars, and hold their hands above their car doors, pointing pistols at Gamma squad. A multitude of drones exit from the back of their vehicles, their sirens can be heard from Zaylee's position. Her radio buzzes as a voice pours into her ears, "Commander Zaylee, police have arrived outside the Nettle building. They are attempting to apprehend Gamma squad." a soldier tells Zaylee through the radio.

Zaylee turns around and looks at Rayna, "How long until detonation?" she asks Rayna. "Thirty seconds." she responds. "Rayna, tell the snipers that, after detonation, they are to run immediately. Everyone else is to throw chlorine bombs or carbon tetrachloride at the police; it will leave them stupefied and it will be the perfect opportunity for the soldiers on the ground to escape in their cruisers while mitigating death." Zaylee tells Rayna. With a scrunch on her face, Rayna replies with "Yes sir."

Zaylee surveys the scene occurring on the ground below. The drones have begun attacking each other, but the cyberpunk squad ones have the upper hand as they begin tagging the other drones and launching exacto rounds into their enemies, homing in and not missing. Tommy flies out of the crowd of drones towards the Electric Squad leader, while the other drones continue to do aerial maneuvers to tag and attack the approaching drones. Bullets fly through the sky, piercing into their respective armor. Bronze casings and plastic coverings from the drones drop onto the floor. Tommy flies forward, firing off eight rounds.

The bullets fly, flowing through the air, until they find their targets. They hit their targets dead center, dropping the drones to the floor. Tommy flies in a cheerful motion as the police drones fall to the ground. Their hardware guts spread out near the officers. The rest of the drones regroup near the center, looking into the building. They fly in and gun down the remaining workers before exiting and staring back at the police.

An officer begins to shoot at the Electric Squad leader, the bullet ricochets off towards another police vehicle. She turns around, turns on her electric power to full, and propels a multitude of bullets in return fire. They land into their vehicles, creating decent dents in the side of their armored cars. A few cops are shot; a bullet goes through a cop's chest, tearing a hole in her chest. Another cop takes a bullet in the thigh, right near the femoral artery, causing it to squirt blood a fair distance away from him.

The remaining police hide behind their vehicles. The captain grabs his radio, which makes Zaylee grab her monitor and turn it back on. "We're going to need SWAT reinforcement. There is a combatant here with a minigun. And several illegally ascertained police drones with military grade exacto rounds." he says as the voice comes through Zaylee's monitor. A bullet ricochets off his car and he clicks the radio again, "Location is" he says, but is interrupted as more bullets fly towards him, causing him to look up and fire again. Zaylee grabs her tablet, commanding Tommy to fly over at the captain and take him out. The drones fly up over the police and begin firing.

The officers continue to stare up into the blinding sky and fire at the drones. Zaylee's drones retaliate accordingly, as they begin to take cover from each other's fire. Tommy angrily approaches the captain and puts two rounds in his head. He falls on the side of his cruiser, blood pouring out of his head, messing up his hair, until he finally thuds onto the asphalt.

Zaylee picks up her radio again, clicking the side of it, giving her the ability to talk to two squads at once: "Gamma and Zeta squad, try to keep the police causalities to a minimum. Only kill those that get in your way. I have taken out their captain before he gave our location and my hacks on the police network should still be in effect, redirecting police to different areas across L.A."

"Yes sir!" Gamma and Zeta squad reply. Zaylee continues commanding through the radio, "Throw out your chlorine bombs to distract the officers and, as soon as the explosion occurs, take the police cars and leave the area. Gamma squad inform Bravo squad to do the same." Both leaders simultaneously reply, "Affirmative."

Suddenly, an overpowering explosive noise rattles the entire block. The snipers get up from their position and start running. Zaylee picks up her binoculars and watches from a few blocks over as the top of the building begins to crumble. The buildings remaining workers die as the building falls over, creating pillows of smoke and debris all around the street. Zaylee scans down with her binoculars, the squads are throwing out their chlorine bombs. The police forces begin to cough and fall to the ground. After passing out the squads put on their masks, and slowly begin dragging them away.

Zaylee scans her binoculars towards the freeway. She notices SWAT cars approaching off the 134 freeway and knows that they pinpointed the captain's location before he was terminated. Back, near the Nettle building, the police cars are being filled with Electric and Mantis Squad members. As soon as the cars are filled, they zoom down the street at a fast rate.

Zaylee sighs in relief, "Ah." She watches them drive off into the distance and puts her binoculars down and looks at Rayna, "Lieutenant, bring me a drone cam." Zaylee commands. She runs over and hands her a tablet. On the tablet is drone three, giving a view of the Nettle building from the street level. The buildings letters had fallen in front of the lobby, and the rest of the building had fallen in the distance. The support beams, are all broken and mangled.

The top half of the building was gone and the falling rubble had destroyed most of the lower levels, killing almost everyone inside. The top levels had been completely obliterated upon impact, killing all of the executives, if they remained on the top floor. Zaylee and Rayna nod at each other, staring at the debris all over the asphalt, proud of what they had accomplished.

"Lieutenant, begin packing up. Give the drones commands to meet us at the rendezvous point. I will tell the squads to abandon the police cars somewhere remote. Then we will pick them up and head back to base." Zaylee says, handing Rayna the tablet. "Yes sir." she replies, grabbing the tablet and beginning to command the drones.

Chapter 20: Epiphany

Police cars rush down the street, sunny skies turn black, rain pours down. Thunder strikes across the horizon. They break formation into a street armada, going northbound onto Vermont. After dodging real police and SWAT swarming East down Los Feliz boulevard, the police head towards Glendale and the Nettle building. Their faux police cars go unnoticed by the oncoming response team. They make their way to the top of the hill, winding around, looking at the landscape.

It starts to drizzle, and then pour, but the trees block most of the droplets from getting through. Finally, the cyberpunk squads enter a parking lot and park next to several average looking vehicles. Out in the distance is a massive building with three large domes overhead; they are at the Griffith Observatory.

They exit their vehicles, carrying their weapons with them into their new vehicles. The Electric Squad leader pops the trunk on a small four door sedan, plopping her gatling gun inside. Another electric member places her bag marked 'Tesla grenades' next to it. They enter the sedan and drive off with the other squads, following shortly behind them. She leads them down the hill and back onto Vermont Avenue. The streets remain residential for a couple blocks with different painted apartments and houses on both sides. They stop at a red light on Franklin and look at the businesses in the distance. "Disgusting." the Electric Squad leader comments. The other members in her car nod in agreement, rolling down the windows.

Someone in the back notices the sign for Melbourne Avenue and shouts, "Melbourne bounce! Crank up some of that electronic dance." The driver clicks the radio and turns it to a satellite station labeled 'Jumpstyle'. A hard, but upbeat electronic beat flows from the speakers. The driver continues down the street, towards Koreatown, but one vehicle goes down Vermont until they reach Sunset, where they turn right. Noticing this maneuver, a soldier in the back asks, "Yo, Lazarus, where are we going?" Lazarus grips the wheel and says, "A little detour boys, so we can see the fruits of our labor." Lazarus affirms. His mini-Mantis-blade hangs over the steering wheel; his gauntlet sits atop the center console, denoting him as an experienced member though.

Palm trees line both sides of the street. Buildings pierce the skyline. The street below is bold and brightly lit with neon signs that stare into their souls as the rain drips down the windshields. People walk on along the sidewalk, lost, searching for meaning, searching for happiness, unaware of the chaos these soldiers had just wrought. Most of the neon signs are attached to restaurants that line the street.

The private companies, liquor stores and mom and pop restaurants, remain intact on the lower level. They continue down, until they reach a block that was once occupied by countless corporate restaurants. They are now craters in the ground of Los Angeles, the robot corpses still standing within them.

Rolling down the block past the buildings of Los Angeles they see more scorched remains left by the fires of the rigged Salt robots who were meant to take over and lower costs for businesses across the nation. They relish their victory as rain pours onto the robots' charred remains, curing the flames they had set and destruction they had set upon on the lands of California.

Soldiers roll down their windows so that they can stick their head, their weapons flush along the window-sill. Their metal mantis weapons lay cold and turned off from their previous acetylene powered attacks. Rain speckles their weapons, dripping down to the asphalt below.

Broken robots still lie in the center of a MacNeil's, their pieces mixed with the building's rubble. Their vehicle goes unnoticed by an oncoming police car and continues West, towards the Ocean. They see a sign for the Beverley Hills Hotel, which the driver pulls closer to, eventually parking near the red curb. Lazarus looks at the passengers in the back, and tosses them a spray can each, "We're going to let these franchise owners know who not to mess with." Lazarus states, opening his car and exiting. The rest of the Mantis members follow his lead, following him onto the grass in front of the sign.

"Jackie, Bobby, and John, spray down the sign. Make it completely red. John, you kneel down so Bobby can get on your shoulders" he orders. He looks at Hank and points down the street, "And you, Hank, you stand watch." Lazarus kneels down next to John, allowing Jackie and Bobby to wrap their legs around their respective shoulders. They stand up and begin spraying the sign down, until the sign is completely red.

A bus boy runs out from under the awning, noticing their activity, and attempts to approach them. Hank meets him before he can reach, "Stand down, we are here to protect people like you." Hank claims. "What do you mean? Like me?" the bus boy asks.

Bobby and Jackie drop their red spray cans and grab white ones from John and Lazarus. They begin spraying the words 'Leave your franchises or DIE' on the sign. The bus boy looks back and Hank, his finger pointing wildly at them, "My dad owns a MacNeils! You guys are those terrorists!"

Hank gets in his face, "If you do not leave, I will slice you in half." he says clicking a button on his blade, activating the acetylene and turning his bladed hand bright whitish-orange. A look of fear strikes across his face, "I'll leave, I swear!" he shouts, stumbling over the curb trying to run away. Hank watches him run up the driveway and out of view. Bobby and Jackie finish their spray painting and hop off the shoulders of their partners. Lazarus looks at them, "Time to get home." he says to them, they all get in the vehicle and drive off.

As they drive down the street, they can see the burnt remains of the fancy homes that once stood there. "It's California. You'd think they'd be used to fire by now." Hank says. Lazarus nods, "Yeah, but they're power tripping morons. They needed to be taught a lesson."

Slowly, they make their way back to the Citadel.

—

Vero stands behind a microphone at the front of the Citadel. Zaylee, Rayna, and the rest of the cybersquad leaders stand behind him, "My people, we have won this day, we have triumphed over the corporations." he says solemnly to the crowd. They begin to cheer wildly, throwing their hands into the air with various weapons attached to them.

"We must now repair our broken engine with the right parts; floating farms will feed Los Angeles and its outskirts for eternity. Nothing can stop our purity from returning to these lands. The outlying cities in our county that used to grow oranges, strawberries, and other fruits, the cities of Glendora, Covina, San Dimas, La Verne, and Claremont, shall grow them once again. Our neighbor counties, Riverside, San Bernardino, and Orange County are sure to follow our lead, returning the farms and ranches to Corona, Lake Elsinore, Norco, Rancho Cucamonga, Fontana, Rialto, Colton, Highland, Tustin, Irvine, Anaheim, and Santa Ana. The only exceptions being cities like Oak Glen who were wise enough to maintain farms, ranches, water sources, and their beautiful Apple orchards. They were the only intelligent cities left in Southern California, but no longer shall they remain alone. For the farms will return and the new technology of floating farms will be given to all; we will return all of our cities to their former glory!" Vero claims, the crowd roars, raising their hands up in agreement.

"We will need to find and train botanists, scattering them across the states." Vero says. "Orange fields shall, once again, grace the Eastern side of Los Angeles County. We will bring them botanists and floating farm agriculturists to help them expand their horticulture into apricots, cherries, grapes, pears, peaches, pumpkins, and even vegetables. Then, they can finally be self-sustaining cities without having dependence on Los Angeles' corporate greed."

Vero pauses, putting his hand out towards the crowd, "And while the botanists work their magic, we will suppress any return of their political corruption. We will balk the Cartel. End the rich's reign of terror. Stop the diplomatic immunity. And our various local governments will no longer fund asinine projects, like ridiculously expensive maintenance of ridiculously useless sports fields and gymnasiums. And, if they fail to abide by the new law, philosophy, and understandings of science, then the people will gun them down, drag them through the streets, and show their sins to the populace!" Vero yells. The crowd roars with excitement.

Eager to speak, Vero continues, "Their tyranny will never return, for we have shown them what we are capable of. A group of our small size has cleansed their society, and that is how simple it is, when you have the Lord on your side. And with a massive population like California, we will only need a pittance of the state's support and this will never happen again." Vero claims, as Zaylee

171

begins to cough, holding back her vomit.

Vero looks back, noticing her coughs. She goes down to her knees, unable to hold the vomit back, and throws up on the stage. Rayna rushes to her side, putting her arm around her, "What's wrong?" Zaylee continues looking down, "I don't know, I've been tired lately and queasy lately." Zaylee replies, wiping the vomit from her chin. Rayna continues asking, "Are you sure? What else could be wrong?" Zaylee pauses, a thought goes off in her head, "I think I know what's wrong. You need to drive me to the drug store." Zaylee demands, trying to get back onto her feet. Rayna grabs her shoulder, helping her until she's stable on both feet. Zaylee closes her eyes and breathes deeply several times. Zaylee looks at Rayna, "Okay, let's go."

Zaylee walks on her own with Rayna by her side, in case she falls again. They meander through the crowd until they reach the phone booth elevator on the opposite side. They enter, and Rayna pushes the button to type in the numbers 7243747 in order. The elevator activates and a neon logo, signifying that the Hydraulic Squad designed it, lights up.

"What's wrong Zaylee?" Rayna pesters. Zaylee looks at her, "Well, I've been tired lately and throwing up lately. Plus, my appetite is all off; I'm hungrier than usual." Rayna looks at her, puzzled by the comment, "I don't understand." she replies. Zaylee persists through her comment, "You don't have to, I just need to get a test okay." The elevator dings as it arrives at the top. They look through the glass door noticing the trees and fountain visible in the center of the courtyard. Rayna continues thinking, "Oh," she finally says, putting everything together. The elevator sits in the center of the lobby. Rayna opens the doors, but Zaylee stays inside.

She looks at the glass and ponders aloud, "Rayna, have we been too cruel? I am a terrorist now, full-fledged. I had innocent people killed. I slowly regretted it and said to minimize all causalities but I killed a ton of people." Zaylee states, causing Rayna to reenter the elevator and stay inside, "Where is this coming from?" Rayna asks. Zaylee begins to articulate, "I hate what I have become. I've participated in many totalitarian actions I sought to prevent." Rayna rejects Zaylee's words, "We are not totalitarian. We are doing the right thing." Zaylee ponders again, "But are we doing it the right

172

way? I don't think we are."

"When injustice becomes law, resistance becomes duty. Jefferson gave us this truth and it's the only way we'll survive." Rayna answers. Zaylee utters, "But we both know that humanities greatest traits are endurance and cognition. If we were persistent against them and used more effective cognitive methods, we could have changed them without violence. I don't want children to grow up in a world where our only solutions are violence." Zaylee continues. Rayna spits out a retaliation, "But that is the way of the world, Zaylee. Ms. Schesis has reminded us that the world was built from violence. Our cognition has allowed us to avoid our natural morality. Thus, the world suffered. Did you even pay attention to any of her videos?" Rayna queries.

"Of course, I did, but I don't want my children growing up with violence all around. I want a world of peace, where everything can be solved through words and kindness." Zaylee attests. Rayna clears her throat and assures her, "That's not going to happen. If you want an Empire like the Romans, you must fight for it. Alexander the Great didn't build his Empire through peaceful negotiation." Rayna declares, staring into Zaylee's eyes.

Zaylee chuckles slightly, "He also enslaved entire nations to achieve his goals, just like the corporations enslaved us. The problems are still the same, it's just a new face of the same tyrant." Zaylee responds, looking back at her. Rayna leans back into the glass, "Zaylee, I don't know what's gotten into you. For technology, for progress to continue, we must be in control. We must have God at our side. It's the only way, and it's a long path. You know that." Rayna replies. "Well, I just think there is a better way that we could have followed. We didn't have to do this, my anger about what happened to Trey and Ciara led me astray but deep down I've always known what's right. I should have just pressed the government more, not attacked them and the corporations, that wasn't right." Zaylee explains, walking out of the booth.

Outside, in the lobby, is her car. Its coat of white paint shimmering from the leftover rain. The sun peaks out, hitting Zaylee's eyes. They walk over to her car and Zaylee pulls out her keys, unlocking the vehicle, and, then, throws the keys to Rayna. She catches the keys and opens the driver door, putting one foot in the vehicle.

Zaylee looks over at Wilshire Boulevard, a shiny red vehicle sits with yellow and red flames along the hood. "Whose car is that?" Zaylee asks, pointing over at it. "Huh?" Rayna asks, before turning her head and looking at the vehicle. "Oh no." Rayna says, backing up. "Get back into the elevator." Rayna demands. Zaylee turns and looks at her walking back to the telephone booth in the center of the lobby, right near a beautiful fountain.

"NOW ZAYLEE!" Rayna screams. Zaylee begins to freak out, "What's going on?" Zaylee asks, walking towards her. Rayna grabs her arm and pulls her into the booth, smashing the button and quickly pushing the buttons 7243747. "Are you going to explain yourself?" Zaylee asks. "That car is known as the F-mobile. I thought it was taken apart, but it's back. Fuego is back." Rayna confirms to her. Zaylee asks, "The Spanish fire is back?"

Rayna's body begins to shake, "Fuego is the man who put a bomb in King's Memorial. Dekima's father." Rayna answers. "You mean that thing that used to be in Compton's old Civic Center?" Zaylee asks. "Yes, that lunatic thought it was a perfect spot to hold up a dirty A-bomb, with the little points and the ring holding them together." Rayna explains, using her hands to show the points. Zaylee queries, "So? Why can't we handle it?" Rayna sarcastically replies, "He left an eleven-kilometer zone of radiation in the ghettos of Los Angeles. Yeah, sure, go handle him."

Zaylee straightens her posture, "Well, let's rally the forces and take him out." Rayna looks at her with a face full of fleeting hope, "He might not be after us." she says. "Okay, then why is he sitting outside our Citadel?" Zaylee asks. Rayna replies "I don't know, but we should just wait it out. Monitor him and hope he goes away." Rayna replies.

The booth finally touches the bottom and its doors open, allowing them to exit. Zaylee looks out and sees groups of cybersquad members cheering in a circle, raising their hands and throwing money out into the center as two people fight.

Chapter 21: The Fire Returns

Toxic Celebrations

A mantis soldier swipes right diagonally, missing the hydraulic soldier. The hydraulic soldier steps forward, slamming her right fist into his shoulder. "Go Alyssa!" a soldier shouts, throwing a dollar into the pot for the Hydraulic Squad. Alyssa pulls back, watching the mantis soldier grab his wounded shoulder, popping it back into place. He runs forward, swiping with his free hand, causing her to dodge right. He moves his blade, shoving it into her right side. She clenches the wound; blood drips down onto the floor.

"Yeah! Go Hank Mountain!" someone screams, dropping change into the mantis pot. Alyssa smiles, turning the dial on her arm, throwing her hydraulics into full power. The red LED blinks at full power through the air, her arm flies towards Hank's face. He stealthily dodges, side stepping to the left, and launching forward, binding her in a bear hug. Bound by his arm, she flies backward onto the floor, Hank laying on top of her. Immediately Alyssa tries to squirm out, but he continues to hold her tightly.

He maneuvers his free arm, the blade attached to it glistens in the air, slamming it into the concrete, cracking it. The blade gets stuck in the floor, allowing Alyssa to roll out from under him. He activates more gas from the acetylene cylinder, lighting up his blade with an even more intense heat, allowing him to pull it out of the concrete. He stands up, noticing Alyssa staring directly at him with her hydraulics embedded arm in the air. He instinctively reacts by lifting his arm. The shiny chrome blade, heated orange, cracks upon her impact. Pieces of it drop onto the floor until his bare arm is shown, the hair on his arm stands on edge.

Alyssa pulls her fist back, along her waistline, and smiles at Hank. She thrusts her arm forward into his stomach, knocking him three meters out of the circle and into the crowd. His body flies through knocking the members of the crowd out of his way until gravity pulls him down to the floor. She puts her hand up into the air, clenched in a fist. The hydraulics click, releasing built up air pressure from its pneumatic powered cylinders.

The hydraulic soldiers rush in, circling around Alyssa. They

175

lift her up, cheering wildly and spilling their drinks. Vero picks up the money bowls, bringing them to a table off to the side. He drops the money out, counting it out and separating it in intervals of twenty-five dollars. "They cheated!" a Mantis Squad member yells. "Yeah! Why is Hydraulic Squad doing all the counting?" another demands, walking over to the table. Vero puts a hundred dollars aside in a pile for Hydraulic Squad and looks over at the Mantis-blade sitting on his hand.

Vero continues to count the money as he speaks, "Electric Squad charred up the last hydraulic soldier bout; the fights are fair." Vero claims. Rayna arrives beside him, her long coat flowing, as she approaches. They bicker among themselves while Rayna whispers into his ear, "We have a problem. Fuego is back." His face turns from listening ardently to shock. He leaves the money on the tablet and walks with Rayna to the control room. Desks line the north end of the room; ex-police sit, watching the monitors in front of them.

Zaylee comes in behind them and asks, "What's the report?" Rayna stares at the screen, "Nothing so far, ma'am. It's status quo." she replies. Zaylee looks at Rayna, "See, nothing to worry about. It's just a fluke." The monitors flash, an override program takes over. Haskell code strings across the screens before they turn completely black. A blonde-haired man fades in on the screen, his hair spiked up, and a grin on his face.

Odysseus' Return

"Ah, Los Angeles, my old but familiar home. You didn't think you could hide from me, did you? With the power at the NSA's disposal, we easily spotted your sign. Why, oh why, did you label your hideout?" the blonde man asks through the speakers. The drones at the back of the room turn on and begin flying around. "Someone used my code to hack these little puppies. Interesting." the voice continues. Zaylee looks at Rayna with ponder. Rayna shakes her head, "That's not Fuego." The face looks back, almost as if looking at Rayna, then the enceinte's speaker system activates. "Oh, it's me. I had facial reconstructive surgery again. The name's Nova now." he replies through the citadel.

He grins, "But don't worry, I know you won't say anything."

Nova attests. Zaylee's face turns hostile, "And why is that?" He chuckles, "Because I have a gift for you." Nova's voice continues, his face almost staring at Zaylee. "What, you thought I was going to say because you'll be dead?" Nova says to only the control room. "I'm not like that, I simply have a gift for you." Nova declares. Rayna walks closer to Zaylee, her coat hitting the back of her shins as she stops beside her.

Rayna urges Zaylee, "Do not trust him, Zaylee! Whatever it is, I fear sociopaths, especially those bearing gifts." Rayna states. Nova gives a look of displeasure to Rayna, "There's no need to worry, my gift will fix it all." Nova claims. "I just need all of you to exit, now." his voice echoes through the citadel. The drone's sirens activate, their loud squeal complimented by their spinning lights. Their weaponry drops down out of their compartments. The ex-police type away on their keyboards, attempting to take back control of the drones. Zaylee walks closer to a monitor, placing blue tinted glasses over her eyes, pushing the officer to the side. "Leave." she commands, looking at the screen. The glasses blue tint lessens the brightness with an amber like hue.

He obeys her command, stands up, and walks behind the chair, staring at Zaylee near the computer. She hits 'ctrl+R' and quickly types in 'CMD' and hits enter. A black box with white letters appears on the screen, she types in 'tasklist' and hits enter. Every executable lists off, she scrolls down and finds 'haskell.exe', just to the right of it is a string of numbers and a memory size. She types in 'taskkill /IM haskell.exe /F' and the drones immediately drop down to the floor. Zaylee stands up, knocking the chair backwards. Her glasses remain firmly on her head.

"You'll need administrator privileges to restart your program." Zaylee claims. Nova looks surprised, "Finally, someone competent. It was hard enough getting into your system; figures you would have another failsafe. Most people would have just pulled the plug, which would have turned off your defense, but I would have still had control of your drones. See, I left a little Trojan in your server so I could just keep my protocols running if you did pull the plug." he says, pulling out his keyboard, "No matter, there's always another way." he professes. Zaylee stands over her keyboard, putting her fingers back on the keys.

She types 'netstate -a' on the same program as before. Strings of numbers under the label 'Local Address' appear. A look of deep thought crosses her mind while staring at the numbers. "Ah." she exclaims, selecting a string of numbers on the screen. "But ma'am, we're using the latest encryption protocols. Isn't that the most secure?" an officer asks. "How did he hack us?" he asks.

Zaylee's voice become monotonal as she focuses on the task at hand, "Anything can be hacked. I even enabled enhanced protocol filtering but if he's hacked the Admin of our router, neither Ztorq encryption or PLT address filtering matter at that point." she argues, continuing to type quickly on her keyboard. "Gotcha!" she shouts, terminating his internet protocol from accessing the network. Zaylee smiles looking at the monitor, her eyes relax despite the monitor's glow.

She looks up and sees his face still on their televisions. "Hah, you think that's all you need to stop me?" Nova articulates, through his laughter. The police monitors flash, activating the Haskell program once again. "How?" Zaylee inquires, astonished by his capabilities. The drones start to fly up again. "It's a fatal flaw within your operating system, the automatic updates. A sinful, illegal device forced upon their consumers, but oh so wonderful and government approved!" Nova exclaims. Zaylee exclaims, "Oh. But how did you forge your IP for theirs? Wouldn't you need to have the exact server and website information to send an update?" Zaylee asks.

Nova looks at the camera, "A child can fake their IP, you know that." he answers. Zaylee pauses for a second but then replies with, "Yes, but to do it properly you need a denial-of-service attack. Our servers have been running non-stop." She removes the glasses from her face and places them in her pocket. "Hah. You really do know your stuff. The legendary blue glass general! Leader of the grey hats. What a lucky a day." he says, as he unlocks the elevator. "Now, get outside so we can continue this conversation face to face beautiful." Nova states, as the drones move closer in on them, urging them to enter the elevator. But they ignore the request and remain where they are. Nova looks at the camera, annoyed. The drones fire several warning shots into the monitors, cracking their screens. Zaylee leads the way to the phone booth. Rayna, Vero, and the ex-police following behind her.

Zaylee and Rayna enter the phone booth. She presses the buttons 7243747, the smooth exterior gracing her finger while she pushes in. It makes it way to the top, giving them natural light as the lobby becomes visible. Zaylee watches Nova run his fingers along her supercar, tracing it with his smudged fingers. Zaylee and Rayna exit the phone booth, pulling out their weapons. They shoot at the crimson dressed soldiers. Their hands jerk back after firing. Immediately, the crimson dressed soldiers return fire. Behind them, the ex-police start firing at the drones. They circle around, dodging the drone's bullets.

The Mantis Squad exits the crammed booth. They pull out their weapons, extending their blades. One of the mantis soldiers rams his blade into the drone above, slicing it in half. The heated hardware drops on the ground, broken into pieces. A group of three of the mantis soldiers rush towards their adversaries but the crimson soldiers place bullets into them, causing them to fall over, dead. Lazarus heads towards Zaylee, Rayna, and Vero who are now are hiding behind Zaylee's vehicle. Both Zaylee and Rayna are holding their pistols up towards the sky.

Zaylee tips her head over the vehicle, and notices the Electric Squad exiting the booth. By turning her head over to the crimson soldiers, she sees them tying up the remaining members of the Mantis Squad. Zaylee turns to look at Lazarus and Vero, "Lazarus, help Vero and the Electric Squad escape. I can't have more bloodshed on my consciousness." she declares. Vero shakes his head, "We can't leave you here to die." he states, rejecting her idea.

She places her hand on Rayna's shoulder, "I will not be alone. We will hold them off while you run." Zaylee declares. Rayna smiles and nods, "We can take them." Vero and Lazarus look at each other, slowly creeping around the vehicle. Zaylee and Rayna stand up, their weapons already pointed at their enemies. They fire every round in their magazine, taking down several of the crimson soldiers. After running out of ammo, Zaylee drops out her magazine, while Rayna tosses her gun to the side, eager to put her mechanical arm to work.

After slamming a new magazine into her pistol, Zaylee starts to fire again. On her left, Rayna presses a button on her arm, activating the hydraulics. It dings, notifying her it's ready. She jumps up, crushing a drone with her fist. The guts of the drone spread out across the floor. One of the pieces falls into Zaylee's hair, but she hastily brushes it out with a quick flick of her head.

Off to the side, Vero and Lazarus lead the entirety of the Electric Squad out. Nova, unaware of their escape, continues focusing on Zaylee and Rayna. He sprints towards Zaylee, smacking the weapon out of her hand. Then, he turns towards Rayna, punching her in the stomach. The hit causes her to grab her stomach in pain. During the punch, the crimson soldiers grab ahold of Zaylee. A single soldier grabs Zaylee's hands, binding them together on top of her head while another points an assault rifle at her.

Another crimson soldier picks Rayna up off the floor, then binds her hands together on top of her, just like they did with Zaylee. The soldier holding Rayna slides her on the concrete, moving her closer to Zaylee. Both Rayna and Zaylee notice the rest of the cybersquad that stayed to fight are now on their knees with their hands behind their head with soldiers dressed in crimson pointing assault rifles at them. The remaining hijacked police drones circle up high, pointing their weapons at them from above.

Nova looks at Zaylee and Rayna, as if waiting for them to attempt to escape. They remain still in their confined state. Zaylee is even confident enough to insult him, "You're shorter than I envisioned." Zaylee claims, looking at Nova. "And you're prettier in person." Nova replies, "I'm getting shivers just looking at you." he continues, walking towards her. He stops in front of her, she must tilt her head slightly down to see him. Rayna is at eye level with him, "You are kind of tall for a girl though, Zaylee." Rayna adds. "Not now." Zaylee replies quickly.

"Zaylee Ross, I remember you vividly now. Leader of the blue glass armada. But, where are your blue glasses to protect your eyesight from the LED's?" Nova asks. Zaylee remains quiet, but looks down at her pocket. Nova notices her glance, "Ah, I see, in your pocket." he says, reaching down and pulling them out. He puts them on his head and looks at Zaylee, "It's too bad that you're not very talkative, I was planning on having some fun. No matter, you're still talented, but you're a grey hat and I'm a black hat. There are more options for me." Nova explains, reiterating a bit. Zaylee gives him a look of disgust, but does not retort. Nova looks at her, "What, all you do is protect and hack illicit servers. We hack, violate, and destroy everything for our benefit. More options means more money." he continues. Zaylee ripostes quietly, "But I don't need to use Russian or Chinese virtual private networks to circumvent federal investigations."

Nova gets a touch annoyed, "Yes, yes, untraceable, anonymous, IIRC, blah blah blah. We're intelligent people here, no need to explain what we already know." Nova says, attempting to derail her. Zaylee looks at him, "It's a valid point and you know it." she says. Rayna looks over at him, seeking a way out of his clutches, "But the IIRC and anonymous hunted down pedophiles, rapists, and animal abusers. Aren't we fighting for the same things in a way? Dispensing justice against those that escape the law?" Rayna asks. "We are trying to stop evil just like you do." Rayna continues. Zaylee leans over and whispers into Rayna's ear, in a quiet enough tone that the soldiers behind them can't hear it: "What are you doing?"

Rayna leans back over to Zaylee's ear, "I'm negotiating by appealing to his ego." she whispers back just as quiet. Nova pauses, "You don't know what evil truly is. I'm the chaos this world deserves. And you can't stop them all with actions like yours. You need to bait them out of hiding and then kill them all." Nova claims. "What do you mean?" Rayna asks. "This world is full of cruelty, but also ignorant. When I was at the end of my reign as Kasai, I promised myself one thing before I became Fuego: If people are cruel and stupid, I am going to put them all down at once and stop them from destroying reality." he proclaims.

"So, all this is to, what? Abide by your promise?" Zaylee asks. "Nope." Nova replies, beginning to pace back and forth. "I learned when I was Fuego that cruelty isn't enough to kill them all, you have to go a step further, invent some technology, battle with the baddies, you know, grow a little. It's why I took the name Nova; a supernova is the most beautiful explosion. And I'm the star, ready to explode and take all these heinous people with me." Nova declares. He stops to look at Zaylee, "You know you are going to die right here, right now." Zaylee, with fear filling her, looks at the drones flying above.

Nova looks at the drones and then back at Zaylee, the amber tint reflecting off the glasses he's wearing, "You think this is some video game, some novel, or movie that you can just win the day? No, this is reality. I have bested you, there is no return. You will die, as protagonists should, since you are all side characters in my grand scheme to protect us all." Nova declares. Zaylee wiggles her hand out and lifts it up, swinging it at Nova. He grabs her hand and twists it, breaking the carpals in her hand. The crimson soldier behind her backs off, allow her to fall and grab her broken wrist. "Tsk, are you really afraid of death? It's a release from this dreadful place. Embrace it." he claims.

He looks at his soldiers, "Tie them up." he instructs. Several crimson soldiers run over to them. They place Zaylee on her knees and start binding her with rope. Rayna jerks a hand free and grabs Nova's arm, crushing it under the hydraulic pressure. "Why are you doing this?" Rayna asks, quivering in fear, but not easing up on her grip. He uses his free arm to rip off Rayna's mechanical one and stares at her, "You have done this to yourself." he replies. The crimson soldiers finish binding Zaylee and leave her on her knees. They walk over to Rayna, then hand the soldier behind her a zip tie. He loops it around her arms, before tightening it. He pushes her down to her knees, tears streaming down her face.

Rayna looks at Zaylee, "I'm sorry. I should have never fought with you, you were right. Violence breeds violence and we are faced with it ourselves, by someone with no reservations." she states. Zaylee responds, "It's not your fault, we all need to learn."

A soldier approaches Rayna, pressing the barrel against her head. He pulls the trigger, her brains splattering onto the citadel floor behind her. "NO!" Zaylee screams, falling over on her side, the tears rushing down onto her commander outfit. The soldiers pick her up, setting her back on her knees. He presses the barrel against her forehead. "Stop." Nova commands.

The soldier drops his weapon back to his side. Nova approaches Zaylee and kneels beside her, his lips next to her ear. "I have watched you Zaylee, through the NSA feeds. You passed our evaluations, devote yourself to the Crimson Rose Cause and I will let you live." Nova says. He licks her earlobe causing her to pull away. Zaylee scrunches her face, "What is wrong with you?" she says through her tears. He stands back up, looking at Zaylee still on her knees.

"Nothing is wrong with me. I simply want to sentence all the brainless and cruel people to death, leaving only the amicable and intelligent. Think of how wonderful the world will be without them. With the believers of God. If only people like us remained, it wouldn't be such a bad place to live." Nova explains to her. "I will never join you." she says, spitting onto him.

Nova swiftly pulls his pistol from its holster and fires. The bullet travels through Zaylee's skull causing her to fall onto Rayna. Their blood mixes, slowly draining out of their bodies and into the gutter.

"The more you fight who you are, the more you become what you hate. Understand, love, and be confident in who you are. Intertwine with the facts of nature and ascend; if you are intelligent enough you can shape the world into what you want, but if you are one the most intelligent humans you realize both simultaneously. The road is long, but those with a brain will eventually become water; the future awaits only the greatest of humanity. Your path begins today.

Will you make it to understanding the meaning of life?"

Ms. Schesis, Leader of the Schesis Project

The End

Thank you for reading the first novel in the Tales of a Schesis World
If you enjoyed this opening novel the next in the series is titled:
Social Destroyers

Author's Note

Zaylee wants to fix the world properly, she, sadly, can't. Their world is unsuited for a peaceful revolution, while Trey and Rayna understand that's not possible (I pronounce it Ray-na, and if anyone was wondering she is Vero's 'Reina', which is the Spanish word for Queen; it was a King and Queen setup) It's impossible for them because they have done it for so long. They understand the corruption already but have the wrong solution. Zaylee had to learn it through pain and she learned the right solution through violence. Everything builds up towards her inevitable destruction of the corruption. These actions lead Zaylee to slowly become angry with the people she thought were helping society and eventually seek violent retribution against them, again part of her path. But these are necessary flaws that she has to overcome to reach a purer outlook. It takes getting pregnant to do so, but it does happen, albeit at the last second.

I wrote about violence because it stems from nearly every crevice of humanity. There is not a single nation on this planet, that I know of at least, that did not start from some form of violent overtaking. Even if some countries didn't, many did, and that's what I was trying to channel.

Onto a happier portion, there are some literary devices wedged in. I don't know if they are of any particular use though. You see, I labeled Chapter 5 as 'The Chemist' because it's followed directly by Chapter 6 'Chrematistic Popularity'. These words, chemist and chrematistic, are similar but they mean completely different things. If someone were to read this book, I'd like to dive into their mind and see if they realized that or they just presumed that Chapter 6 would be an extension of Chapter 5 without reading them. Just some bit of curiosity, since, ultimately, I don't believe the chapter names are of any particular use, other than to serve as stop-gaps in storytelling.

The concluding chapter shows similar little games, it's the 21st chapter and the first portion is titled toxic coronation. The legal drinking age in the states is 21, hence the reference to intoxication. Subtle, and probably just another weird thing I like to do. There are little things like that all over the place. Like one of the lines in

Chapter 20, referring to fires. Then, if you know the story of Odysseus you'll recognize that Chapter 21 gives you the timeline for Nova. It has been ten years since he left his kingdom in Los Angeles, just like the story Odysseus. In this case, the past kingdom.

Some of it is foreshadowing though. If you don't like spoilers, skip this paragraph and continue onto the next. Chapter 4 has importance to the story and the name is a clear reference to the third book, The Historian. The cultural remarks allude to the second book, Social Destroyers. Anyway, just know that there is a reason/reference to a great deal of what I write. Like why would a phonebooth be in the year 2052? Why the year 52? Well, 52 weeks in a year, this is the year where everything changes, etc. So, yeah, I'm one of those writers your English teacher talks about when they ask you what every little fact meant. However, I don't do this with everything, like colors, names, objects might be the way they are because I think the name is cool. Like how I like the name Zaylee, and how I created the name Vero by switching the N in Nero for a V. And some things like that.

Something that many probably won't agree with is the names of restaurants, corporations, and/or politicians: none of these companies are real. They are fictitious figments of my imagination in a fictitious Universe. If a company, politician, or restaurant chain declares defamation, I'd like to refer them to the many books, videos, and media posted with truths that do the same thing, while using their name. There is no defamation if it's true, so I could have literally written about real companies and real politicians if I so desired but I didn't because that's part of my humor and writing technique. Not everyone agrees with this style, but I enjoy it, and it's why I wrote it about. Regardless, at the end of the day, these are entirely fictitious stories and they are supposed to be about characters, philosophy, morals, and learning.

Several chapters in here go over medical terminology and medical experiences. I did this intentionally to help the readers learn something new. The same goes for my command prompt codes at the end of my novel, even though they are not technically what would happen in such a scenario (most likely). It's just enjoyable for me to read a book and learn about things and new words, so I put them in my own book, hoping others will like it too.

So, about the deaths, the character Nova will stick around and some of the cyberpunk squad members. But, as you learn at the end of this novel, Nova is a unique character, with a non-delineated goal (until book three). He is one of my favorite characters to write, Ms. Schesis is the first and easiest to write about though. Although I do very little published writings about her, I do write hundreds of pages of scratch work and world-building around her. Anyway, Nova is eccentric, talented, brilliant, and hauntingly evil but he has a good side. You won't see the good side till you've read book three (and you can read the series in any order). Here's a hint though, there's a reason he appears bored. If he wasn't evil, he would, undoubtably, be smarter than Ms. Schesis. However, he is like a parallel antithesis, a reminder that things can be way worse. Still, this is not his book, it is Zaylee's book.

Zaylee and Rayna were characters I loved in the very first book I wrote. I felt like they didn't get enough attention, so, I started developing stories based upon the scratch work I was writing before. Zaylee's path to help society is similar to Ms. Schesis, but she's not as capable. So, Zaylee eventually comes to terms that Ms. Schesis perspective is the only superior method of "helping" society, but she enforces it poorly, taking a good thing and turning it into something horrific. Which is what I intended, but I'm still unsure if it comes off like that. You see, religion is supposed to be a good thing, and so is science, but both have negatives when used improperly. These types of insurrections never end well, and that's the point.

Each commander gets their influence from death. Rayna's isn't told directly, but she says her parents' killers got off free. I felt like adding it in wasn't necessary though. I wrote lots of these little details, trying to only let the one's I thought were worth keeping remain, after all, this is mainly Zaylee's story. But anger and coincidence cause Rayna and Zaylee to go to Koreatown, where her partner, Vero, is about to be arrested by Zaylee for doing what the law fails to. So, Rayna steps in to protect him against her best friend. These are stories about family, friendship, and revolution. Everything is interconnected; families and friendships are the cornerstone of humanity for we are communal animals. The same thing goes for the next story in the series: Social Destroyers.

One of the main protagonists (antagonist, depending on the

viewpoint), Kyro, takes up his mantle. I won't ruin that story, but it's just another example. The next story has more of a Roman vibe to it, whereas this novel was heavily based on Greek mythology. It's not a copy of their stories, but I like to have nods to them. I like to think it helps people learn a little about history. There are several references here and there, like how Zaylee is Atlas, Nova is Odysseus, they talk about Greek mythology, etc. There are also modern references, to pay homage and it's part of my humor, like some of the names of the individuals (see Captain Kiff for one) and so forth.

I could go on, but I've been sporadic enough, so I'll leave you with some final thoughts: If there's anything to remember about my novels it's this: there's a reason for most things I write. then there's a reason I left the Electric Squad leader nameless. Mantis and Hydraulic Squad had their own undoing in this book. Although a few of them escaped Nova's deathgrip. They will all be a part of the next novel, given their briefly mentioned escape in Chapter 21.

Lastly, the last chapter signifies Zaylee's failure to complete the missions on behalf of her veneration of the Schesis Project. Her transformative experience would have, most likely, caused her to stop the cyberpunk squad from doing so. Still, it is of importance to mention this given how quickly the last chapters happen, since they definitely had more plans left, but not enough time.

So, I guess, if you liked this novel, you can look forward to Social Destroyers when it eventually comes out. There's plenty more to come and plenty more technology left. In fact, Social Destroyers has, probably, the most pieces of technology. Kyro and the rest await! As a final parting point for this book, I felt like it would be nice for the reader to have the opportunity to read the Caustic Corruption parts, as they were big motivators. I will leave those here for the interested reader (they are videos done by Ms. Schesis), but, unfortunately, I won't do this for the next two books because they aren't as necessary for those books and these are my unedited drafts/notes:

Caustic Corruption 1: Politicians

Politics. A system several millenniums old. Its corruption has aged with it. No government is free from the Malpais of humanity than any other system. The rapacity of our species has perpetuated itself into our psychology. I am here to tell you about actual senators, actual members of congress, and your representatives that have manipulated the system to their advantage.

To some of you, this is nothing new. You understand that our politics are corrupt. What we lack is finite evidence. And we lack a proper implementation within our government to prevent corruption. We have continued embezzlement's, continued violence, and continued sexual assaults perpetrated by our leaders. I believe everyone understands the reasoning behind stopping these problems, so let's jump right into who your corrupt representatives are.

1. Senator Logan

The Senator from Virginia, Mr. Logan. On the screen we have video proof of his crimes against females. He is seen vacating a strip club with two girls. We have interviewed each of these girls. They did not want to release who they are, so we have blurred their face. Mr. Logan has put two females in the hospital to satisfy his hedonistic desires. Whether it was casually consensual or paid consensual, he must be subject to review. If it is the latter, the people should impeach him.

Although I believe these documents will be enough proof for his impeachment anyway as he used government funds to pay for his strip club visits. Your tax money is being used on strippers. That is a gross breach of protocol. If you do not stand up to impeach Mr. Logan, as classified by the law, you are an accessory to his crimes.

2. Senator Dwyer

The other Senator from Virginia, Mr. Logan's partner in crime, Mr. Dwyer. We have documents containing information of Mr. Dwyer's astronomical embezzlement of government funds. She helped set in motion development projects, only to siphon the funds.

Her embezzlement is unmatched by any other politician.

One such project was a school in Henrico County. She presented the project as the first and largest county school, he presented it with beneficial factors. If she had done what she said, it would have been a great addition to the state of Virginia. But she did not. She took a cut of the project's money and they built a tiny building no bigger than a house, and labeled it as a school.

Senator Dwyer is not exempt from public bribery either. We have documentation regarding bribes she took from businesses to implement laws in their favor. On multiple occasions she willing promoted monopoly of the market. She prevented other companies from rising up by restricting usage to the parameters of only a few businesses.

This is the same woman running for President. She has a predicted winning chance of seventy percent. The people have basically decided that she will be their next President. Did no one look into her actions? Did you just look at her and say "Oh we haven't had a female president, let's try that."? I find it foolish. A President should be elected by their accomplishments and their proven abilities.

When Dwyer was previously part of the cabinet, she let the embassy in the Middle East get attacked, killing our soldiers. The people are aware of this. It's been a widely known fact for a few years. It's why she was booted out of the cabinet. So why would you allow her to be President? That is the most ridiculous thing I have ever heard.

The people have the power to stop her embezzlement and prevent any further damage she has done. You, citizens of the United States, have full rights to remove her from office. She does not deserve to work in politics any longer, she has proven to be extremely damaging to the business and public sectors of our country. I have given you the proof you need. It is up to you to decide what you want to do with it.

3. Judge Kinon

Dwyer could not have done it alone. Kinon helped her pass laws and influenced the supreme court to rule in her favor. Kinon is

191

an accessory to Dwyer's crimes. She has been rumored to have been similarly bribed by the large corporations into passing laws. There is no confirmation of this but the likelihood of it being true is significant. Her and Dwyer are together constantly.

4. Vice President Malkovick

He is the leader of a bunch of corrupt senators, being head of the senate, it's not surprising that he is part of the corruption. In the previous documents encompassing the bribes Dwyer took, he was mentioned to receive a cut. (Flesh this part out more maybe?)

5. Ambassador O'Conner

O'Conner has been supplying weapons to the Middle East, at a high price. Some of greatest military technology is produced in Saudi Arabia. She took the contract and gave a portion of the technologies to our enemies. Providing they equally compensate her for the goods. And, of course, they did. As you can see in this invoice, she has made eight figures from her illegal conduct.

She has not only provided our enemies with a stronger arsenal, but she has increased the mortality of our troops. They go hand in hand. If our enemies have stronger weapons, they can more effectively kill our men. She is part of the increased deaths in the Middle East that have been so widely televised.

Her husband and herself have both asked astronomical amounts of money to give speeches too. I understand that if the people are willing, they should be able to ask any amount for their speeches. I disagree though, I think they should do it as a service to the people. We pay them through taxes and they both hold political positions that pay decent amounts of money. Why should we have to pay them more?

6. Ambassador Crocker

The man in shades himself. We have promoted him on television for his ground breaking efforts to decrease tension with Russia. His picture is synonymous with hero. What we failed to realize was the technology he provided Russia for the contract. What he has done is not necessarily evil. The way he did it was evil though. He did not let the American people know what he was doing; he did it behind our backs.

Our people are not privy to dirty politician tactics; they actively try to make the people uninformed. We should not be made aware of classified dealings but we should be made aware of where our money and resources are going. The politicians have no rights to remove our knowledge of political dealings. We should be made aware of each Ambassadors efforts with other countries and what they are making the American people agree to.

7. Senator Tan

The Senator from Colorado. The widely renowned Senator who participated in the legalization of marijuana. We are going to ignore the drug. It is not the focus of our topic. Why is he important though? Well, I think the American people would like to know of his affiliation with the Mexican Cartel. Here are pictures of Senator Tan and the Cartel's leader.

From what we have attempted to decipher from the routing information of the marijuana being moved from Mexico, we have come to the conclusion that Senator Tan helped legalize marijuana as a deal with the Cartel. He would, more than likely, get a portion of each delivery's profits.

8. Mayor Antonio

The Mayor of Los Angeles, one of the most populated cities in the United States. His corruption peculiar case of extension of the police bribery. Mayor Antonio has worked closely with the police for several years; working with the police is part of his job. It is, however, not in his job description to allow the police to accept bribes from local gangs.

The majority of gangs are hindered by the police force still, the opulent gangs continue to thrive. Their ostentatious violence spewed onto local businesses. Their brutal murders continue. It is because they have enough money to pay off the police. The police chief and, by extension, the mayor's salary are increased greatly from gang funds.

Here is the proof needed to incriminate him.

9. Governor Clestor

We all know her from her acting career. She was a talented actress but a mediocre politician. I will never understand why we elect celebrities as politicians, there are significantly more qualified people out there. Why don't we elect them instead? Particularly the ignorance of electing lawyers as presidents when their main job is commander and chief – a heavily military and ambassadorial job.

Her corruption is not as significant as the rest. She has just implemented asinine restrictions on the people. Her state is going through a drought so the water laws make sense, but why allow non-agricultural businesses to continue their water for aesthetic purposes? She had the ability to heavily tax their usage.

She let them get away with it instead of doing the more appropriate thing: build towards a solution for the drought. The money she could get from heavily taxing their overuse of water could be used to fund to more adequately seed the clouds for water or create an easier means of importing water to her state.

10. The Supreme Court Justices

Yes, not just one supreme court justice, all of them. For our final spot on the list, we have the most corrupt, the most widely known, and most totalitarian of them all: The entire Supreme Court.

The proof of them overriding the people's proposition in California is widely known. The proof of them doing the same in Texas is similarly known. They have done this in many states besides California and Texas. Yet still no one tries to stop them. They create laws for the entire population of a state. Still, no one tries to abolish their laws. And any threat they receive to undermine their power is nullified and ignored immediately. They will use the law to their advantage if you threaten them. There is no free speech with them. You cannot say certain things to them without being imprisoned.

A board of nine members removed the freedom to vote for over fifty-five million people in California. Disregard any opinion on one view or the other, and just realize the fact that less than 0.000001% of the population decided if homosexual marriage was legal for the entire United States. They have decided that their small panel knows better than millions of people. They have given themselves more power than any amount of people in the United States. They can override anyone and any amount of people just because they have been given that power.

They have decided that these nine members have more power than one hundred senators and four hundred thirty-five members of the house of representatives. If either of them passes a law, they can revoke it. And if the Judicial system can pass any law they want without opposition from the executive or legislative branch. Yes, the Judicial branch has more power than even the executive branch. If you want unlimited power, I'd suggest becoming a Supreme Court Justice. You will be unstoppable.

They have zero opposition from the people or others in the government, due to the unlikelihood of actually rallying congress to balk them. Opposition is how we grow. It is how we develop more efficient and effective ideas for living and coinciding with nature. The initial setup disregarded all of this. They did not setup a system of checks and balances. And now there is no one that cannot stop them. They have corrupted themselves with power. They have damaged our world with their power. The United States is a world power and anything they do also damages the entire world. Their lust for power has the potential to effect over seven billion lives. A small panel like that, who isn't even subject to trial and error, should not have that kind of power. They have done irreparable damage to nature, the people, and many governments other than our own.

The people and the people's desires for their nation do not matter to them. The people's votes mean nothing. They have made voting pointless, other than for representatives. The Supreme Justices have decided that they know better than you. They have made themselves omniscient over the people. They can deem whatever we vote on as against the constitution and reverse it if they so choose. They can just create a law or disobey any law they choose. Every single foundation for our government can be twisted by them.

The Judicial system setup is flawed. It cannot be properly balked by any other branch of the government. They need a proper system of check and balances like the others do. We need to develop a new system to check them. And we need to remove the current power-hungry monsters rampantly destroying our nation. If we can do this it will help prevent the majority of their corruption and it will help protect the people and their rights. The Supreme Justice isn't the first of the three branches to openly strip the people of their rights, but they are the first that cannot be balked or overturned.

Every part of the Judicial system is massively corrupt with power. The same corruption in the Judges is also within parts of our police force.

We should not fear cops. We should enjoy their presence. They should be there to help us in our times of need. They should constantly be trying to help their citizens like firefighters and emergency personnel do. A cop should not hide in attempts to criminalize us. They should be out in the open to psychologically reinforce the law to protect and help the citizens of our nation. They shouldn't be trying to aggravate or vilify us with tickets and their violence like they currently do. They should be there to help us. Right now, the police force acts like a criminal organization and not a government service.

The American police force has become like a gang. Except this gang is unstoppable. They cannot be stopped because they have the entire corrupt Judicial system backing them. Although, I know some of the police force, like in California, has already started to rally against itself, as they should do, because your management is corrupt.

Police officers embody the law. They do so because they need to enforce it. They have to be the law and they have to abide by its every rule. So, if the law is corrupt, they will be too. It is the nature of the beast.

We fear them because we fear our own law. That should not be. They should not be given power over the people. They are here to enforce our rules. Not drive tanks, wield assault rifles, and victimize the people. They shouldn't have any more power than what we give them. We should be able to stop them. We should have the rights to stop them from abusing their power.

We the people do have the power to stop them. It is as Roosevelt said:

"Let us never forget that government is ourselves and not an alien power over us. The ultimate rulers of our democracy are not a President and Senators and Congressmen and Government officials but the voters of this country."

Roosevelt was one of the politicians that the world should aspire to be like. We should not have to deal with the atrocities committed by our current government. Nor their greed. We can learn from Roosevelt's example, actually we can learn from all of the politicians in that era. They would give free speeches, host radio shows, and talk directly with the people. They didn't charge outrageous amounts for a speech nor did they demand the people to accept their views. They wanted to work with the people. We can return to a time like that. We are the rulers of this nation, not some pitiful man in a suit trying to tell us what we should do.

We can overthrow this tyranny. We can stop the justice system from turning our nation into a totalitarian disaster. Each citizen has the power to remove any person from office, we have to work together. We need them to recognize our voice. We can show them how we want our government to be. We are unified country. What we want, should be what we get. If it is plausible. And regardless of plausibility or desire, there is no person that should have to tolerate the atrocious effects of Judicial corruption. It should not be a priority at all.

Our people have their own sufferings to deal with. We can alleviate the political stress they have. We have to apply our efforts to the fullest extent if we are to stop political corruption. There is no way around this. We must use our power as a unit to overthrow the corrupted politicians. We must put in place restrictions on politicians. We must give the Judicial system a more effective check and balance system with the Executive branch. No one branch should be able to pass laws or prevent passing of laws that the people have voted on. For now, we can be their system of check and balances. We are the true owners of the power they have.

These politicians have let the power go to their head. Their greed has adversely afflicted our nation. They are using our money and our resources to benefit themselves instead of the people. They also bend the law to fit their malice lifestyle. They embezzle, they steal, they kill our citizens, and destroy our nation. They are in positions where they are supposed to help us and they do the opposite. We cannot allow this continue. If we are going to stop these afflictions, we must first cut off the head of the problem. Then we can bandage our wounds. We can help create a more desirable environment to live in.

We need to circumvent all the destruction of politicians. We need to apprehend and remove the Judicial members that plague our enforcement of law. We need to take our nation back from these conniving, deceiving, and malevolent tyrants that push us down. Only when the evil is removed will our nation have a chance at truly thriving and developing itself.

We will do this without government. They are not our ally. They do not want to help us. But we will not be alone. We will have each other. And together, together we can stop them. Thus, I will leave you with my parting thoughts on the matter:

"The people need to remember that politicians are our servants. They are not our leaders; they are the catalyst for our ideas. Nothing more and nothing less. The strength of the people's idea decides the strength of the politician."

Caustic Corruption 2: Oligopolies

The United States market is dominated by monopolies, duopolies, and oligopolies. The laws and efforts to prevent only a few firms from controlling a market have failed. The United States has failed to maintain a widespread market and our anti-trust laws need to be reformed. This is because, as the population increases in size, the need for more companies to have patents to innovate on becomes necessary, lest those few companies begin working together to control the market.

Our Judicial system, corrupt as it is, has failed to prevented us from having this limited market. Since the late twentieth century Judges have allowed the majority of competing companies to be bought out and owned by a single entity. Our Judicial system stimulated the markets limitation into what it is today. Now almost every company is owned by two massive companies which, in turn, has affected the markets for cars, drinks, candies, frozen foods, chips, and much more.

Not every area is dominated by a monopoly so they haven't been completely idle in regards to enforcing laws to stop monopolies but they have failed to stop duopolies and oligopolies. Every market is dominated by two to three companies now though. The economy has effectively become run by omniscient oligopolies. In oligopoly situations the consumer suffers but the illusion of a wider market spectrum and wide choice of products is maintained. The people have suffered under the illusion of this mocked wide spread market. We understand and recognize the fallacy of duopolies, so why not oligopolies?

We know that a duopoly prevents a constant innovation from being maintained. A company will only have one competitor to compete with. They only need to innovate enough to defeat the other company. In current duopoly situations the destruction of innovation continues exponentially. Usually, one company suffers more than the other because one of the companies has convinced the Judges to give them exclusive rights to specific patents. They use this exclusive right to keep the other company down and prevent any new company from rising up. They prevent another person from using or contributing to their patent in an innovative way.

The large companies try their utmost to remove innovation from the equation. Namely, if they cannot stop you, they will swallow you. They will buy out any company they can; if a company was overly large, they will try for a merger. They cannot stand competition because it effects their sales. So, they have made it so that smaller businesses, like a Ma and Pa setup, a contractor, a construction company, or such, stands no chance against them. They are the undefeatable beasts of Wall-street. All of the smaller companies are shoved down by the conglomerates trying to reinforce their domination of the market.

"If they can't beat you, they'll buy you."

The actions done to keep the little companies out is against the law. Yet no one attempts to make them abide by the law. The large companies know that the easiest and most effective way of winning is to bend and break the rules. Since they have the law behind them, they cannot lose. Their influence is so massive they can reshape the rules to their advantage; their influence allows them to keep the people uninformed about their shady business tactics. And as long as they maintained their clout, the general population would still be caught in their illusive snare. The general population would still be caught in their snare, if I wasn't here to tell you all about it.

I will tell you and show you all the corruption inside the United States market. I will show you how they are oligopolies. I will show you where and when they have abused the Judicial system to maintain their dominance over a market. I will show you how they have stripped our nation of innovation. I will show you why their actions are caustic and destructive. I will uncover their illusion and their lies and show you the truth.

The companies who the majority of people believe are separate are not, we are led to believe these products come from different people, yet they are truly under one company. They try to fool us, try to keep us under their thumb, while they reap the benefits and we stay ignorant. They label other companies differently than their products. Even on the back of their product where you should be able to information about the real owner of a product, they simply label it with the manufacturing area, or the parent company, instead of the head company that owns the rights to the product.

I'm not talking Illuminati or some conspiracy, these are legitimate business practices that people are, for the most part, unaware of. If you were to ask around, to someone that has worked at a restaurant, a grocery market, or any place that works with the most popular of products, they could confirm to you how much these companies own. They try their best to hide it from us but I am here to tell you about their malicious business practices. I won't let their despicable actions go unnoticed for another day.

I will give you some examples because I just want to give you a taste of the monopolies, duopolies, or oligopolies that are currently dominating our market. Some of these you may know already and those that have researched, fixed, or worked in the fields with these products will know how large these companies are and how much they dominate their respective industries. I apologize in advance if this information is repetitive for you. Anyway, here we go:

Craft – We've all seen their advertisements for their macaroni. However, that's not all that they own. They own Kadbury Candies, B. J. Hunz Sauces, Nibisco, Feet Peanuts, and much more. They have swallowed and own so many companies it is a jumbled-up mess. It would take hours to go over all that they own. The largest merger would definitely have to have been their one with Common Foods.

Some of their most notable products include: GOne Steak Sauce, Jell-E, Chocolate Ahoys, Carica Duilliers, Pennsylvania cream cheese, Ores, you know those delicious filled chocolate cookies? What a weird name for them. Anyway, they own Writz Crackers, Less-than-ambient temperature Whip, Bear Grahams, Frosty-Aid, Velveta cheeses, Tillas, Kutter Butters, Exclusive Crackers, Joggin' Gum, Quadscuits Biscuits, and Wheat Slims.

There is some weirdness going on though, they were under a company called Mondez International and for awhile they tried to claim themselves as different companies, but they ended up becoming one again. They are Craft foods again. They just kept swapping names around trying to fool the people. They eventually realized the people weren't really paying attention anyway.

Several class actions lawsuits have been placed on them,

mainly for false advertising. However, they allowed them to do two massive mergers: Kadbury Candies and B. J. Hunz Sauces. Both were humongous companies that are now under the Craft umbrella. Not a single person stepped up when they absorbed and merged into a single entity. They maintain a monopoly in certain markets and a duopoly in other markets but because they still separate the titles of their products as Hunz or Kadbury, they have maintained the illusion that they are still separate companies.

Duolever – Duolever is a simplistic company. They monopolize but to a certain degree. They are probably the least worst on this list. They have many laudable services they provide and they donate. At the end of it all, they still monopolize though.

Notable products: Pigeon Soap, Hammer male spray, Mouthton tea, Devilman's, Bechel, Redband, Content, and Knar cooking products. They are a single large conglomerate. It's interesting how they own Hammer and Mouthton. Those are two very different products but given their size, they could easily afford to pay for marketing both products. They do have Pigeon soap which is similar to Hammer and they do have Devilman's and Knar which could be considered similar to Mouthton. So, they have just diversified what products they make. They do make a bunch of chocolate and ice cream too but it's not as important as the others that I mentioned.

Their chief executive officer, Parry, makes roughly twenty million each year. Same as the Nettle's chief executive officer but Duolever is not even close to one fourth the size of Nettle or even one hundredth as evil. We'll get to Nettle eventually. I still think that twenty million a year is too high of a salary. Why does he need all that money?

Tycon – Just like Craft they have too many products to list, I don't want to keep you here all day. Unlike Craft though, their products are usually in the meat market. The majority of people will already know which products they do own, but they may not know which companies they own. So I will name the companies instead of their products:

ICP Inc, Gunners poultry, Licoln's creamery, Franzies Foods, Gold Prospect Farms, Crispy Kitchens, Ocama Foods, Volleyball

Foods, Honeyboo Foods, Vatrac Industries, Inheritance Valley, Molly Farms, and Bright Brand Foods Inc.

Just like Craft, no one stepped up and decided that these guys own too much. They own many farms from coast to coast, yet despite owning a whole valley, their chief executive officer makes a lowly fifteen million salary. Much less than the Craft chief executive officer. Maybe he learned a thing or two from oriental culture and how they dictate their salaries, I highly doubt it though. He still makes quite a bit more than the oriental company's chief executive officers but I'll get to them. I keep saying that don't I? Well, we will soon enough. There is lots of information about these oligopolies.

Their chief executive officer is a very religious person. He regularly attends church and teaches children about the gospel. It is admirable. His job is stressful and takes up a good amount of time, and he still finds time to spread the gospel of Jesus Christ. So maybe he could be called a good man as well as a chicken killer. He can definitely feed people like the prophets of the past, their leaders did give fish and bread to people too, he's just more effective. He decided to mix the breading with the fish.

Fishsticks. Get it? Fine. I know I'm not funny. I won't joke again.

Peptri – You have probably seen their main product, Peptri cola, they have advertised it all over the world and they constantly pay to have it subtly advertised in media. But did you know that all of Chip-Lay Inc is owned by Peptri Inc? Chip-Lay Inc alone encompasses forty percent of the savory snacks United States Market and thirty percent of the entire world's savory snacks market. The monetary gains are even more mind boggling. Did you know that twenty-two of their brands generate over one billion a year?

Their Chip-Lay products include: Layed, Doritas, Tostitdas, Rufflas, Walkars, Fritas, Cheetas, and Rald Gold pretzels. Their Quacker-Lay products include: Rice-a-ronald, Chewy Granola bars, Greck's Super Yogurt, Yogurt Bars, Quiisps, Aye Aye Crunch, Live cereal, and of course Quacker oats products. Their soft drink market includes: Brawndo, Waterfina, Gravelstar, Nude Juice, Propeller, AMPED, Tropican Fruit Juice Blend, Smug Root Beer, Isse, and Valley Dew.

Their chief executive officer is Indya Noyu. I find it ironic that her name is similar to the name of the country she is from: India. Anyway, Indya makes over fifty-five million a year, meaning she makes roughly a dollar and seventy-five cents a minute. You are so close to two dollars Indya, increase that salary and you can be a part of the exclusive one dollar a second club. Well actually, given the cash bonuses and stocks she receives along with the pension money she's probably over two dollars a second.

Indya has been chief executive officer of Peptri Inc for over thirty years. She is pushy eighty years old; she has made tons of money and she will continue to until she finally relinquishes the monopolized throne she sits on. She has helped Peptri Inc greatly. She has helped expand their company greatly. She was part of the team that helped Peptri swallow Quaker. What else will she help them swallow in the upcoming years?

In regards to the law, Peptri Inc has faced no consequences for their destruction of many rain-forests and murder of many of their inhabitants. They likewise faced no charges for pushing many farmers into a state of poverty because of the land they own. However, they did face charges in the past for discriminating against specific race applicants. It was a small charge of three million though. Overall, they have by no means adequately made up for the destruction they have wrought.

Original Cola's – The Original Cola Company likes to eat up other companies too, they have swallowed Second Maid, Tums Up, Bark's, and Okwalla. So much for a widespread market! They are basically a duopoly with only Peptri Inc really standing a chance in the soft drink market, mainly because both their gross product sales keep rising annually and anyone who stands in their way they swallow, like Original Cola's attempt to swallow the Heyyan Juice Group, luckily this attempt was stopped. Heyyan came to their sense.

They own over five hundred soft drink products alone. They have over two billions servings of their products around the world. Some notable products that Original Cola owns would be Dacani, Intelligent Water, Superade, Nutrient Water, Nitrous Energy, Full Pistons, Beast Energy, which they just recently acquired by the way,

Fantasmo, Second Maid, Spritz, PHD Pib, Freska, Super-C, Gold Mountain Peak Tea, Fuse, Bachardi, and Barks.

Their chief executive officer, Mr. Kanta, is one of the richest Middle Easterners in the world, even though he doesn't even make the top ten list, he still garnishes over forty million a year, which used to be sixty million in a few years ago. Maybe he gained thirty three percent of a conscience over the last few years. He's by no means poor either way though.

His salary increased during their acquisition of PHD Pepper & Snaps Group. They own A&U, Deja Clear Water, Diet Right, Desert Plant Cooler, Crushed, Islander Punch and a few other brands. They acquired over fifty brands during their acquisition. They made themselves a force to be reckoned with. Yet only Peptri can truly compete with them. They share many despicable similarities with Peptri. In the past their company consistently rejected specific applicants because of their race and they similarly stripped farmers of their land. However, they are even more despicable than Peptri in other areas. They paid many scientists and researchers to declare sugar as healthy to sell their product. They have promoted obesity on several occasions. Their Nutrient water claims to be healthy yet contains copious amounts of sugar. They were associated with a death-squad in Guatemala and Columbia, they of course denied the association in both.

Original Cola is evil but they are not the most evil on this list; I have saved the worst business for the last spot on the food list:

Nettle – The Nettle family holds some of the grossest, if not the grossest, people in the entire world. This is the company that has told the government and the public that they have no rights to clean water. They have supplied free baby foods to Africa, got the baby off the mothers natural feeding, the mom stops lactating, and then they stop providing the food. They knew the parents would have no choice but to buy their products afterwards.

Notable products include: Arrowtribe water, Kinderger Baby Foods, Protein Booster, Heat Pockets, Mean Pockets, Mean Cuisine, Stuffers, DiGiovani Pizza, Purryna Cat Food, Fiskies Cat Food, Benitful, and too many others to name. They have over eight thousand brands in total. Fifty of the eight thousand make them one billion a year. They are without a doubt the largest food company on the least. And the way they sell their product makes me sick to my stomach. Almost every single one of their products is deployed on the premise that their consumer will become dependent on their product.

A good majority of their products are stolen from third world countries that are dependent on the resources they steal. The major thievery is water. They will not allow any single person, group, or government to have access to free water. They will siphon it out or poison it if they need to. It is said that they were the ones who released the methane pockets at the bottom of a few bodies of waters because the people refused to give them it.

The Nettle family removes their board of executives if they do not agree with their perspectives. Their most recent chief executive officer only make a paltry twenty million a year. It is paltry because Nettle is double if not triple or quadruple the size of the other companies on the list.

There is proof that the others were fired because they made too much. Although their officer and his salary has stuck for quite awhile. They are content with him. Maybe it's because of his statement about water. And this is a direct quote:
"Water is now a privatized asset. It is, and never was, a human right. We just happen to own the most clean water in the world. If you have a problem with it, that is your issue to work out. No law or country will stop us. We can pay them off. We are big enough to own your government. So, tell me, why would your government or its people's opinions matter to us?"

Essentially, since your body is mostly water and you depend on water, he is saying he has the right to end your life by depriving you of water. The sadistic nature of the Nettle corporation does not end there either. In monetary gain their family makes the combined salaries of every single chief executive officer on the list. They pay their employees, their managers, and everyone else at least one half of the equivalent salary they would be making at another company. Any extra money they do not have to spend goes directly to the Nettle family. They will garnish and cut salaries by cycling through employees. If an employee demands a higher salary, they get denied.

They ask again, and they get fired.

The malice of the Nettle family is unparalleled in the world. Their atrocious business practices have no limit. If they haven't come for you already, they will soon.

Now that we have tackled the food industry, how about we tackle a new industry? The automotive industry. Want to see how corrupt they are?

General Autos – General Autos makes GAC, Chevi's, Buckies, and Caliliacs. Their chief executive officer, Marge, made a little over sixteen million. Just a tiny bit over. And also, two hundred and ninety times that of the highest paid Union worker. I wonder what she needs the money for, to feed her family Bugattis? Oh, and she does have her Masters in business, her bachelors was in BS. That's bachelors of science, not masters of, well you know, what she actually does.

Given all the car recalls they have and how often the government bails them out. It's a marvel that they are still in business. Oh wait, it's not a marvel. They forge the paperwork. Their cars are faulty but they blame the drivers. Maybe they will try to recall humans next for being ineffective at driving their cars. Given the governments tendency to bail them out whenever they need it, instead of letting them die and giving others a chance to build better cars than them, they will probably be able to legitimately recall humans if we allow their business practices to continue.

Folkswagons – Chair, Sodas, Porcha, Linguini, Buscemi, Susuki, Ducat, Audo, and Bensley.

Who names all their products? A child? Regardless. They absolutely monopolize the sports car market. They are part of a duopoly on supercars. They advertise it, they flaunt it, they claim to make the fastest cars in the world.

Now the question is: are they really the fastest cars in the world?

They would need to be a little more than five times faster to have the land speed record. So, they definitely aren't the fastest cars in the world. But what about production car?

That is their claim to fame. Their Buscemi Venular is renowned as the fastest production car.

The Buscemi Venular has held the record for years. And when they were beat, they ended up paying off the world record companies to keep their car as the fastest production car. The problem was that these small companies had legitimate production cars that obliterated their records. They both had a production line, which was a requirement for the record, and they followed all the guidelines the world record companies required. The smaller companies legitimately beat them.

The nice and generous workers at Folkswagen accidentally dropped some cash and knowledge to the world record companies, informing them delicately that they broke this rule and that they should change the rules to maintain their high record standard. They basically had them create a new standard to declare their records illegible. The workers and Folkswagen pointed out that they had two more production units than them and used that to their advantage over the smaller companies. So, the world record folks edited the requirement to be exactly the amount of the Buscemi Venular for that year. And then, every year after, they repeated it again and again so that the Venular won. They still continually modifying the requirements so only the Buscemi Venular could win.

The mastermind behind it all was their chief executive officer Mark. He acquired his PHD in metal research and metal physics, and makes a paltry twenty-five million a year. His yearly income only allows him to able to buy twenty five of the fifty Bugatti's they make on average every year. Step your game up. You should be able to buy them all Mark. Well, actually he could probably get a hefty discount and buy them all anyway.

Fita – This is the other part of the supercar duopoly with Folkswagen. Fita owns Horse, Horse two, Dodgem, Crysler, Beep, and Alfu Romeo.

Both supercar companies have terrible names for their companies, I think. You could have used Jets, Rockets, you know, something that is a motif for speed? Horses aren't fast anymore guys.

However, Fita isn't just part of the supercar duopoly, Fita also owns the most out of the four major car developers that dominate the market. They are definitely the largest conglomerate on the list. It's not because they own the most products, it's because they make the most common products. Dogem and Crysler are multi-billion business on their own. They have even made offers at Toyada to buy them. In a few years, they will probably buy them.

Fita is the only direct competitor with Folkswagen in the supercar market. General Autos makes a few, along with a few of the other companies, but Fita and Folkswagen are the two most popular and dominating. There are only a few competitors outside of them. And they will probably buy them out eventually anyway. Fita has a nasty habit of buying every company in sight, as I said before.

Their chief executive officer, Sarge, makes a good seventy-three million every year. He is the second highest grossing chief executive officer on the list. Which is even more baffling when you begin to actually look at how much each of them make. They don't have a shortage of money that's for sure. And Fita is even more rapacious. Sarge may make great money but the Agnalli family that owns Fita makes the most. Their family worth well over fifty billion dollars.

If you are listening Sarge, I have a suggestion, you should put one of them supercar engines into one of your tiny Fitas. I wanna see some sports cars lose to those small smartcar looking things. Watch the racers cry as a tiny Fitas stomps on their custom race-car by running a seven second quarter mile.

Toyada – Lexas and Csion. They also own a portion of Usuzu. While Toyada doesn't own the most, they make the most. Their company as a whole makes well over eight hundred billion every year. For the company that makes the most money, you would expect them to have the highest paid automobile chief executive officer.

Nope. Japanese culture wasn't as rampantly greedy as the rest of the world. Things have changed since the AUE has taken over most of Asia, but Japanese culture had it right.

Their chief executive officer made only five million a year. The Japanese were quite good at removing excessive greed. Culturally, they wanted to provide service to their people but at lower salaries than any other chief executive officers in the world. It's admirable.

Quick fact: The highest grossing automobile maker is Mr. Sluski. He makes well over two hundred million every year. His company doesn't make the most money though. Mr. Sluski makes almost five dollars every second. It's deplorable. There are only thirty-one million five hundred and thirty-six thousand seconds in a year. So, Sluski is making one half the median hourly minimum wage in the United States in one second. He is making their entire years' salary in almost an hour. Is that okay? He claims that he uses that money for good and that he would get rid of his company, but that's just him getting good publicity.

He is an innovator but so is Toyada. Culturally, Toyada does not abuse the system like Mr. Sluski does. He is the worst kind of innovator. I don't care if he released his patents and allowed the other automakers to use them. He still makes more than all of them.

Now we can tackle the media. There are only a few companies that run almost every single form of media. I know you guys are getting bored, so I will keep this one shorter. There are six companies that own ninety percent of all the media. Just a few years ago it was fifty companies, but that number has dwindled. Now they are just conglomerates. They act like they are still separate companies, even though they are owned by one head company. I will only go over three, to keep it short.

Dradni – The animated company turned super entity. They own the largest sport news network. They own several animated stations. They own XYZ and Bruana Vitra media. Two massive companies that own enough companies to fill several books. And Dradni owns them both. They also two massive companies for their films: Larcul Arts and Spectacular. The acquisitions of both were widely known but their impact was not fully realized until years after their acquisition. They have made insane amounts of cash from both. And they continue to bleed their viewers for more cash.

Ubiquitous Electricities – CameraCasters, CBC, and Galaxy Pictures are their largest assets. Once again, you could fill several books with just what those three own.

Time Harry – RNN, TBO, and Harry Brothers. The first two dominant cable and the last creates films. They helped film several multi-billion dollar movie franchises and continue to do so. They compete with Dradni now. Since they have Investigator Comics and produce all their movies, they compete directly with Spectacular Comics. But they are both in the film industry, so they were competitors already. Just now they are a duopoly. Time Harry and Dradni are practically the only two companies producing comic films.

Their growth has been astronomical in recent years. They show no sign of stopping. They are the omniscient media powers that run every piece of information on your television and computer. They continue to buy out each other and become even larger conglomerates. The media is a definite oligopoly. Most of these companies have over-ridden the law on several occasions to increase their sovereignty over the media.

One example would be the fact that some of the media companies own way more radio stations than what the Federal Communications Commission allows. And they do nothing to stop them from buying more radio stations. These companies are oligopolies in all forms of media.

You can find out more about these oligopolies for yourself. Pick out any product and I bet there is a super-company that owns them. There are of course others that I did not mention, Natural Foods, General Factories, Chaqut Branded International, Autogill, and many more. Our United State markets is quite varied but each market usually has two companies that run the roost. If the market is even larger, then there will be a few more companies trying to dominate the market.

The problem is that while the United States prevents singular monopolies, companies are allowed to create duopolies and oligopolies in single markets. And every company can dominate multiple markets too, if they can. Many of these companies dominate lots of areas instead of just one too, but their very best to make people think they don't. They do this by creating new companies with different names to try and further alienate the people from their business practices.

In the world there are roughly seven hundred companies that

own ninety percent of all assets, products, and wealth.

In each of these seven hundred companies, the chief executive officers are typically not the highest profiteer. The owners and the highest shareholders are typically making anywhere from two to one hundred times as much, depending on how much ownership and stocks they have. The owners and stockholders usually own big portions of multiple companies and not just one. Their pay adds up exponentially. They make money from their assets by abusing the stock market. And there is not a single government entity that attempts to stop them.

The Nettle family makes the most out of any of the other owners mentioned on the list. They are also the evilest too. However, none of these companies are absolved from malice and destruction, these traits are necessary for making exponential profits. They need to continue shady business practices to continue making the inordinate amount of cash that they do. They aren't going to stop overnight. And the people will have to slowly gain back the power to stop them.

Each of these companies has instated laws and restrictions on competitors to make sure that their domination will continue throughout the years. They are building towards a future where just one of them will be the sole provider for every necessity. There is no innovation in the market anymore.

The rich conglomerates shove us down. They keep us poor, uninformed, and addicted to their product. They will continue to drain our accounts until we want to stop it. They have severely damaged our markets but it's nothing we can't remedy.

When Gandhi enacted his version of non-violent revolution, he neglected the fact that economic turmoil also results in causalities. That is what these corporations are doing today. By controlling the market and forming oligopolies, they gain control of millions of lives. Their prices, their employee wages, their effect on the market, everything can cause death or hardship for millions of people. It's the way of the world and no one is doing anything to stop it.

More specifically, our government is doing nothing to stop companies like Nettle from destroying our world, harming our people, and even killing us. No government in the entire world is trying to. We are stuck in perpetual motion feeding into their malice.

I will not stand in this perpetual motion any longer. I will strive for a paradigm shift. I want you to strive for this paradigm shift with me. Together, we can stop these companies. Together we can end this tyrannical corporate dictatorship.

There are laws that can be put into effect to prevent corrupt businesses from thriving but the government is not willing to listen to reason. This is the flaw with a representative government, corporations can bribe them into doing whatever they want. Sometimes people have to send a message to get them to listen. The people have already removed the majority of the superior courts that have allowed these companies to continue their domination. You have removed one problem. Another has presented itself. What will you do? Will you allow them to abuse you, keep you in the dark, or will you stand up to them? Will you stop their tyranny?